Altered

MARNEE BLAKE

This book is a work of fiction. Names, characters, places, and incidents are the product of the author's imagination or are used fictitiously. Any resemblance to actual events, locales, or persons, living or dead, is coincidental.

Copyright © 2015 by Marnee Bailey. All rights reserved, including the right to reproduce, distribute, or transmit in any form or by any means. For information regarding subsidiary rights, please contact the Publisher.

Entangled Publishing, LLC
2614 South Timberline Road
Suite 109
Fort Collins, CO 80525
Visit our website at www.entangledpublishing.com.

Embrace is an imprint of Entangled Publishing, LLC.

Edited by Candace Havens
Cover design by Louisa Maggio
Cover art from iStock

Manufactured in the United States of America

First Edition December 2015

embrace

To George and our boys.
The three of you taught me everything I know about happily-ever-after.
I love you.

Chapter One

The motorcycle was almost sideways.

Seth leaned hard into the curve, not braking as he hit the gravel at the edge of the road. His tires skidded, sending his bike careening. It took all his strength to bring the machine under control. He slid to a stop next to the metal barrier that was the only thing between him and the rocky cliff's steep drop. But as he stared over the edge into the darkness, he waited. And waited…and waited.

No rush of adrenaline, no blood-thumping wave of panic. Nothing.

He leaned forward, studying the craggy rocks and silence below, detached. Hell, he studied everything detached these days. He bungee jumped, BASE jumped, skydived. He used to love long drives on his motorcycle. Now? Even the wind in his hair and the feeling of flying along the open road didn't touch him. It all used to work.

The moon was high above him, and the night was clear. The empty air in front of him beckoned.

He got off his bike and dropped the kickstand. At the

edge of the road, he gripped the metal barrier, the only thing standing between him and the open sky. It was no barrier, really. He could hop the bit of steel and be free-falling in a heartbeat. Less than a heartbeat.

His breath quickened, and his fingers chilled on the cold metal, the sharp edges of it biting into his palm.

His phone vibrated in his pocket. He didn't step back as he answered it. "Campbell."

"Where are you?" Nick didn't waste time on greetings. Said caller ID made pleasantries unnecessary.

Seth looked over the side of the cliff again. "Nowhere."

"Nowhere near San Antonio? For your sake, I hope that isn't true."

"Relax. I got held up in Denver. I'll cross into New Mexico in a half an hour. Be in San Antonio by tomorrow night."

Nick snorted. "No rush. Training only starts in five days. In North Carolina."

"I'll be in time." Like he'd miss it. Special Forces training, the army. This was why he still bothered polluting the air with his breath.

Nick must have recognized the defensiveness, because he backed off. "How's the ride?"

"Good." Seth grinned. "You know, we could take the bike to Bragg. Probably shave time." Nick could be such a stiff. Seth couldn't help razzing him sometimes.

His friend's chuckle floated over the airways. Seth could almost see him smiling, glancing down with his hand in his pocket. "No way, man."

Seth's grin widened. "Fine. I'll get the rental car." Something with a V8, maybe German engineering.

"My ass. It's not the car, it's the driver. Love the speed, hate the death potential. I drive."

"Cars have seat belts, asshole."

"See you tomorrow."

"Later."

Seth pocketed the phone and noticed the blood on his hand for the first time. He found a gash in both palms, perfectly straight. Streaks of blood glistened on the metal in front of him. The sting of it didn't even faze him. He removed his handkerchief from his back pocket, careful to keep the blood off his pants. He bit the fabric, right in the center, and tore it in half. Wrapping one half around each hand, he secured them with the efficiency of a man well trained in field dressing.

Which he was.

After all, though the pain didn't bother him, there was no reason to bleed on his bike.

As he stared at his bandaged palms in the moonlight, exhaustion crashed over him.

He hadn't lied to Nick. He had been held up in Denver. He'd stopped to see Linda. But it hadn't been the visit that stopped him. No, that had only taken a minute. Linda had refused to speak to him.

It had been two years since Bobby died. Apparently that hadn't been enough time for her. Of course not. He'd lost a good friend; Linda had lost her husband.

Maybe he should stop for the night. He woke every day at dawn anyway. He could easily cover the hours to San Antonio before dinner tomorrow. A sign a mile back promised a bed-and-breakfast. He only noticed because the town's name had made him smile.

Glory. Population twenty-three.

Seth chuckled as he threw a leg over the motorcycle. Only twenty-three people? Sounded glorious.

With a stomp, he deftly started the engine. Then he spun the bike around and sped toward Glory without a backward glance.

When Blueberry Michaels let herself in the back door, the clock on the stove read 2:53. She rubbed her palm against the headache forming in her forehead. Even after a year, she wasn't used to the late hours.

Once a morning person, always a morning person.

She dropped her messenger bag and bartending apron on the kitchen table before taking a peek in the fridge.

Ah...Gran left her dinner. Nice.

She could have grabbed food at the bar, but their menu was pretty standard bar fare. Read: meant for carnivores. She usually had to settle for fries, grilled cheese, or mozzarella sticks. Not much by food pyramid standards.

Blue warmed up the whole wheat pasta with veggies and tofu and grabbed a glass of tap water. As she dropped into one of the retro kitchen chairs—celery green, courtesy of the seventies—and dug in, she kicked off her black orthopedic work shoes and wiggled her toes, smothering her sigh of bliss.

She really needed a new job.

Problem was she needed the paycheck. Not many jobs paid as well as tending bar, especially with no college degree. Gran's Social Security check didn't begin to touch their bills. With the mounting number of prescriptions Gran needed and the increasing doctor bills, Blue was barely making ends meet for them working six nights a week.

God knew how she'd pay for it all when Gran's health really started to decline. And at seventy-six, Gran wasn't getting any younger.

Gran had brought up moving first. Two years ago, right after Blue's high school graduation.

"Blue," she'd said. "Why don't we move to Santa Fe or Albuquerque? Even Denver. There are plenty of personal care homes. And you could go to school, come visit on weekends."

She'd shut Gran down right there. Because neither of them would be happy in a city, any city. Gran barely tolerated the people in Glory. She hated crowds. A jam-packed personal care home would be her idea of hell.

And Blue? She didn't trust anyone else with Gran, especially a corporate-run personal care home. Corporations didn't care about people. They cared about money. After all Gran had done for her over the years, she refused to hustle her into some unfeeling institution. They only had each other. She wasn't going to leave the only person who'd ever loved her in some home that smelled like bad TV dinners and urine.

Blue smothered the tinge of all too familiar resentment, followed by the also familiar shame. This was her choice, one she made every day. Gran had taken her in when her own mother had fallen apart, too consumed by her grief and pain after her husband died to mother anyone. She'd never seen any bitterness on Gran's face, only unconditional love and acceptance. She would give her grandmother the same. Even if that meant picking up another job to stay here, in Glory, where they belonged.

Maybe someone in town needed help. She already drove thirty minutes to Raton every night. Adding more travel time appealed to her like greasy chicken wings. Besides, she'd prefer to stay closer to Gran during the day, to keep an eye on her.

Blue finished off her dinner with a swig of water. Then she put her dishes in some dishwater and scrubbed them down. Gran beat her awake every morning, and Blue didn't want her to have to clean up her mess. That's when she noticed the pill organizer and the empty water glass next to the rooster salt and pepper shakers.

Damn. Gran missed a dose of medicine again today. Blue mentally ran through the list of Gran's prescriptions. The most vital was for Gran's blood pressure. It looked like she'd taken her dose the night before, so she should be fine until morning. Blue reached into the drawer nearby, jotted a note to remind her grandmother to take the forgotten meds, and scrubbed down Gran's empty glass, setting it in the strainer to dry.

She needed to get someone to check on Gran while she was gone at night. This sort of slipup shouldn't happen as often as it did. Maybe someone in town would barter with her. Blue could do work for them if they stayed with Gran at night. It might work.

She nodded, decided. But the movement made her dizzy. She steadied herself with a hand on the sink. As her head spun, her stomach heaved. She leaned over the sink and threw up her entire dinner. After the retching subsided to dry heaves, she turned on the garbage disposal and rinsed out her mouth with water.

Sweat broke out all over her body, and she stumbled to the hallway, feeling as if her guts were on fire. She'd been tired lately, working too much. Obviously, she'd run herself down and set herself up for the flu.

Great. She couldn't afford to miss work. Apparently her body thought otherwise.

On the way to her bedroom, she faltered outside Gran's door. Usually she checked in on her before she went to bed. But in this state, she'd probably wake her up. Or worse, expose her to the flu. At her age, she didn't recover from illness as fast as she used to. Best to leave her to her rest. She passed the door without going in.

In her room, she grabbed the trash can and emptied the contents on the floor before staggering forward. She collapsed on the bed and pulled the covers over her.

When the shivers started, she knew this was no ordinary flu. She quaked, shaking the bed frame. Her skin seeped even as everything under it felt on fire. She writhed, threw up five more times, six times...so many she stopped counting until all she could manage were dry heaves. As she curled in the fetal position, she debated food poisoning or some kind of exotic disease. The kind no one ever heard about because they didn't live to tell the tale.

The pain went on and on, and she thought she must be dying. She passed out—she was sure—and time became subjective, measured only by twisting and dry heaving. Eventually the light crept through the window, in streaks at first and then in a steady wash.

But the agony continued.

Until it ended.

As quickly as it came, the pain, the fever, the nausea... gone.

She lay still, gasping, feeling her limbs and testing her stomach's fortitude. No way a flu left that fast. Usually she had to sip broth and eat toast, tough it out through endless cups of bland tea. But this...nothing. It was as if she'd never been sick at all.

Impossible.

The only remnant of her illness was the smell of sickness in the air. And the filled trash can.

Gagging, she scurried into the bathroom. She dumped the nastiness in the toilet and rinsed out the sick. She seriously considered throwing the trash can out, but she didn't have the cash to replace stuff because it grossed her out. So she set it aside, deciding to bleach it later.

The door to Gran's room was still closed. Maybe it wasn't as late as she thought it was. The clock on the living room wall read two thirty. In the afternoon? Maybe Gran was resting...

But she held her breath as she pushed Gran's door open.

The shades were drawn, and the trash can had been pulled next to the bed. In the dim light, Blue moved toward the bed. "Gran?"

Her grandmother's gray curls peeked out of the flowered comforter, and Blue almost smiled. Gran loved the floral prints. Blue was more minimalist. She shook Gran's shoulder gently. "Gran?" she called again. When she didn't move, Blue shook harder. "Gran."

Nothing. She rolled her grandmother over. Blood seeped from her eyes, her nose, her mouth, made more garish by its contrast with the flowered sheets. "Oh my God. Gran! Gran, wake up!"

But she knew. By the silence of her body, the lack of air expansion in her chest, Blue knew. A quick press to her neck verified the truth. She staggered back from the bed, shaking her head. "No. No."

In her pain, she scanned the room to avoid looking at the dead body. The full trash can. The shades. Gran must have felt the same flu-like symptoms she had last night. The flu had been bad, but bad enough to kill someone?

The evidence lay on the bed, lifeless. She wanted to cover her, to shield Gran from her eyes, but she couldn't bring herself to move forward. Couldn't bring herself to leave, either. Instead, she stood there, wishing she were strong enough to pull the sheet over Gran's face.

And as if it obeyed her, the sheet rose in the air and dropped over the dead body on the bed.

Chapter Two

Blue stomped on the brakes in her beat-up Chevy Cavalier outside Murphy's Gas on Main. The street was abandoned, unusual at this time of day.

A phone, to call 911. She didn't have a cell—didn't have the money to pay for it—and the electricity and phone were out at home. Strange time for a power outage.

Gran didn't need immediate medical assistance, but Blue needed to tell someone, to have other people know that Gran was there—dead—in their home. And the Murphys were the best sort of people. She bounded up the stairs to the gas station convenience store.

The CLOSED sign hung on the door. At three in the afternoon? Officially, the station opened early, closed late. But Blue had seen them open in the middle of the night for travelers who passed through Glory and needed to fill up. The Murphy family lived right upstairs. Either Jenna or Max could be down in the shop most of the time. And when they couldn't see to the shop, another local girl, Carmen, did it.

Ignoring the CLOSED sign, Blue twisted the knob—

unlocked, as expected—and went in. She'd grown up with the Murphys' four kids, and the door had never been closed to her, even now that all of them had moved away from Glory.

"Is anyone home? Mr. Murphy? Mrs. Murphy?"

The store was deserted, and there was no sign the place had opened today. The card table in the corner, where Mr. Murphy and Mr. Schumacher played cards, was clear of clutter. That was odd in itself. Blue had never seen that card table free of newspaper pages and coffee mugs. It was the first thing Mr. Murphy did every day—separate the paper into sections, drink his coffee, and read through the happenings. Everyone else who passed by would browse as well, as if the Murphys' card table was their portal to the outside world. Her stomach sick, Blue rushed through the store to the stairs at the back, taking them two at a time, calling for the Murphys as she went. But there was no breath of movement above her.

Dread coursed through her as she hit the top of the stairs, like it had when she opened Gran's door. She rounded the corner and stopped cold.

Jenna Murphy lay on the floor, blood trails from her eyes, nose, and mouth—same as Gran. Her body curled next to her husband, and Max's face sported the same gore. But they held each other, as if they'd known their last moments had arrived and their last thought had been to reach for one another.

"Oh, God." Blue covered her mouth, gagging. Not them, too. How could this be?

She reached for the phone, her hand trembling. *Please work.* Silence greeted her, the line dead—the same as at her place.

She needed to get away from here, from the bodies and the blood of the people she cared about. As the walls closed in on her, she stumbled back, tore down the stairs and out onto the porch. She tripped down the porch steps and out into the middle of the deserted street.

"Help!" Her yell came out a pathetic squeak. "Oh, God, help." The summer heat had sucked the air from Glory, and she gasped and panted, suffocating.

But there was no one around. Their tiny town was barely populated, but this was ridiculous.

"Someone…" she whispered. Then she tilted her head back and screamed, "Help!"

The sound of breaking glass broke the silence, as loud as machine-gun blasts. She covered her ears, falling to her knees. On both sides of the street, every visible window had blown out. The huge pane of glass that used to boast the insignia of Mr. Schumacher's hardware store had been reduced to jagged pieces.

What the…

A soft *click* sounded from the Keilmans' bed-and-breakfast. She froze.

"I want you to turn toward me, slowly, with your hands where I can see them." The unfamiliar voice held enough grit for her to know he meant business.

Her eyes widened in disbelief. Seriously? Someone was going to rob her now?

"Is this a stickup?" Laughter bubbled from her, and she swallowed it. Why laugh at a time like this? Better than crying, she supposed.

"Get up."

She stood, her heartbeat speeding, and wiped her dusty hands on her black uniform pants. God, she hadn't even changed. Of course not. There'd been no chance. She got sick as soon as she had dinner last night, and then she'd found Gran…

And that sheet stunt.

Blue shook her head. Things only moved by themselves on the Syfy Channel. She must have covered Gran herself. There was no other option.

Turning, she lifted her hands and faced him.

He wasn't what she expected. She'd expected a stained-T-shirt-wearing, unshaven slob with a beer belly. A drifter looking to capitalize on someone's low moment.

Like hers.

What she got was a tall man in excellent shape—if his muscled arms and trim waist were any indication—probably only a year or two older than she was. Twenty-one, twenty-two? Dressed in camo pants and sporting the look of a soldier, he was fit and bronzed. And good-looking. Very good-looking.

What was a soldier like this doing in Glory, the morning after Gran and the Murphys had been killed by the plague?

"It was you." She stepped toward him, her hands up.

"Don't move." His gun hand didn't waver.

She stopped, but she didn't shut up. She glared at him. "It has to be you. Glory never gets visitors, and suddenly you're here, obviously a soldier, with a gun, and Gran and the Murphys are dead."

"Listen, sweetheart"—he smiled the sort of smile that said she was crazy—"I spent the last hour tripping over dead bodies. Being alive makes you suspicious to me."

"No, you listen, G.I. Joe. I live here." Her hands curled into fists, and she stepped the last two feet toward him. She stood close enough to see that his eyes were steely gray. "You're the suspicious one. My grandmother was killed last night. I think you know what happened."

"Whoa, whoa. I don't know anything about your grandmother. What I do know is that I stopped in this piece of paradise late last night and checked in to that bed-and-breakfast." He motioned to the side with his gun, indicating the Keilmans' little lodging. "I took a shower, got sick like I'd been on the worst bender of my life, and woke to complete carnage."

"My God." Blue covered her mouth. She glanced at the

Keilmans' B&B, its crisp white shutters and its cheery yellow porch. "Not the Keilmans, too." Was she the only one left?

"If you mean the little chatty woman who runs the B&B and her silent husband, yes. I found them a little bit ago, when I could move again." His tone had softened, as had his eyes. He dropped his gun but didn't put it away. "I'm sorry. I'd imagine you knew them."

"Yes." In a town the size of Glory? Everyone knew everyone.

"And a family. Over there." He nudged his head behind her, toward a farmhouse in the distance. "I found a couple, early forties, and two children. All the same."

The Barnetts, too? "No, wait. They have a son, too. A year older than me. Jack."

He shook his head. "Wasn't there. Just the four of them."

She studied him before allowing her gaze to scan the quiet street. What the hell happened last night? She rubbed her temple, trying to sort it out. They'd all been sick, that was clear enough. Had they been poisoned? Who would poison them? More important, why poison them? Glory was small, barely warranting a dot on the map. They weren't worth killing. And why had she and this soldier lived when everyone else…didn't?

Too many questions and no good answers. None of the questions or answers would bring Gran back to her, anyway.

But where was Jack? He came home for the summer a couple weeks ago to help out on his family's farm. Maybe he'd spent the night in Raton. He had friends there. She hoped that was the case. Being the only survivor—at least, the only one she knew—left her empty, completely ungrounded.

She narrowed her eyes again on the soldier. The gun now rested at his side, and he ran his hand over his head. He looked as tired and worn as she felt. Maybe he was being straight with her. Maybe he was a victim of circumstance. But she still didn't trust him. "Who are you?"

"Seth Campbell. Specialist, United States Army. You?"

"Blue." She crossed her arms over her chest. "So what now?"

"Blue?"

She sighed at the familiar confusion. Curse her parents for this weird name. "Yeah. Blue, short for Blueberry. My mom…a bit of a free spirit."

"Ah. Got it." He glanced around at the street covered in broken glass. It looked like there had been a tornado. "How did you do that thing with the windows?"

Do what to the windows? "What are you talking about?"

But he didn't get a chance to answer.

A helicopter rose out of the west, over the Sangre de Cristo range. It covered the ground low, much lower than the few medical helicopters that serviced the area and much faster than the even fewer news-reporting aircrafts that visited them.

Maybe it was the National Guard, responding to their emergency. She lifted her arm to flag them down.

Seth grabbed her elbow and half pulled, half dragged her toward the Keilmans' porch. She lurched up the step behind him. He tucked them behind the double rocking chair, crouching low. When she didn't squat, too, he yanked her down beside him.

"What are you doing?" she hissed, tugging her arm out of his grasp.

"That's a military helicopter," he whispered back. He didn't add the "duh," but she got it.

"Yeah, I know. Probably the National Guard, right? This is an emergency." Why were they whispering? The helicopter couldn't hear them. Then again, maybe it had something to do with their close proximity, with the feel of his hip touching hers.

The helicopter swept the town, swinging low and hovering, kicking up dust as it flew over the sparse gathering of buildings in her town. She could see men hanging out, their hands shielding their eyes despite dark sunglasses, assault rifles hanging at their hips. The weapons made Blue fold closer to Seth as they hid there, on the porch.

Why did they have their guns out? They wouldn't need weapons to respond to an emergency, would they?

The men scanned the area, still searching for something and obviously ready to use force if necessary. Then the helicopter turned and continued east. She listened as it slowed, as if to land.

Finally, Seth turned, eyes narrowing on her. "Do you think it's a coincidence that a military chopper shows up here after everyone dies?"

And suddenly, it didn't seem coincidental at all. Whoever killed her town was here to see how it worked out. Nausea that had nothing to do with the flu tugged at her stomach.

Seth cursed under his breath. She scowled at him. Something wasn't right here.

"What is going on?" she asked. He shook his head. "No. You're going to answer me. What do you know? You're in the military, and there's a military helicopter circling over us. But you didn't want them to see us. So what's going on?"

"It's complicated."

"I'll try to keep up."

He sighed, standing up from their hidey-hole. She stood, too, and put some space between them for good measure. He glared down the street, after the helicopter. "Those aren't army men. My guess is they're Goldstone."

"Goldstone? Like the security firm, the one with all the government contracts?" Blue didn't catch the news much these days, thanks to working ridiculous hours and sleeping even stranger ones. But she'd have to live under a rock to not know the name. Soldiers for hire in the Middle East, willing to do what the government couldn't do legally. Whispers of civilian murders and unethical torture.

Mercenaries.

"That's the one."

"What are *they* doing here?" She fired the words at the helicopter. The last thing they needed was more death.

"I don't know."

Blue studied him. He had the kind of face that kept secrets well. "I don't believe you." She stood up and hustled off the porch.

He caught up with her easily. "Hey, where are you going?"

"I'm getting out of here. Can't you hear? They're landing." If he thought she'd stand around, waiting for a bunch of mercenaries, he was nuts. And if she was honest with herself, she wanted to get away from him, too. He made her uncomfortable. The gun, the closed face, the fact that he was an outsider…the fact that he was good-looking. It was all too much.

He grasped her arm. The move was unexpected, and she lost her balance. Her momentum spun her, and she found herself pressed against his warm chest. He held her loosely, and her breath caught.

"They'll be waiting for you," he gritted.

Gazing up into the serious look on his handsome face, she knew he was right. That helicopter was looking for something, and it was probably them. She had no desire to be found. She pulled out of his arms, needing to put some space between them. "What do you propose, then? We can't wait here for them to come and get us."

"No. I'd prefer to be left alone."

She nodded. "Agree."

He inhaled slowly. "I think we should stick together."

The way he said "together" made a shiver skate down her

spine. "Why?" Being alone wasn't an attractive option, but she didn't know this guy.

"So I can murder you." He rolled his eyes. "Christ. Are you always this suspicious?"

"Yes."

"We're alive, and everyone else is dead. We should stay together is all, until we figure out what happened."

She gritted her teeth. She hated how logical he sounded. "Fine."

"Don't sound so psyched." He offered a lazy grin before he was all business again. "Are there any other ways out of town? I came in on 25, but they'll be watching that."

She thought. "There's a road. It's barely a road…" She shook her head. The road that passed Kitty's house was more like a trail, a roundabout way to get out of town. The kids used it for quadding, mostly. It was steep and in bad shape. "It's not an easy drive."

"Perfect. Let's go."

Of course something like that wouldn't deter someone like him. She sighed. "All right, Rambo. My car's that way." She nodded down the street to her Cavalier.

"That's your car?" He wrinkled his nose as if he smelled something bad.

She looked at her car again. Okay, so fine. Even she had to admit it looked pretty shabby, with its blue paint pockmarked with rust. But his disgust irritated her. "That's it."

"Right. Come on." He grabbed her arm again. He started toward the Keilmans' again, rounding the corner of the building. "My bike is around back."

"Wait. Bike? Like motorcycle?"

He nodded, still towing her along.

Her heart picked up, like the rev of a Harley's engine. No way. No motorcycles. She'd fallen off a dirt bike a couple of years ago and broken her collarbone. Even now, years later, the thought of riding without car walls made her palms slick. "I don't think so, pal. Unless you want me to ride on the handlebars of a ten-speed, I don't do bikes. Ever. Besides, you don't know the road. If we're going anywhere, we go in my car. And I drive." Blue yanked her arm out of his grip. "And please stop pushing me around. Your excessive testosterone is showing."

He dropped his hand. "Right. Sorry."

She paused, taken aback. With his short-trimmed hair and tanned, lined face, she hadn't pegged him as the easy apology sort. More the chest-thumping, crush-a-beer-can-on-his-head type. The miscalculation softened her. "It's okay."

"No bikes, though?"

"No. An accident..." She tilted her chin up. She didn't have to explain herself to him.

He searched her face, like he was reading her mind. Then he nodded. "So we take your car. But I drive." He started running toward the car. Surprised, she picked up her pace to keep up.

"Fine." She fished the keys out of her pocket and pressed them into his palm, not letting them go immediately. "But take it easy on her. She's vintage."

He snorted.

As they reached the car, Seth kept glancing behind them, toward the east where the helicopter had landed. They slipped into the Cavalier's front seat. Hurrying, Blue gathered the trash on the floor of the passenger seat and tossed it in the back—two empty Big Gulps, five Babybel casings, and a dirty pair of socks—so she had somewhere to put her feet.

Seth chuckled, and the sound did something strange to her stomach. But he didn't comment as he started the car. She scowled at him. "Don't judge."

He grinned, the sight of his straight, white smile irritating her. He shifted the old car into drive, and they peeled out, heading west toward the mountains.

She stared in the rearview mirror until the buildings in Glory got too small to see.

"Did you check the whole town?" she asked him, looking straight ahead. "You know. For…survivors?" She tried to sound casual. Failed.

In her peripheral, his fingers tightened on the steering wheel. "I found eight bodies. Eight."

"Eight?" So many. And if they looked anything like Gran and the Murphys, she knew exactly what he wasn't saying.

"Yes." He swerved to miss an exceptionally large pothole before jerking the car back on the path, spitting gravel and dust behind them. "The bed-and-breakfast. The hardware store. And the farm. Eight."

"And I saw Gran and the Murphys. Three." Three. It was a small number. It didn't sound big enough to hold all the pain she felt.

"You were close to your grandmother." It was an observation, not a question.

"Yes. She raised me." Except that was too simple. Gran hadn't only raised her. She'd been her everything.

"I'm sorry." His words were soft. "I lost a good friend, a couple years ago. It was horrifying. I can't imagine losing someone I'd loved my entire life."

Blue hazarded a glance at him. His eyes remained on the road, necessary to navigate the trail's massive ruts and ditches, not even looking at her. He hadn't shared his story to see how she'd react.

He'd shared so she would know that he understood.

That sympathy squeezed past her strong facade. In this car, with his understanding, everything pressed in on her. The aching loss, the bone-numbing pain. Her fingers trembled. To stop the movement, she pressed them in her thighs until it hurt. She *had* lost someone she'd loved for her entire life. She didn't have many people she loved, and now one of them—the most important—was gone.

She gazed out the window again, blinking hard, forcing the tears to stop. When she was confident her voice wouldn't shake, she finally said, "She was amazing. She didn't deserve this. I don't know what happened, but she didn't deserve this."

"No. She didn't."

He maneuvered the car through a curve, decelerating a bit. That's when she noticed his speed. "Christ. What's wrong with you? How fast are we going?"

"Right now, about forty-five. We were going faster a second ago, but the speedometer seems to be broken. What year is this thing, anyway?" He took another turn, bouncing her car through another series of potholes.

"It's a 1993. I don't have a car payment," she defended. Seth snorted, and she scowled at him. "And you're going to kill us."

"We'll be fine. The car, maybe not."

She opened her mouth to school him when he nodded up the road. "Hey. Up ahead. Does that road go anywhere?"

He pointed at the Laughtons' driveway.

Kitty.

"Yes." She patted his arm to get his attention. His forearm was firm, solid. She pulled her hand back. "We need to stop. That's the Laughtons' driveway."

"Not a great time for a visit." Even as he said it, the car slowed, and they barely made the curve.

Her fingers dug into the door armrest. They were lucky her Cavalier didn't lose a tire, making a turn like that. "We need to see if they were affected by this flu. Don't you want to know how far the killing spread?"

When he didn't readily agree, she added, "Besides, this is my friend Kitty's house. I need to see her. Before we go." They both knew she meant she wanted to see if she was still alive. "It'll only take a minute."

He didn't argue, and she was thankful.

They hit another turn at breakneck speed, and she bit her lip, pressing her pink Chucks into the floor and gripping the seat. "Hey, maybe you have some sort of death wish, but I don't. How about we slow down a little?"

"I don't have a death wish," he grumbled. "I just like speed." But he eased his foot off the gas anyway.

She grinned, the first one of the day. It felt good.

"Right," she said and stabbed at the radio. Death Cab for Cutie erupted from it like a phoenix from the ashes, stopping their conversation.

They finished the harrowing drive up the mountain in silence.

Chapter Three

Blue's friend's house came into view as they rounded a corner. It was a cabin, barely visible where it sat tucked in the trees. Good. Goldstone's helicopter would have a hard time seeing it from the air.

Goldstone's helicopters. Christ.

What the hell had happened back there? Why was Goldstone all over some dinky town in Colorado? And how the hell had this pixie girl blown out all those windows?

He studied Blue next to him. He'd caught sight of her after he'd found the bed-and-breakfast owner and her husband. It wasn't the first time he'd seen dead bodies. He'd returned from the Middle East two months ago. It had been different there, though. They dressed differently, lived differently. It had been a different planet. These people…

He clenched his jaw. The image of those twin girls—the Barnetts, Blue had said—in side-by-side twin beds…it would stay with him forever. Their little bodies in matching Cinderella nightgowns with matching blood trails from their eyes and mouths.

As he'd returned to the main street, he'd felt like he'd been tossed into a horror movie. Or like he might be the last person in the world alive. The town was a ghost town. Silent. Eerie. Full of dead people.

That's when he saw her. This girl—Blue—standing in the middle of the street, arms outstretched, her eyes bouncing all over the street, like a caged animal. She was short. So was her blond hair, shorter than the way most girls he knew wore it, but it looked great on her. Like a shaggy Peter Pan, it seemed to go in every possible direction. Makeup smeared under her eyes. She looked fragile. Until she opened her mouth.

Then she'd tilted her head back and cried out. And broken everything. Like something straight out of a comic book.

That's how it looked, anyway. Glass shattering everywhere. He'd covered his head and ducked, waiting for it to end.

When it did, she'd fallen to the ground, defeated. He'd instinctively wanted to go to her. She'd looked broken, like she needed someone. But after what he'd seen her do, he'd approached her cautiously.

She didn't appear dangerous, though. In fact, he liked her. She had a smart mouth and spoke her mind. Those were some of his favorite qualities in people.

And he liked everything about the way she looked. Compact, a bit edgy, and curves in all the right spots.

Maybe it hadn't been her that blew out the windows. Goldstone could have done it with some sort of bomb. Electromagnetic or something. He'd seen a few pretty messed-up weapons. Never this, but that didn't mean it wasn't possible. Anything was possible.

Besides, she hadn't moved. He hadn't seen her do anything. And she'd seemed confused about it when he asked. He shook his head. Nah, it couldn't have been her. Probably a weird coincidence.

Seth stopped the car under a tree, out of sight of the sky,

and they slid out. He joined Blue on the other side.

She rested against the car, crossed her arms over her black polyester uniform shirt. "I guess we should go knock."

But she didn't move, only stood, staring at the quiet house. A long moment passed while she did nothing.

Not wanting to push her—she'd been through a lot today already—he stalled. "Anything I should know about the Laughtons?"

Her eyes remained trained on the quiet house. "Parents. Dad—Mike—works in Raton. See him at the bar where I tend sometimes. Mom—don't know her name—stays home. Daughter, Kitty, a year younger than me."

He sensed her anxiety, her worry for her friend. "You and Kitty are close?"

"We were close in school. We've drifted some since graduation. Her parents…they're strict."

The front porch light was on. They had electricity here. All the power had been cut to Glory.

He checked his phone in his pocket. Still searching for a network. He'd lost cell service as soon as he'd driven into Glory last night. No internet, no phone. He hated being disconnected. Maybe the Laughtons had somewhere he could at least plug his phone in, to rejuice it. Maybe they'd get internet closer to civilization. He needed to know if anyone else was affected. What if the entire country had been wiped out?

Then again, those guys from Goldstone looked pretty healthy to him.

On a whim, he pressed the button that released the phone's battery. Phones with batteries could be traced, and he preferred to remain untraceable. Maybe he was paranoid, but better safe than sorry.

"What's wrong?"

He tucked the phone back in his pocket and glanced at

Blue. "What do you mean?"

"You wrinkled your nose."

"Nothing."

In front of them, the house felt peculiar. "Maybe they aren't here," he offered, even though he didn't believe it for a second. They were in there. They both knew it.

Blue turned to meet his eyes. She didn't buy that, either. But she nodded and started for the porch anyway, her back straight and her hands steady.

He followed. In that moment, he admired the hell out of her.

She banged on the door and yelled, "Mr. and Mrs. Laughton? Kitty? It's Blue Michaels. Are you home?"

No one came. The swing next to them swayed. After long moments, she knocked again. Nothing.

It was now or never. Seth reached for the doorknob.

She grabbed his sleeve. "Hey. What are you doing? You can't just go in."

"I think we can. Should, actually." Because they had to know. And what if the Laughtons were in there, dying, right now? He twisted the knob, and the door opened. "Lemme guess. No one locks their doors around here."

"Yeah. Not a lotta crime," she whispered back. Their eyes met, and neither missed the irony. He stepped inside onto gleaming ceramic tiles.

"Mr. Laughton?" he called, taking in the neat living room with its comfortable furniture and obviously used fireplace. Magazines lay on the coffee table—*Seventeen*, *Better Homes and Gardens*, and *Men's Health*—along with an iPod and a half-eaten muffin. This was the kind of living room he wished he'd grown up in. "Mrs. Laughton?"

Blue turned right, through the living room and into what looked to be the dining room. He followed the hall in front of him, and it opened into the home's warm kitchen. The scene should have been domestic bliss, with the bananas on the counter and the coffeemaker open, cleaned recently.

But the dead body on the floor ruined the coziness. The remnants of sickness were apparent in the sink. The hair on Seth's arms lifted. Damn, not another one…

Grim, Seth dropped down next to the middle-aged woman—Mrs. Laughton, he assumed. A quick feel at her neck confirmed her death, though he probably hadn't needed to check, what with the blood trails on her cheeks and from her nose. She was cool to the touch.

He looked up to find Blue, her hand over her mouth and her blue eyes as large as quarters. He shifted, trying to shield the body from her sight. "I'm sorry."

And he was. He hated seeing this, and he hadn't known this woman or her family. This must be so much harder for Blue, stumbling across friends and relatives.

She nodded, her eyes watery. But she dropped her shaky hand. "Let's find the rest of them, then," she whispered as she headed to the door, giving Mrs. Laughton a wide berth. Her movements were jerky, as if her limbs weren't working properly.

He had the strangest impulse to reach for her as she passed him. To squeeze her hand or…something. But he didn't.

When she'd gone down the hall, Seth swiped his hand over Mrs. Laughton's eyes, closing them. She looked slightly less gruesome, though the blood on her cheeks didn't help. Then he stood and followed Blue upstairs, determined she shouldn't come across anyone else without him.

Blue halted at the top of the steps, in front of the bathroom. Turning, she looked down at him, her lips white. "Mr. Laughton." Then she nudged her head behind her, indicating the bathroom.

Sure enough, Mr. Laughton lay in a heap on the tiles in

front of the toilet.

His stomach sick, Seth took Blue's hand, unable to keep from reaching for her this time. Together, they left the man there, continuing deeper into the upstairs. Ahead of him, she opened a door and peeked in before moving on. He glanced in as he passed. The master bedroom. Empty. The next door swung open, and Blue stopped. She gripped the doorframe, her knuckles white.

"Kitty?"

A chill crept down his spine. He had no idea what to expect, but he stepped behind Blue anyway, determined that she not face whatever it was alone. He rested his hand on her shoulder, so she knew he was there. The feel of her under his fingers comforted him. He didn't pause to examine his sudden surge of protectiveness.

Because Blue was so short, he searched the dark room over her head, looking for adversaries. It took a moment for his eyes to adjust to the darkness. Then he saw her. Curled in the corner, her legs tucked up to her chest and her head resting on her knees, a mass of dark hair falling around her. She appeared to be wearing a pale dress of some sort.

Until she spoke, he thought she could have been a ghost.

"Please," she whimpered. "Please go away."

Blue stepped in. "Kitty? It's me. Blue." Her voice cracked with emotion, as if being rejected by this girl was the last straw.

The girl's head lifted slowly. All Seth could make out was long dark hair and an oval face that shone white in the otherwise dark room. "I know. I know both of you."

What? He'd never met this girl before in his life. He was sure of it.

She looked right at him, brushing her hair out of her face to reveal big pale eyes. "I know I've never met you before, Seth. I can hear your thoughts."

That's impossible.

Blue's shock shouted through the room without a sound. It hurt Kitty's head.

She'd thought the same thing around midnight last night. She'd clutched the toilet in her parents' bathroom—Dad had quarantined himself in the other one—and thrown up so many times she'd thought she'd die.

Then the flashes began. Explosions behind her eyelids, like fireworks, followed by the worst headache of her life.

That's when she'd heard them.

Her mom, tinged with her mother's signature meekness. *This is my fault. Mike is sick, Kitty, too, it sounds like. I bet that meat was bad.* Upstairs, there was Dad's ranting. *Who didn't wash their hands properly? Why don't they listen to me? There are ways to do things. The two of them will be the death of us.*

Later, as her mother's breath became shallow and her head throbbed, she worried for her, Kitty, her daughter. *I'm dying. I can't leave Kitty alone with Mike. He'll smother her.*

She'd worried for nothing. Her father had already died, his last thoughts filled with an old girlfriend and regret.

Kitty's throbbing and aching ended, then, and her stomach stopped revolting.

That's when the tears came.

She crawled into her room, left the lights off, and rocked herself. The stillness of the house filled her, the silence.

What had happened? What should she do now?

Mom couldn't tell her the right thing to do, and Dad couldn't ridicule her for doing the wrong thing. So she'd stayed there, with the corpses of her parents in the other rooms, for hours, probably, until she heard Blue and Seth arrive.

Even before they came in, she could hear them on the porch, wondering what they would find. Blue's hope, her wish to find Kitty living and breathing. Her memories of her grandmother, of the Murphys, the heartbreak and guilt. Seth's stoicism, his admiration for Blue, his flare of jealousy at their home. If only he knew…

All the while, as they crept inside, she'd huddled in her room, trying to breathe and block them out. Trying not to be a horrible freak.

She can't hear thoughts.

"I thought the same thing. Yet there it is." Kitty's whisper broke the silence.

It took Blue a second to realize she'd been speaking to her. "Don't do that."

"Do what?"

"Talk to me when I haven't said anything."

"Sorry." Yeah, that probably would be annoying.

Blue turned to Seth. He wasn't looking at her, though. He was too busy staring at Kitty as if she was naked and on fire. Kitty pulled her knees closer to herself.

Seth's thoughts jerked from military men he knew to the flu he'd had last night. Then he focused on Blue and remembered the windows exploding along the street in Glory.

Kitty turned to Blue, too. "Why did the windows in Glory blow out?"

"What?" Blue's eyes widened in horror. *How does she know about the windows in Glory?*

"He's thinking about it." Kitty nodded to Seth.

Blue glared at him. "Why are you thinking about that?"

He stepped back from them both. "Christ."

"You asked me about the windows back in town. Why?"

He sighed. "Because it was crazy timing. You yelled. The windows broke. I blamed a bomb or electromagnetic pulse or something. But, now, after seeing this"—he nodded toward Kitty—"I wonder if you didn't have something to do with it."

Blue shook her head. *No. No way. That couldn't have been*

me. The sheet stunt was strange, but the windows, too?

Kitty glanced at her. "What sheet?"

"Stop it, Kitty." *How is she doing that?*

"What sheet?" Seth echoed.

Blue swiped her bangs from her forehead, somehow managing to look chic and punky even in distress. Kitty hadn't even changed out of her nightgown.

Shaking her head, Blue shifted from one foot to the other. "Gran. I had the flu. I woke and found her...well, I couldn't go to her." *God, I sound like such a coward.* "Anyway, I wanted to stop looking..." *And the sheet covered her by itself.*

"You moved the sheet by yourself?" Someone else had the flu and woke up a freak. Kitty didn't want to be comforted by that, but she was.

"Yes. I mean, no. I don't know." Blue dug her hand into her hair. "The sheet moved. I don't think I did it."

This is insane. This can't be happening. Seth glanced around the room. "Try now. Pick something and move it."

Oh, right. Even as Blue thought it, she focused on the bed, and it lifted off the ground a half a foot.

No way. Just no way. Blue skipped back, her hand to her mouth. The bed dropped to the floor with a crash.

Kitty got to her feet, her bare toes cool against the hardwood. "You did it."

"No way."

"You already said that."

Blue scowled at her. "No, I didn't."

"Oh." *Yeah. Guess not.*

"This is insane. It must have been that flu." Blue's voice shook with anger, and she began to pace. "If I could have done this yesterday, I would have caught that extra tray of glasses at the bar instead of making another trip. And Clay, oh, Clay." She growled. "That guy pinched my butt again after I warned him not to. If I could do this, he would have woken up this morning with more hurting that his usual hangover."

"Do it again." Seth put his hands on his hips, a scowl on his face. "Move something else." *There must be some logical explanation.*

Blue's face darkened, and her thoughts followed suit.

Kitty stepped back. Suddenly, she was bombarded with all sorts of thoughts from both of them, and it was too much. She hit the wall behind her and dropped to the floor again. She covered her ears and tried not to hear.

She needed something, anything to distract her.

A prayer, said a million times, popped to her mind, and she chanted it in her head mindlessly. Her mother said her religion had saved her. Kitty never knew from what, but after a lifetime with her father, she could guess. So, she took her mother's advice and dived in.

When she finished the first prayer, she began again. She couldn't remember the order of the rosary, but the exact configuration couldn't matter that much, right?

She'd get credit for trying, wouldn't she?

Chapter Four

Blue stared at him, with his defensive posture and his firm jaw. He wanted her to perform. Like a circus monkey.

As if finding out she could move things without touching them was hard on *him*.

Anger flooded her. She didn't need this right now.

"Oh, do it again, huh?" She glanced at Kitty's dresser. A jar of cream jumped and zipped across the room. It crashed against the wall, making Kitty jump and white goo splatter everywhere. A brush followed it, connecting with a thud. As Blue got the hang of it, she let her gaze fly, and the contents of the room exploded around her. The blankets, the pillows, a stuffed bear. She spared the television—those were expensive—but everything else tumbled and twisted as if on a breeze, with barely any effort at all.

The rage was heady, and it filled the empty spots. Heat rushed to her face, warming her where she'd been cold. She wanted to curse, to scream. To curl in a ball and cry. To be home, where she belonged, in the place where she'd smiled with her gran and felt loved and whole.

She turned on Seth and gave him a mental nudge.

"How'd I do?" He stumbled backward, his eyes wide, his hands coming up as if to defend himself. A flash of alarm passed over his face.

In light of his fear, she froze. What was she doing? This wasn't her, not at all.

When she allowed herself to meet his eyes, he met her gaze with his steady gray one. There was no frustration or judgment there, only understanding and concern. The anger left her. Slowly, seeping out, not in a rush. In its wake, all she had was her loss and uncertainty.

What would happen to them now? They had nowhere to go. Maybe her life hadn't been perfect before, but she'd known where she belonged. She'd had someone who loved her.

He continued to watch, his eyes searching her, as if he could see every emotion racing through her.

She dropped her eyes, and the huge expanse of his chest stretched before her. He smelled good, despite the stress of their situation. Like shampoo and mint. She swallowed, suddenly awkward.

She had the strangest urge to reach for him. To let herself fall forward.

"Yes. That's fine." His whisper swept over her, and she closed her eyes. He didn't say any more, but he didn't have to, it seemed. She felt like he got it, her loss and heartache. Everything.

He wasn't the enemy, after all. He'd seen all the bodies, too. He'd had the flu, too.

He'd had the flu…

Her brows dropped, and she looked him over. He didn't look any different. But she and Kitty didn't look different, either. "So what are your new superpowers?"

"What?" He stiffened. That obviously hadn't been what

he'd expected her to say.

"If you had the flu that caused this, then why aren't you moving things with your mind or hearing thoughts?"

His eyebrows dropped. "You think I lied?"

She shook her head quickly. "No. I didn't say that." And she didn't mean that, either. She didn't have any reason to believe him, but she realized that she did. The thought terrified her. "I only mean, have you tried?"

"Tried what?"

"To touch your nose with your tongue." She rolled her eyes and folded her arms over her chest. "What do you think? To move things with your mind."

"No. I haven't."

"Maybe you should."

Seth stared at her, then at Kitty, studying them, a crinkle forming in his forehead. Then he nodded, as if he convinced himself. "You know, you're right. Maybe something is different about me, too." He squared his shoulders and scanned the room, his brow furrowing. Then he took a deep breath. "So, how do I do it?"

Blue considered. "I don't really know."

"Helpful."

"I focus on something and…ask it to move." Really. That sounded ridiculous. It *was* ridiculous. Ask it to move. Lovely.

Seth's look told her he agreed. "Right. Ask it to move." He turned to the desk chair. He squinted and grimaced. He moved his hand.

Nothing.

In the awkward silence afterward, Blue couldn't help herself. She mentally picked the chair up and twisted it in the air.

Seth spun, his eyes widened in horror and awe. "My God. Did I do that?"

She set the chair back down, immediately feeling bad.

"No. That was me."

His face stormed over, and he stalked to the doorway. "This is stupid."

He slammed the door behind him. Blue listened to him go before meeting Kitty's eyes.

"That wasn't nice," Kitty said as she flitted around, picking up things Blue had sent flying. The room looked like there'd been a burglary. Guilt swept through her. It hadn't been cool to wreck Kitty's room like this. She'd lost her stuff there for a minute. No need to take it out on Kitty.

She focused on the contents, trying to remember where she'd gotten all the pieces. As she recalled, she sent them back with her mind. Strange as it was, this gift could definitely come in handy.

"Sorry about your room," she offered.

Kitty shrugged. "It's fine."

No, it wasn't, but it was nice of her to say so. "And you're right. That wasn't nice."

"But you were feeling a bit self-conscious and lashed out."

That deserved a scowl. "Yes, Kitty. I was. Thank you for reminding me."

"Sorry." Kitty looked much younger than eighteen in her long nightgown. "But I've known you for years, Blue. It didn't take mind reading to know that."

Blue sighed, feeling bad for snapping at Kitty. She was winning friends and influencing people left and right around here.

She watched Kitty tidy. She understood the need to do this, but they didn't really have time for cleanup. "We should go, Kit."

Kitty's hands paused. "What do you mean?"

Instead of explaining, Blue allowed her memories of the helicopter to play across her mind along with Seth's explanation about Goldstone.

"He thinks they did this to us?" Kitty's eyes widened. Her hands shook as she clutched her elbows, seeming to fold in on herself.

"Yes. But we can't figure out how." It didn't make sense. None of it.

"We're far from town. At least ten miles. I can't imagine they'd look here."

"I don't think we should chance it." Blue motioned to the other girl's nightgown. "You might want to put something else on."

Kitty looked down. "Right. Can't be running around in my nightgown, can I?" She opened her dresser and sifted through again, pulling out a pair of jeans and a T-shirt. She seemed so casual. Maybe she was in shock. Losing her parents, reading minds… It might be too much for her.

Blue stepped toward the other girl, thinking she should say something. "Kitty, you know…"

Without turning, Kitty answered. "Blue. I don't want to talk about it."

"Whatever you say." All righty, then. No talking about it. That was fine by her. Changing the subject, she motioned at her ruined work clothes. "Hey, could I borrow something clean, too? I haven't changed since…" Her throat tightened, and she couldn't seem to continue.

"Sure. Here." The other girl tossed her another pair of jeans and a tee.

"Thanks." Blue turned away to give them both some privacy. She kicked off her Converse and stripped out of her dirty clothes. The jeans were a size or two too big, but Kitty tossed her a belt without a word and Blue cinched them closed, folding the bottoms up once. She yanked the clean tee over her head, feeling almost human again.

She gathered her dirty things and left. Kitty deserved a

moment to collect her thoughts and finish up in her room, alone. Blue would have liked the same before she had to run. It hadn't happened like that.

Besides, she should find Seth. Apologize. That had been a pretty cruddy thing to do.

But Kitty had been right about her being self-conscious, as much as she hated to admit it. She'd always been the weird kid. The kid whose father committed suicide to avoid jail time for tax evasion. The kid whose mom left her behind.

Growing up like that in a small town hadn't been easy. Over the years, she'd convinced herself she didn't care what anyone else thought. She'd had Gran, and Gran loved her. But now Gran was gone. And this—being different, being strange again—brought all those elementary school feelings back. She'd stopped being the confident girl she'd grown into and gone back to the days when she'd punched Jack Barnett in the nose when he said her parents had left because of her.

That was her baggage. It wasn't fair to take it out on Seth.

She scurried past the bathroom, not looking at Mr. Laughton. There'd been too much death today. She couldn't deal with it all right now. She took the steps down two at a time, calling out, "Hey, Seth," as she went, trying to figure out how to patch things up with him.

But a rhythmic beating, like a swarm of bees, filled the air, becoming louder.

The helicopter. Goldstone.

"Kitty! Now!" she yelled up the stairs, panic making her voice higher. Her heart picked up as she dashed through the hallway, scanning the little downstairs for Seth. Nausea swept through her. He'd probably been pissed and gone out to the car.

"No." It came out on a whisper. She didn't know when in the past few hours he'd become so important to her, but he had. Maybe because they were in this together. Maybe because he seemed to get how she felt about losing Gran. She didn't know. But she sure as hell knew she didn't want Goldstone to get him.

Kitty joined her. "Seth's outside."

Blue nodded. One benefit of having Kitty around: no need for chatter.

She slid the door open, peeking out. The steady beat of the helicopter's propellers sounded above them. It must be directly overhead. "They found us."

Kitty shook her. "No. They don't know we're here."

"You can hear them?" From so far?

Kitty wasn't listening to her, her eyes closed and her mind in the sky. "They know my house is supplied by well water. There was something in the water in town. A chemical, a drug. Something to change us. They think our house is safe because we don't get water from town." She opened her eyes, pain naked on her face. "That's true. But my father insisted on dessert at Murphy's last night. He wanted Mrs. Murphy's pie."

Blue didn't have time to soothe her. "What else?"

She looked back at the sky. "They need to catch whoever's left. To contain us, keep us quiet." Their eyes met again. Kitty's brow dropped. "They're looking for someone else, too. The doctor who did this. He's on the run."

What? She didn't have time to think about that. "Where is Seth?"

She followed Kitty's eyes across the porch, out into the middle of the driveway. What she saw chilled her.

The helicopter became deafening. Seth, in his camo pants, black T-shirt, and shorn hair, stood squinting up at the sky, a glare on his handsome face. His legs were apart, his hands at his sides clenched into fists. Even from the porch, Blue could tell every muscle was tensed, as if ready to fight.

Which was crazy. Just nuts.

"My God," Blue breathed.

"He's angry. So angry," Kitty said. She sank to the porch floor. "I can't...there's too much...so violent..." She covered her ears.

But Blue didn't check on her. She stumbled forward, tripping down the steps. "Seth, you have to move!"

The helicopter dropped, getting closer to the ground, and the buzzing of the rotors intensified. She froze. The wind picked up, stealing her breath, and she braced herself against it. A man hung from each side of the black helicopter. The way they held their assault rifles spoke to an intimate familiarity with the weapons.

The men moved, working quickly, and a rope dropped from each side of the aircraft. If she wasn't so terrified, she'd admire their efficiency.

"Seth! Get away from it!" The first man rappelled down, right above Seth, but he didn't move. If anything, he braced his legs apart, as if he planned to take the guy on.

Why wasn't he listening? He'd lost it. No other explanation. "Christ, Seth! Go!"

She stepped toward him. He was going to get himself killed.

No more death today, she decided. And definitely not Seth.

But before she managed more than a step to help him, he exploded into the air, soaring toward the helicopter, at least three stories high.

Seth couldn't hear thoughts or move things with his mind. But he could fly.

He didn't know how he did it.

One moment he was paralyzed with fury. He'd watched the Little Bird crest the trees and felt pursued.

Hunted.

Since joining the military, he hadn't felt so helpless. It was one of the reasons he'd joined up. Even in Afghanistan, he hadn't felt outgamed. They'd always had the upper hand. They were better trained, better equipped.

Just better.

But now? Seth had no weapons, nothing to protect himself. These guys were tracking them like criminals. And worse? It wasn't only him. Inside, there were those two unarmed girls. Two civilians, like Bobby.

They would be killed. Like the people in Glory.

Like Bobby.

As the Goldstone soldier rappelled down that rope, his rage became unbearable. These guys couldn't come in here and take them out. He wasn't a victim, and he sure as hell wouldn't let Kitty and Blue be victims either. He would save them all, if it was the last thing he did. This time, he wouldn't let anyone down.

He didn't know what he planned. But his body needed to do something.

And like that, his brain supplied that something to him.

It played out like a movie. He'd jump above the incoming soldier, drop down with one arm, secure the other man's knife, and cut the line. The guy would drop like a stone. Then Seth could shimmy up and take out the pilots. The helicopter would fall. And he would jump away to safety before it hit the ground.

Except no one could do that.

Even so, he sprang up, jumping higher than humanly possible. As the distance between him and the soldier closed, time slowed. No, that wasn't right. Time didn't slow, but his mind ran through the possibilities so quickly that he could make the minutest movements necessary to adjust his trajectory with no difficulty. A tiny shift of his hip to account for wind, considering the downdraft from the propellers. He landed exactly where he planned, gripping the rope right above the mercenary's head.

He used the momentum from his body—about thirty miles per hour, if he had to guess—to swing around the rope and kick with his legs. While he moved, he snagged the knife out of the other man's holster and cut the rope directly beneath him, above the soldier's head.

He didn't watch the other man fall. Instead he overhanded it up the rope.

Why was he so strong? He'd been in great shape before, but this? This was sick.

He pushed that aside as he shimmied up. One of the pilots leaned over, working the line, probably trying to unlatch it. Why didn't the guy shoot him? Would be much more effective. Didn't make sense. But his unusually adept mind seamlessly worked through the possible implications of the detaching rope. As the rope dropped, Seth lunged, grabbing the skid with both hands. He hoisted himself in an effortless pull-up and swung into the helicopter in one fluid movement, facing the stunned pilot.

He punched the guy in the face.

The pilot lifted off his feet and slammed into the back of the helicopter, sliding down into an unconscious heap.

Two steps brought him to the other pilot. Pilot number two had more time to prepare for the attack, and he dived at him with knife at the ready. As Seth grappled with him, the helicopter lurched, dropping fast.

In a far recess of his mind, he wondered why he wasn't freaking out. But the logic made so much sense. He could do this. It was irrefutable.

As they tilted, and he gained control of the remaining pilot's knife, a bright pink blur caught his eye.

Blue.

She stood in front of Kitty's house, staring up at him, and the starkness of her face registered even from this height.

As the helicopter lurched and dropped, it took only a split second to realize she would be hurt when the helicopter went down. Maybe even killed. The cockpit would land safely in front of her, but the propellers would break. He knew it, the events so certain it was as if they'd already happened. Fear twisted everything in his head.

His priorities realigned.

That wasn't acceptable. He knew it with an unfamiliar fierceness. Blue, with her sassy mouth and unpredictable vulnerability, could not be hurt. Definitely not because of him.

His brain supplied what he would have to do, almost without him thinking.

He followed the instructions.

Relieve pilot of his knife: check. Smash his nose with heel of hand: check.

Jump from helicopter, now thirty-two and a half feet from the ground, give or take an inch or so. Check. Bend knees at an exact forty-five-degree angle to absorb the majority of the weight from his fall, tilt to roll to the left and tumble into somersault to distribute his velocity.

That part hurt worse than he'd expected. He knew he'd sprained his left ankle. He'd chosen the left, because he wouldn't need his left foot to drive them out of here.

But it still hurt like a mother.

It wasn't the first time he'd felt pain, though, so he rolled to his feet in one smooth motion and was running instantly. He tore off toward Blue, who stood staring at him as if he was some sort of circus freak show.

Which, he admitted, he was.

He scooped her up without breaking stride. She seriously was a scrap of a thing, and her added weight did nothing to his speed. He tried not to think how good she felt against him or how much his ankle hurt. He picked up the pace and hauled ass away from the helicopter crashing behind him.

As he rounded the house with Blue in tow, the aircraft hit the ground with a deafening crunch, kicking up dust and knocking him off balance. He pitched forward, falling to his knees and dumping Blue unceremoniously onto the ground. He managed to roll to the side, but he couldn't halt his momentum completely.

She grunted as he landed half on top of her.

She was okay. His relief was overwhelming.

He shifted off her, wincing when he put weight on his ankle. Shit, that hurt. Something tickled his upper lip. He swiped at it, coming away with blood.

A nosebleed?

Blue rolled away to cough on her knees.

He crawled to her side, checking her over gently, looking for bruising and blood. "Are you all right?"

"Christ, Seth," she answered through a sputter, shifting away from him. He'd never been happier to hear someone growl at him. "Why'd you let them see you? Why didn't you hide?"

Why didn't he hide? Not feeling like answering that, he scowled at her. "I saved your life."

"No, you almost killed yourself." She got to her feet, glaring at him. Her blond hair stuck up in every direction, and this close he couldn't help but notice how blue her eyes were. The sun was hitting them just right. He could make out the darker blue circle around the outside. They were gorgeous.

Distracted, he missed what she was saying. "Sorry?"

"How'd you do that?"

"Do what?"

She smirked and waited. Right. He'd dived into a helicopter. From the ground. "I don't know?" It sounded like a question. Because he wasn't sure it was a good enough excuse or that he had a good answer. He tried again. "I just knew I could, all right? I knew the helicopter was right there. I knew I could stop it."

"You knew you could stop a helicopter."

"Yes." He ran a hand over his head. "Hey, you move things with your mind. Don't be so judgy."

She snorted.

"I watched it arrive, and suddenly, I knew I could do all those things." He glanced over at the now destroyed helicopter, where it smoked and creaked behind them. "Listen, we don't have time for this. I took out the helicopter. That makes you happy, doesn't it?"

"Are any of them…dead?" She gazed at the wreckage, her back straight and her lips tight.

He followed her gaze. At the time, all he could think about was saving Blue and Kitty and himself. This helicopter was against them, so he was against it. It was that simple. He fought people for a living, protected people with his hands and his skills. It was what he was trained to do. Them or us. And he preferred to be the last one standing.

Now, witnessing how disturbed she was, he thought on that. "Yeah. Probably. I threw one out of the helicopter from almost forty feet up."

She nodded with her eyes still on the mangled heap.

"I'm sorry." Why was he apologizing? He'd done what he had to do, hadn't he? "They were going to kill us," he defended, not understanding why it bothered him so much to see her upset. They were running from these guys, weren't they?

"No, they weren't." From the porch, Kitty cut into their conversation. "They wanted to take us prisoner. Take us with them."

He threw up his hands, gazing at the sky. God grant him strength. "Oh, well, even better. Prisoners. Of Goldstone."

Hell, no. He wasn't going to be anyone's prisoner. "Listen, I did what I thought was best."

Blue nodded again, but her jaw was set as she pushed past him. As if she was pissed that he'd saved them from being taken hostage. He turned to Kitty, looking for sanity in this chaos. "I did what I could."

"I know." The way she said it sounded tired. This wasn't the reaction he'd hoped for. Where were the thank-yous and the great jobs? Instead, he got attitude from one and creepy understanding from the other.

Well, whatever. He'd done what he thought was best, what had made sense in the moment. He'd thought they were in danger. Excuse him if getting rid of the guys who were after them wasn't a good thing.

"It's not that it isn't a good thing," Kitty added. "It's complicated. We need to leave, though. They called in our location. The other helicopters will be here in ten minutes."

"You know, it's really freaky when you do that."

"I know." Kitty nodded toward the shed behind him, tucked back from the house. "Ever driven an ATV?"

Finally. Some fun. "Hell, yeah."

All four of them: dead.

Blue hadn't tried to sort through the rubble, because Kitty hadn't sensed any thoughts or dreams there. Blue had seen enough dead bodies today. Any more might be her breaking point.

As they loaded the meager supplies they'd gathered onto Kitty's family's ATVs, no one said much, working quickly, consumed in their thoughts and all aware of the helicopters looking for them. Even Kitty left them to it in silence.

Blue tucked a jug of water on the grate behind the seat on

Mrs. Laughton's ATV, securing it with a bungee cord next to the bag of nonperishable food and spare clothes she'd thrown together. She tightened the strap around her supplies with too much force, and it made an unnecessarily loud snap in her haste. She'd rushed through the kitchen, intensely aware of Mrs. Laughton's body in the center of the room. They'd covered her with a blanket but agreed they didn't have time to bury Kitty's parents properly.

She'd regret that later, she was certain.

Next to her, Seth readied his own ride. His ATV had been Mr. Laughton's. Blue got the impression Mr. Laughton had been trying to compensate for something. Or a lot of somethings. His ATV's engine was beefed up something fierce. Green flames streaked along the sides, and the seat was tricked out with nail-head studs. Blue could taste Seth's eagerness to get his hands on the souped-up thing, to get going again. She gritted her teeth, her disappointment intense.

She'd been wrong about him.

Blue hated guns and violence. After all, her father had shot himself. To her, a gun had caused a lot of her problems, not solved them. But military men—men like Seth—believed guns and bloodshed fixed everything.

She'd certainly never thought she would be attracted to someone like that.

And she admitted that she was attracted to him. Very much.

Stupid body.

The sun was setting, casting fingerlike shadows through the trees. With its retreat, the heat had seeped out of the forest and had been replaced with a chill that lifted goose bumps on her arms. She returned to the car and grabbed the beat-up jean jacket from the passenger seat's floor. She swung it on, not bothering to button it.

Was she missing anything? She ducked into the backseat

of the Cavalier, inhaling the musty scent and squashing her nostalgia. She'd never see the pile of garbage again, and that bothered her for some reason. It wasn't like the car was reliable or even nice. It was stupid to care so much about it.

She grabbed her iPod, having forgotten she'd tossed it back there after work last night. Candy wrappers still littered the floor, and a handful of old paystubs were scattered on the backseat. She didn't think it mattered to leave those things. They were dealing with a high-level security company. They would know all there was to know about her by now. She slammed the door closed and walked around to the trunk. She popped the key latch and smacked her palm against the middle of it. The lock had broken a couple years ago. She probably could have had it fixed pretty cheap, but she'd felt kind of cool being able to open it with her hand. Like Fonzie on the *Happy Days* reruns Gran watched.

Trying to stave off the unexpected tears, she opened her eyes as wide as she could. The contents of her trunk swam in and out of focus, and she held the hatch open, because it wouldn't stay up by itself. Finally, her vision cleared, and she glanced over the handful of trash inside. As an afterthought, she removed the screwdriver and wrench she kept back there, in case, and allowed the trunk to slam shut with dull finality.

Turning from the car she hadn't realized she cared about so much, she joined Seth and Kitty.

"You ready?" Seth's face was unreadable. With his dusty camo and soldier chic, he managed to look hot in spite of all of this.

She gritted her teeth. "Yeah."

He nodded, retreating to his ATV and swinging a leg over it in a practiced move. Right, he drove a motorcycle. He'd know how to do this. Not that he didn't do everything with an easy grace. It was a little irritating.

She turned away, needing to focus. Needing to stop

thinking about him.

Beside her, Kitty did nothing to hide her misery. Her eyes were red, and tears still streaked her cheeks. Though Blue had always thought her family was strange—after all, they'd been friends for years, but she'd only been invited over a handful of times—this had been Kitty's home, and her parents still lay inside. Blue knew too much about how that felt. She'd run from her own home this morning, leaving her loved one behind, too. She squeezed her friend's arm. "You okay?"

Kitty nodded, glancing at the house once more. Fresh tears slid out of the corner of her eyes, and she didn't bother to swipe at them. Instead, she pressed the ignition switch, and the ATV roared to life beneath her, effectively ending any conversation they might have had.

Blue met Seth's eyes, and he only shook his head. The message was clear. *Don't press. She needs space.*

He was right. Pushing her friend wouldn't be fair. She'd talk when she was ready.

She held Seth's gaze for a moment. Who was this man who could kill people one moment and then intuitively understand what someone he didn't even know needed?

They stared at each other long enough for butterflies to set up residence in her stomach.

He broke the eye contact first, starting his machine with a lazy kick of his foot.

Still unsettled and conflicted, Blue mounted up as well. As the ATV rumbled to life beneath her, she couldn't help casting one last glance at her Cavalier. Leaving it felt wrong, as if she was abandoning the last bit of her normal life. Which maybe she was. People were hunting them, and she had no idea what would happen if they found them.

She might never return to Glory again.

She couldn't count how many times she'd dreamed of leaving Glory. Crummy jobs, too many bills, and worst, the fear that her grandmother wasn't getting the best care. But she'd never imagined she'd leave like this, running like a rat from the light.

Beside her, Kitty started off, leading them into the woods, and Seth followed closely behind her. In the distance, Blue could hear the beat of helicopter propellers. Letting up on the brake, she eased the ATV into motion. God, she hated open-air riding.

As she followed her companions, she refused to look back at the Cavalier.

It was only a car, after all. She was still alive. Most of Glory couldn't say the same.

Chapter Five

The trip down the mountain took less time than the trip up had taken in the Cavalier. Thank God for that. They heard helicopter propellers constantly at first, but they became less pronounced as the minutes passed. Instead of returning to the road, their little caravan made for the winding creek that fed into Trinidad Lake. They would camp near the lake until morning and then make the short trip from there into Trinidad, where they'd catch the Amtrak out of Colorado. Kitty insisted the Amtrak train didn't come through until midafternoon. She'd taken it to see her grandmother in Chicago a handful of times.

"Your grandma lives in Chicago?" Blue asked when she mentioned this. "How'd your family end up here?"

Kitty had shrugged. "Dad prefers seclusion."

Blue didn't doubt that. Mr. Laughton had been a weirdo. She tried to keep that thought to herself, and if Kitty heard it, she didn't respond.

They'd driven for a half an hour and darkness had fallen completely when Seth halted. Thank God for the nearly full moon or they'd probably have killed themselves riding through the night. They stopped in the thicker trees that covered the mountains and seemed to be resting in a valley of sorts. "I think the creek is right below us."

Seth glanced at Kitty, who nodded, but her brow was furrowed and her head tilted to the side. "What's wrong?"

Her eyes widened, and she waved, frantic, glancing over her shoulder. "Get down!"

"What?" Down? Did she mean on the ground?

Something burst from the trees beside them. It dropped at least fifteen feet out of the branches to tackle Seth. Blue's heart pounded in her ears as she screamed, scurrying from her ATV to hide beside it. She scanned the supplies strapped to the ATV, trying to see if any of it would help Seth.

It had to be a coyote or a bear. Nothing else moved that fast or could jump so far. But as Seth rolled away, Blue realized he was grappling with a large man, not an animal. Then she heard Kitty yelling like a maniac.

"Jack!" she screamed, swinging off her machine and rushing toward the pair as they wrestled in the dirt. "Jack, it isn't like that!"

Jack? And what wasn't like what?

Then Blue placed the name with the body she saw tangled with Seth. Jack Barnett, another boy from town. They'd found his parents and twin sisters dead this morning.

"Oh, shit."

As Blue watched, Seth slammed his fist into Jack's jaw. The connection's dull *thwack* made her wince. Jack took the punishing blow and then punched Seth in the ribs. He followed that hit with another to the kidney, causing Seth to stumble away.

Seth's jaw tightened and…there. His new talent. It was there, in the look of concentration, of extreme focus. He moved with strategy and calculation, as if his actions were part of an intricate choreography. He'd done the same against the helicopter back at Kitty's place.

He was trying to protect them. Again.

Warmth spread through her stomach. That intelligence, that protection. It was incredibly hot, even as she was terrified for both of them.

The two adversaries squared off, circling each other. Blue searched the area, trying to think of a plan, to find a way to separate them before someone really got hurt. All the while Kitty screamed from the sidelines, "Jack! He didn't kidnap us, you jerk. He's like us!"

"Wait." Blue reached over to snag Kitty's coat sleeve. "Jack's like us, too?"

Kitty shook her off. "Jack!" Then she spun, studied the trees, and tore off into the woods without any more explanation.

Blue took up where she'd left off—watching Seth and Jack try to kill each other.

Jack crouched and dived at least twenty feet across the forest floor, tackling Seth to the ground. In response, Seth grabbed him and threw him sideways. Jack tumbled through the air at least the length of two cars to slam into a fallen log. He rolled away and struggled back to his feet.

Seth grimaced at him and glanced up, considering. Then, from flat feet, he jumped straight up—insanely high—landing softly in the upper limbs above them.

As Blue watched, Jack followed Seth, jumping high into the tree, and settled on the limb a few feet from him. She might have been impressed if she wasn't so terrified for them. They were using these new skills as if they'd been born with them.

Seth tensed, preparing for Jack to dive at him. Her heart in her throat, Blue remembered they weren't the only ones with a new skill set. Jack looked pissed, and she wouldn't let him hurt Seth if she could help it.

Unsure if she was doing it right, she reached out with her mind. Focusing on two different points was more difficult than focusing on one, but she couldn't stand by while they killed each other. She didn't need to move them. She only needed to stop them from moving.

She closed her eyes, directing her attention toward the two men at the top of the tree. She willed them still with all of her might and hoped she was doing it correctly.

When she opened her eyes again, they remained where they stood in the top branches, in the same positions, like statues of gladiators. In a tree.

"I'm going to let you go in a minute," she called out. "But Jack, you need to stop. Seth is one of us, as you can see. And Seth? This is Jack Barnett. You found his family, the twins?" She gave them a moment to process that before she said, "Okay, here goes."

She dropped her paralysis and watched them both take deep breaths, gasping. They shifted, regaining their balance above her.

"What the hell?" Jack hissed. "You know we can't breathe when you do that, don't you?"

"Oh, God." She covered her mouth in horror. "I didn't know. I just didn't want you to kill each other."

Her nose tickled, and she swiped at it. Darkness on her hand caught her eye, and she lifted her fingers in front of her face. Blood. She scowled at it. Her nose was bleeding? She hadn't had a nosebleed since elementary school.

"Why, because you wanted to do it yourself?" Jack dropped through the tree, limb by limb, until he landed on the ground with a graceful leap.

She scowled at him, swiping at her nose again. Jack could be so difficult. "Watch yourself, Barnett. I look small, but I could take you." With these powers, anyway.

"You wish, Blueberry Muffin."

She rolled her eyes. What were they, in middle school? "Gee, Jack, you thought of that all by yourself? That college education must be really paying off."

"Whatever, Blue."

Seth fell to the forest floor next to him, giving him a shove. "You're real charming."

Jack addressed her again. "Who the hell is this?"

Seth crossed his arms over his chest. "Seth Campbell. Specialist, U.S. Army."

"The army?" Jack addressed her, not even looking at him. "I knew he was a stranger, but you got involved with someone in the army? After all of this? Are you an idiot?"

Was she?

She looked at Seth, and his gaze was unreadable. Her immediate instinct was to defend Seth. But she didn't know what to say. She didn't know much about him. He'd helped her get out of Glory, and she knew that he'd toss someone from high up if he felt threatened. She also knew that he made her heart beat a little bit faster, made her trust him when she probably shouldn't.

That wasn't much to go on. She finally said, "He saved my life. And he helped Kitty and me escape."

He snorted. "Oh, you remember that, do you?"

She scowled back at him. "Hey, you killed some people, too. Sorry if I'm having a hard time with that."

Jack turned on the other man, his fists clenched. "You killed people?"

"I took out the helicopter that was following us," Seth sneered. Then he turned back to her as he continued. "When I thought Blue might get hurt, I got her to safety." Something vulnerable flashed in his eyes. Seeing that, the chink in his armor, her heart clenched. He had done that. He'd protected her.

Impulsively, she joined him, taking up residence at his side. When his eyebrows dropped in question, she only tilted her chin up and remained silent.

The animosity bled from Jack's face, replaced by skepticism. "You took out a helicopter?"

"Yeah." Seth broke eye contact with her and crossed his arms over his chest.

"And how'd you do that?"

"I saw it," Kitty said, coming out of the trees, her hiking boots crunching the underbrush. Pine needles littered her messy ponytail. "I watched him jump up into the helicopter."

Someone followed her out of the woods, joining their little group.

Blue squinted at him in the dying light. "Lucas Kincaid?"

He waved awkwardly, his hand at his hip. "Hey, Blue."

Thank God, another familiar face. Luke had gone to Raton High with the rest of them. Word was that he helped care for his father. He kept to himself and went straight home after school, never getting involved in clubs or sports. Not that Blue was the sporty or clubby girl, either. But there had never been any hiding for her. Everyone knew who her parents were. She'd always liked Luke, though. As she'd spent more and more time caring for Gran, she thought of them as kindred spirits.

"Where did you come from?" They'd checked Glory. Luke lived on the mountain, though, not directly in town.

"I found him," Jack piped up. "After I found my parents and realized that someone had cut the power and phones to Glory, I took off. I ran up into the hills, to Parker Sinclair's place. Running's a whole lot easier like this."

Blue couldn't help her smile. "Don't you play football at USC?" The kids from Glory knew he did. Jack had been something of a football god at school.

"Yeah. Exactly. I play football. Doesn't mean I like to

run."

"Right."

"Anyway, Parker wasn't there. His wife or whatever she is…"

"Companion." Sue Bowman had been with Parker since Blue could remember. Years.

"Right. She was there. Covered up. But Parker wasn't there."

Strange. Parker was gone? Where would he go? The recluse spent the majority of his time holed up in his home library, reading and writing. He'd retired to Raton to write his manifesto or something like that. Bottom line, he didn't go anywhere. That he was missing was odd.

Seth's brow furrowed. "Did it look like there had been a struggle? Place a mess?"

"No. Looked the same as the last time I'd been there." The corner of Jack's mouth tilted up. "Five years ago, selling chocolate for Boy Scouts."

Awkwardness settled over them. Blue turned to Luke. "What are you guys doing here?"

"Trying to get away from helicopters and out of Glory. Like you guys, I bet. Jack heard you and came to check it out." He smiled and shrugged. She smiled back. It might be impossible not to smile back at Luke. With his glasses, shaggy hair, and warm brown eyes, he was like those singers in sensitive boy bands. Approachable.

"I thought you were in trouble." Jack glared at them.

That was almost nice. At least she would have thought so if it wasn't coming from Jack. "Where were you going?"

"My aunt lives in Trinidad." Jack nodded to the north. "I was going there. Luke decided to tag along."

"Seemed the thing to do." Luke shrugged. "Didn't want to stay home. My dad…"

He didn't go on, but he didn't have to. His dad was gone.

The whole group lapsed into silence, and Blue couldn't meet any of their eyes.

Now, farther from Glory with a little bit of time under their belts, the horror of it all was catching up with her. So many people dead. Jack had lost his entire family, as had Kitty. Luke's parents were divorced, she thought, but he'd still lost his father. And Gran…

All she wanted to do was hide, to get away from all of these people and be alone.

But she couldn't. It wouldn't be safe to be alone, and she knew that. Not now. Not with people searching for them.

After they were away, she'd decide where to go. Somewhere she might be able to breathe again.

She wrapped her arms around her waist and shivered.

"It's late," Seth finally said, breaking the silence, his eyes on her as if he'd been watching. "We should stay here for the night, like we'd discussed." As if it was all decided, he turned to his ATV and pulled the Laughtons' tent off the back. Moving off to the side, he unzipped the bag and began unloading the tent pieces.

The rest of them stared at each other. Blue looked at Kitty, who was gazing up at the sky.

"I'm not sleeping out here when I could sleep inside at my aunt's." Jack crossed his arms over his chest. "You losers feel free to camp with the coyotes. Me, I'm moving on. I'm following the creek into town."

Kitty didn't look at him when she responded. "Seth's all right, Jack. You should give him a chance." Her words were a suggestion, but they also held resignation. She knew as well as Blue did that Jack would do what he wanted. He always had.

True to character, Jack didn't even acknowledge her. "I'm out of here." He paused at the edge of the trees. "Luke?"

Luke shook his head, hands still in pockets, looking a little like he wanted to rub his toe in the dirt. "Nah, man. It's dark.

Maybe we should stay."

Jack stared at him, then at Blue and Kitty, before shaking his head. "Fine." He turned and slipped into the trees without looking back.

Kitty took a few steps after him. "He's upset. He shouldn't be alone." Her eyes flitted around the forest, as if she didn't know what to do. Which she probably didn't. Blue didn't envy her the ability to hear what they were all thinking.

"He didn't have to leave," she pointed out. "That was his decision." She tried to sound like she didn't care. But silently she cursed him out. Why did he have to be stubborn? Now they'd have to worry about him.

"You guys," Kitty pressed. "Jack lost his whole family. The girls." Her voice cracked, and Blue didn't doubt she was close to breaking down.

"I know, Kit. We all lost our families." Blue squeezed the other girl's arm. "But the rest of us are smart enough to know we shouldn't go anywhere alone in the dark." She handed Kitty a bottle of water from her pack. "Jack's a big boy. And you know him. If he wanted to go, he was going to go. We couldn't have stopped him."

Kitty stared at her. In the near darkness, her eyes flitted around, not resting on anything in particular, as if in panic. Or, more likely, listening to all of their thoughts. No wonder she was freaking out. Finally, she grabbed the water out of Blue's hand and opened it, turning her back on them.

"He'll be all right," Luke piped up as she propped her hands on her ATV and her head drooped. "It's Jack. He thinks he's invincible."

He meant it to sound comforting. But the comment only highlighted that Jack wasn't actually invincible. Even with his new powers.

Kitty began to unload, grabbing her sleeping bag, ignoring them. She slung the thing onto her back and headed over to help Seth.

When she was far enough away, Luke whispered, "What's up with her?"

"You probably don't have to whisper." Blue unhooked the bag of extra clothes. "She'll hear you anyway." At his quizzical look, she tapped the side of her head. "She can hear your thoughts."

His look of horror would have been comical at a different time. "No."

"Yes." She sighed. "And I can do this." With a nod of her head, she lifted his glasses off his face and sent them winging into her hand.

He stumbled backward. "My God."

"Yeah. Thanks to that flu or whatever it was." She held his glasses out to him. When he didn't take them, she laughed, trying to lighten the mood but sounding awkward even to her ears. "Crazy, right?"

She placed his glasses on the ATV and turned away, not wanting to see any more of his reaction. Would she ever get used to people thinking she was a freak? Probably not any sooner than she'd get used to being a freak.

She tried to change the subject. "I'm sorry about your dad, Luke."

It took him a long moment to respond. "Yeah. Thanks." He leaned on his hands on the ATV. "Where are you guys going, anyway?"

Where were they going? "I don't know. Right now? Away." Away from Goldstone and Glory and everything that had happened.

He nodded.

At the tent, Seth and Kitty worked side by side, saying nothing. She didn't want to join them—neither seemed in a friendly mood and she would prefer solitude—but she needed some sleep. Gran used to say that everything would look better in the morning.

Blue sure hoped so. Because things looked pretty shitty right now.

As she slung the backpack over her shoulder, she reached for the food bag. It levitated next to her.

She stilled with her hand over the bag, not touching it, and addressed Luke. "Please tell me that's you, because it's definitely not me."

"I didn't know I could do that." He looked as stunned as he sounded. He could move things like her. She wanted to grin, the relief was so intense. It wasn't only her. Not that she'd wish this on anyone else. But it was nice to not be alone with her weirdness.

Luke didn't seem as thrilled. She answered mildly, "Yeah. Sick, right?"

The bag dropped to the forest floor. He shrugged, not meeting her eyes. "Yeah. I guess."

She remembered her first reactions. The shock. The revulsion. The fear. She felt for him, she really did. But she was too tired to be supportive right now.

Together they carried or moved Blue's supplies to the tent.

Since Kitty and Seth weren't being chatty, she and Luke lapsed into silence, too. It was hard going, assembling the tent in the dark, but Seth didn't want to start a fire and alert the helicopters. Kitty took the lead putting the tent together, as she'd done it before. She dropped her silent treatment and offered instructions from memory.

Blue hunched down next to where Seth knelt, fiddling with the tent anchoring system, offering him two pegs she'd located in the darkness. "Here. I found these over there."

He didn't look up. "We're friends now?"

That wasn't fair. She scowled at his bent head. "I guess."

"Friends trust each other."

"Well, most of my friends don't kill people."

He sighed beside her, glancing sideways. "Right. Hey, I said I was sorry. Okay? I didn't think you'd be so opposed to me stopping people who wanted to kill us."

She handed him the hammer next to her, and he used it to pound in the anchor. "They didn't want to kill us."

"They had knives and guns, Blue. I didn't know they didn't want to kill us."

He had a point. None of them would know that if they didn't have Kitty along, listening in on everyone's thoughts.

She paused, studying him in the darkness. He looked pissed, irritated with her. And she tried to see it from his perspective. He'd gone into that helicopter assuming the men inside were trying to kill him. And he'd done it to keep her and Kitty safe.

Why? She got the impression that if it was only him, alone, he would have made other choices. But he seemed to have needed to protect them.

She was equally angry and touched.

"You're right. You didn't know." She sighed, suddenly overwhelmed with exhaustion. "And maybe you're trained to kill people if needed, but I'm not. I don't even eat meat, for Christ's sake."

"You're a vegetarian?" He snorted. "Figures."

She glared at him. "Now what the hell does that mean?"

"Nothing. Listen, I'm sorry. I was...I don't know. Afraid for us, I guess. And mad."

"You were mad so you killed some people? Remind me not to piss you off." She took one of the other stakes to the other side of the tent, wiggling it into the ground. His hand on her arm stopped her. This close, her heart picked up, and her breath caught. His fingers felt warm on her arm, and she found his grip much too comforting. Why was he so attractive?

In the dark, she could barely make out his pleading eyes.

"I'm serious, Blue. I thought they were here to kill us. Christ, they killed your whole town. How was I supposed to know they weren't trying to kill us, too?" He sighed, obviously exasperated. "I don't want to die. And I didn't what you two to die, either. Even if they aren't trying to kill us, they're trying to take us hostage. Who knows what they plan to do with us? I won't be someone's prisoner. And I can't think of anything happening to you. Or to Kitty."

Her throat tightened; she swallowed hard, held captive in his gaze. It had been so long since someone had taken care of her, she didn't know what to say. But she knew one thing for certain. He was right.

She wasn't being fair. He wasn't the bad guy. She was taking their circumstances out on him. But before she could acknowledge that, his face closed and he dropped his hand. "I wish you'd trust me. You trust those guys." He nudged his head toward Luke and Kitty. "You even trusted that jerk-off." She didn't have to ask who he meant. She recognized Jack when he was described to her.

She wanted to tell him she trusted him, but the words stuck in her throat.

"I trust that you'll get us out of here." That meant something, right?

"I mean me. As a person. I wish you'd trust me."

She sighed. "I've known them a long time. That's all."

"So, time wins you over." He tightened a rope with a tug.

She considered. Not time, necessarily. More like familiarity. After all, she didn't like Jack. Never had. But she knew him. And the longer she knew someone, the more predictable their behavior became. She didn't like not knowing how people would react.

Seth? He didn't seem untrustworthy. If anything, her instincts told her she could trust him completely. But stuff like that scared her. She didn't have a history to prove that. In her life, she banked on predictable. After her father died, her mom had gone off the deep end. By the time Gran stepped in and pressed for custody, Blue had spent five years flitting from one commune to another, exposed to things a six-year-old shouldn't see. Gran had brought order to Blue's life, and she'd come to depend on it. She didn't like to be surprised. Seth could surprise her. And she didn't like that one bit.

"I need to know you better, that's all."

"That's bullshit, and you know it." He looked up then, their eyes meeting in the dim moonlight. They were so close, their noses almost touched. She held her breath, her stomach tightening. She felt every inch of her skin. "You're scared. I'm not sure what you're afraid of, but that's what this is."

"Am not." But her voice sounded small and breathy.

His mouth tilted up on one side. In the moonlight, she could see that understanding again, in his eyes. "You can tell yourself that, but I don't believe you."

It should bother her more, how much he seemed to see through her. Usually, when people came too close, she bolted. But right now, all she could do was stare at his mouth. He had a great mouth, a great peak on his top lip and a full lower lip. Completely kissable.

She leaned closer, their mouths only a breath apart.

"I'll keep you safe. I promise." The vow fanned her face, and she closed her eyes.

He was asking her to believe in him. She didn't know if she could. Not yet.

But part of her really wanted to.

She jerked back, away from that thought and from him, lost her balance, and fell onto her backside in the underbrush.

"You okay?" He leaned over her, concern in his eyes.

Good thing it was mostly dark. Stupid fair complexion, she could never pass off a blush. "Yeah. Fine."

She got to her feet quickly.

"Blue..." he said, calling for her. But she moved away quickly, joining the others. Trying to forget Seth's mouth and avoid Kitty's eyes. Did she think she was being stupid, too?

Blue threw herself into setup—anything to distract herself.

By the time they finally had the tent up, the night air had chilled. They bundled in extra layers, sharing with Luke. The tent was made for three—the Laughtons never camped with anyone else—but they managed to squeeze in anyway.

When Seth zippered the flap closed, the inside was snug. As their resident military and survival guru, he arranged them in the best configuration possible based on their body sizes and varied heights.

It was only then that she realized she would be sleeping pressed up next to Seth.

Luckily, it was the back of him. When he lay beside her, she tensed, sure she'd never be able to relax. The minutes dragged on as she listened and felt the steady rise and fall of his breath. He was warm and smelled wonderful. How'd he manage that after a day of running and two fights? But he did. Still musky and fresh. As if the laws of sweating didn't apply to him.

Thanks to his heat and her exhaustion, her body gave out on her, and she dozed off.

Sometime later, though, she woke screaming with dreams of blood-trailed faces and helicopters full of guns. Then, in the dead of night, she knew it was his hands that soothed her, and she calmed.

She drifted back to sleep, her fingers still tangled with his.

Chapter Six

Someone was in the woods.

Not three or four hours after falling asleep, Seth awoke, instantly alert. He knew it had only been a few hours because his body still ached with exhaustion. He'd functioned before on much less sleep. You didn't survive Afghanistan if you couldn't learn how to forget you were tired. So, as always, he pushed his discomfort aside and focused on the noise outside.

Only, the noise wasn't close. Whoever was coming through the trees was probably still a half a mile away.

Apparently he had some new super hearing, too.

And whoever was coming needed some stealth training. They couldn't have made more noise if they tried.

He still held Blue's hand. She'd whimpered, crying out, about an hour ago. After the day they'd had, he figured she was entitled to her nightmares. He'd soothed her the best he could, and she'd softened again, groggy with sleep, and curled back into him. As she fell asleep, the press of her against his back had kept him awake for long minutes afterward.

"Blue," he whispered, shaking the hand he still held. "You awake?"

"No," she grumbled. "Go away."

"Morning person. I like that."

"I am a morning person. It's not morning."

He chuckled. "Right. We're about to get company."

He'd said it as lightly as he could. He hadn't wanted to scare them. It might be a hiker. A fisherman. Someone completely innocent.

His attempt to sound casual didn't work. Blue shot up. The movement woke Luke and Kitty.

"Quiet." What a bunch of amateurs. He rolled his eyes. "Listen, why don't you guys stay here? I'll go see what's going on."

He got to his knees when a hand rested on his forearm.

"Do you want me to come?" Blue asked, her voice all throaty with sleep. The rasp of it killed him.

He studied her in the darkness, the tightness of her body. Now that she was awake, he could feel her indecision. She wanted to stay. After all that had happened yesterday, she was anxious. Afraid. But she also didn't want him to go out by himself.

Her concern touched him. When was the last time anyone had really cared what happened to him? Oh, his teammates cared. But it was different.

"Would you like to come?" He offered her the chance to back out.

In dark silhouette, her head tilted to the side before she nodded. "I think I should."

This girl continued to impress him. So much courage in such a small package.

"Well, then, let's go." He crawled toward the opening. "I'd say after you, but chivalry seems overrated right now." He didn't wait for her answer before he ducked out.

As he got to a standing position, Jack stepped through the trees.

Once again, Seth experienced immediate distaste. The guy had that swagger about him. Like he owned the world. Or would someday. He hated guys like that.

He didn't look quite as cocky now, though. In fact, he looked downright skittish.

Blue must have sensed it, too. "Jack? What are you doing here?"

"You guys can't go to Trinidad." Jack stepped closer, and Seth saw that he was covered in dirt and he was limping. "They're watching the town."

Blue stepped forward to fuss and scold, somehow managing both at the same time.

Seth sighed. He had been afraid of this, that whoever was chasing them would be waiting for them. It's what he would do. When tracking quarry, you pen them in and tighten the noose. He didn't like that he was the quarry in this particular metaphor.

They'd have to go back the way they came. He wished he had a map. Even if his phone had some juice, he was sure he couldn't use it now. There had to be another way out of this godforsaken corner of the world. Maybe they could jack someone's car. Nah. The roads would be blocked for sure.

What did those fuckers want, anyway? Why had they waited so long to round them up? Why hadn't they been standing outside his door, waiting for him to stop barfing, and then brought him in?

Something hadn't gone as planned.

He almost laughed at himself. Yeah, something hadn't gone as planned. Like, he'd bet they hadn't intended to kill most of a town.

"What happened?" Blue asked as she led Jack to the ATVs. His limp was more pronounced. Something had happened to his right leg. Seth absently turned his own sprained ankle, remembering his jump from the helicopter yesterday.

It felt fine. Better than fine. Like he hadn't done anything to it at all. Strange.

"I went to my aunt's house." It must be closer to dawn than Seth thought, because he could see Jack's face in the waking light. "She was surprised to see me. And upset about my parents. My mom's sister…" He shook his head. "Anyway, she was making me a sandwich, and they showed up. Banged on the door. I told her to hide, and I went out the window. She lives in an upstairs apartment. Had to drop three floors. I think I broke my foot."

Seth stepped forward and gathered the front of Jack's shirt in his fist. "Did they follow you?" This idiot could have given them away. This kid was no brain trust, but this was a new level of stupid.

Jack snorted. "Not unless they can fly. I can run faster than some cars. Now get your hands off me."

They stared at each other for a long time. Seth really wanted to punch him in the face. Didn't he know he'd threatened them all? He should have insisted he stay last night, but the guy was a punk.

They didn't have time for this shit. If Goldstone was coming, they had to get out of here. Now. Sooner than now.

He let go of Jack's shirt, giving him a little shove. "What do you mean you can run faster than some cars?"

"I mean, I'm fast. I used to be fast, but this is nuts. These two dudes started to chase me, and I didn't think, I took off. And it kicked in. I hauled ass down the street and out of town. They didn't have a prayer of catching me."

"That was hours ago. Where have you been?"

"I wandered around. I didn't dare go back to Trinidad. I took off north, up the John Kennedy Highway, and doubled back. Took me a while to find you guys, but I finally did."

"Lucky us." Seth turned and found Kitty and Luke watching them. Kitty, as per her usual, looked completely baffled and out of her element. Luke stared at them all, his expression unreadable. Seth'd like to play poker with that kid. He seemed easygoing enough but gave the impression that there was more under there than anyone suspected.

As he looked over their ragtag group, Seth couldn't help his disappointment. Not one of them had any survival experience. The closest he had was Kitty, who could set up a tent. With help.

The rest of them were a huge liability.

If he'd been smart, he'd have left them behind. He didn't grow up in Glory. He wasn't even supposed to have been there. Far as he could remember, Mrs. Keilman, the bed-and-breakfast owner, hadn't written his name anywhere. He wasn't even sure he'd given her his name. She'd smiled, shaken his hand, and accepted the wad of cash he'd given her.

Yeah, if he'd been smart, he'd have run. But looking at the four of them, he couldn't. If he left, he might as well drop Goldstone a note with their location. Did he think Kitty would last one minute against the guys from Goldstone? Or Luke? Jack might have a big college boy attitude, but he was no real fighter. He had a healthy rage going, but if Seth had wanted to hurt him last night, he would have.

And Blue?

She stood back, away from the group, studying him. In the waking light, she looked solid, as if in the past twenty-four hours she hadn't lost the woman who raised her and run away from her home.

Their eyes met, and she waited for him.

Yes. Blue was a fighter. He didn't know all the details yet, but he could tell she hadn't had it easy. She was a bitty thing, but she was a survivor. It was there, in the jut of her chin and the steel in her eyes. Wrapped in her compact and curvy package, Blueberry Michaels was incredibly appealing.

When she lifted her eyebrow at him, he realized he was staring at her. He looked away, only to find that the other three were looking at him, too.

So he'd been elected the unofficial leader of their little posse, he supposed.

He sighed. Yeah, he couldn't leave them. He'd been left with no one to rely on too many times. And after Bobby…

If he left them, he'd be as responsible for their fate as he'd been responsible for Bobby's.

He wouldn't abandon anyone again. Even a ragtag, bungled-together team like this. It's what made him such a great soldier. Leave no man behind and all that shit.

Hooah.

What the hell were they going to do?

He turned, rubbing a hand over his buzzed head.

There weren't that many ways in and out of Glory. He'd already discarded driving out of here.

He also eliminated air escape, for practical, we-haven't-got-a-helicopter reasons, and boat escape for obvious, there's-no-water reasons.

So what did that leave them?

The ATVs might have another five, ten miles of gas in them, give or take. But even if they got to a gas station to refill, they wouldn't be able to carry enough extra gas to get them all to safety. He had no idea how far each of the vehicles went on a tank, and two would be carrying two passengers. If they ran out of gas, they'd be left walking, and he disregarded that. These kids weren't prepared to go days in the wilderness on foot.

The train was their only option.

"It has to be the train."

"Dude." Jack pushed away from the ATV. "I told you. They're in Trinidad. They've seen me now, and they knew who they were looking for."

"I heard you," Seth gritted out, "dude." He snorted as he scanned the materials they'd brought with him, writing off all of it. Nothing here would help them. "But it's all we have."

Blue cut in before Jack could go on. Her eyes narrowed on him. "What do you have planned?"

The words sang through his chest. Not the question, exactly. Not even her tone, which was as straightforward and no-nonsense as he'd come to expect from her.

But that question said that she believed in him. That she had faith that he'd get them out of there.

It meant more than he could have imagined.

"I have an idea. A crazy idea." He stared at each of them, the plan beginning to firm up in his strategic mind. It was a long shot, for sure. But it was all they had. "Blue. I know you can lift a person off the ground, but can you lift yourself off the ground?"

She really hoped this worked.

The train was coming—she could hear it—and there was no turning back now. No other option. They only had one chance at this. And if they missed, they'd die. Probably. Or be maimed. Whatever.

No pressure.

She closed her eyes. No room for doubt now. She'd listened to Seth's analysis of their situation, and she'd believed him. The train was the answer.

Luke huddled next to her in the brush, his jaw set and his knuckles white against his knees. As her safety depended on him being solid, she decided it would be fine to check in. "You okay?"

"Oh, yeah. Sure. Great."

She smiled, despite the sickness in her own stomach. "I trust you. We're going to be fine." As she reached over and gripped his hand, she met his eyes and realized it was true. At least in this instance. She knew Luke wouldn't do anything to hurt her. At least not on purpose.

"It's coming."

She nodded. "Are you ready?"

He snorted with half a smile and shrugged. "As I'll ever be."

"Let's do this, then."

They rose together as the train came into sight. She stood in front of Luke, her feet apart as if preparing for battle. They each took a deep breath and held each other's eyes.

They'd been practicing all day. At first, Seth thought they would be able to lift themselves. Like flying, but not. Blue had proved she could move objects, and she'd shown she could hold someone in a tree. He'd assumed she could lift herself.

But no matter how she and Luke tried, neither could master it. They could move other people, but not themselves.

They hadn't had time to figure out why, though. With time running out, Seth gave up on them "flying" and decided Luke would basically have to throw Blue onto the train and vice versa.

Seth was right. She knew it, deep down. And she believed that this was their best—maybe their only—option.

The problem was that they didn't have enough time to throw each other separately. The train would be here and gone in less than a minute. So she would have to move Luke while he moved her.

Even considering it, she wanted to throw up.

But the train was coming, sick stomach or not. She took a breath and lifted Luke in the air. He nodded, and her feet left the ground.

At least she and Luke had used their practice time to

master holding someone still without making them suffocate. Good thing, too. She liked breathing.

They rose, up and up, as the train trundled closer. When the locomotive passed below them, they cleared it by at least thirty feet.

During practice, they'd talked about the train. How loud it would be. How much it would vibrate. How much it would affect the air around them. But all that chatter hadn't prepared Blue for how the wind whipped against her. As they dropped down, slowly, closer and closer to the roof, the airstream messed with their holds, whipping them back and forth, tossing them in the breeze like feathers.

And the noise. God, the noise.

The train wasn't moving full speed. It had only left the station in Trinidad a few miles away. But it was still fast enough to screw them up.

They hovered, both of them a foot or two above the train. In front of her, Luke pitched sideways and back, and she scowled, concentrating, trying her hardest to hold him steady as she dropped him the last inches to the train. A gust of wind tugged him sideways, and she panicked then rushed to pull him back on target.

Suddenly, pain exploded behind her eyes, taking her sight. She cried out with it, grabbing the sides of her head with her hands. The agony pulsed and throbbed in her skull, shooting down her back like fire.

She was going to die. It wasn't possible to hurt like this without death.

Her stomach pitched as she dropped fast and hard, her knees hitting what she assumed was the moving train beneath her. She rolled, twisting, and could feel herself approach the edge of the moving train.

She clawed, still blind from the piercing pain, desperately searching for a hold. Heart pounding, her nails scratched against the metal roof, and dimly she heard Luke calling her name.

As her foot reached the edge of the roof and then fell into dead air, her fingers finally caught. A metal box of some sort, a vent shaft or something. She didn't question, only grabbed and held on, still struggling to think around the stabbing pain in her head.

"Blue. God, Blue!" She barely heard Luke over the wind and the noise. "Hold on. I'll pull you up."

The pain lessened enough for her to see him instead of the white light that had consumed her vision moments ago. Above her, he knelt, his knees spread apart to brace himself, his shaggy hair whipping across his terrified face.

"No." She shook her head. He shouldn't risk himself if she could help herself. And she didn't want him to try to lift her with his mind again. Not with this wind. Not in the panic he was in. "Wait, I'm fine," she yelled to him.

As she dangled over the side of a train, she tried to see how she *would* be fine. She took a breath, tried to calm down and think through her options. To her left, about three feet out of her reach, was a ladder made of bars. Probably an emergency or service ladder.

"Luke!" She nudged her head at the ladder. "I'm going to let go. You're going to hold me long enough to catch that ladder."

"Oh, shit. No! I already almost got you killed."

"No, you didn't." She could feel her fingers slipping. "Please. I need you to do this."

Luke's mouth opened and closed, and she could feel his indecision, his doubt.

"I can't hold on!"

He nodded once. She didn't wait. "On three. One, two, three."

With a silent prayer, she let go. And when she feared she

would drop like the dead weight she was, she felt the now familiar tug in her midsection that said Luke had caught her.

Thank God.

She barely had time to think before her fingers were on the ladder. But the transition wasn't as smooth as she expected. Her left hand slipped off the rung, and she swung out, her head cracking the side of the train with a sickening thud. Luckily, her foot found the ladder as she slipped down, and she managed to grab on and right herself again.

Shaking her head, feeling dizzy, she crawled up the ladder and Luke helped her at the top. The dizziness intensified, and her sight faded in and out.

As she braced herself at the top of the train, she gasped, trying to catch her breath.

"Blue?" Luke swam in her vision. She clutched her head, opening and closing her eyes, trying to get a grip. When she pulled her hand away, though, she saw blood. Was that her blood? That didn't make sense. Did it?

"Blue?" This time, Luke's voice seemed far away. "Shit, shit, shit. Blue, hang on." As she faded out, she thought she heard him say, "Seth'll be here soon. Hang on. Seth is coming."

It'd be okay, then. Seth was coming.

She gave in to the darkness, more comforted than she should have been by that thought.

Chapter Seven

As much as Seth hated to admit it, Jack had been right about one thing: running like this was sweet.

Having the new gifts was cool, if he didn't factor in the horror that had accompanied it. The jumping, the new super spidey hearing, the added strength, the super healing. Jack's foot had healed up in a matter of hours, as Seth's ankle had. Pretty amazing, really. But Seth loved speed. And this…this was speed.

Even with Kitty on his back, hanging on for dear life, he was fast.

The plan was to run at the train at a forty-five-degree angle. That way the conductor wouldn't see them coming and they could leap up on the roof to meet with Luke and Blue, who they assumed were already aboard, if all had gone to plan.

Which of course it had. It had to have. He wouldn't allow anything else. He'd feel better when he could see Blue for himself, that was all.

As he dodged around some brush and jumped a small

ditch, he tried not to worry about how much he was coming to care about her. Watching her today had been insightful. She'd wanted to fly so badly. She'd tried over and over, never giving up, never losing heart. Even when he told her they needed to think of something else, she'd wanted to keep going. If they hadn't run out of time, she would have gone on.

When he told her that she would have to move Luke instead, pure fear lit her face before she managed to hide her feelings again. Then she'd started in on him. The idea was stupid. Too dangerous. Wouldn't work. She hemmed and hawed, fighting tooth and nail.

But she couldn't fool him. It had been fine when she only had to worry about herself. But she was afraid to hurt Luke.

So he'd given her a lot of leeway. He'd let her rant and bitch. She'd pushed and pushed and finally, he reminded her gently, "You should practice. Luke's depending on you."

Her mouth snapped shut, and he watched uncertainty flicker in her blue eyes. So tough sometimes, and then these moments of vulnerability. She was something else. He'd dropped his voice so none of the others would hear him. Unable to stop from touching her, he took her hands. "I believe in you."

She stared up at him for a long moment and then whispered, "Don't do that."

"What?"

"You don't know me."

He smiled at her, squeezing her fingers. "I think I'm starting to figure you out."

Her mouth snapped shut, and she swayed toward him. Then, as if catching herself, she'd spun away, joining Luke without any more fuss. Seth had chuckled. He was starting to get her, all right. How strong, how loyal. And he liked it all. Very much.

Now, as he and Jack tore across the ground, he forced

himself to stop thinking about her. He shouldn't have been thinking about her at all right now. He knew better. Distractions could kill you.

The train approached in front of them. He relaxed, allowed his brain to easily calculate the distance that remained before he overtook it. A quarter of a mile, less, maybe. He adjusted his trajectory and realized Jack had as well. He increased his speed by a fraction, holding a fairly steady thirty to thirty-five miles per hour.

Kitty clung to his shoulders. They'd rigged a sort of sling to tie her to Seth's back. He knew she didn't like it, feeling completely dependent on him. To soothe her, he sent her his most reassuring thought: *I'll try my best not to kill us. I can do this.*

He couldn't tell if it worked, but again, he couldn't afford distractions.

They'd planned to board at the back of the train. The front was where the passenger cars were. Avoiding detection meant avoiding people.

Of course Jack had to make his leap first. Not surprising. Seth held back when Jack sped up. He didn't have anything to prove. He waited, watching as Jack's feet left the ground and he flew through the air, legs still running, landing on top of the second to last car with two extra steps before he stopped.

Looked straightforward enough.

Seth's feet left the ground and, as before, his mind seemed to slow everything down. He could feel every minute movement of his muscles. Even Kitty on his back didn't present a challenge. He calculated his jump speed, the speed of the train, and the additional weight on his back. And he prepared his legs to absorb the landing shock, managing to board the train as if he'd stepped onto the roof instead of jumped onto it from the ground some sixty feet away.

"Show-off," Jack said, crawling up behind him. Seth

smiled as he dropped down to his knees and untied the fabric pieces holding Kitty in place. The train continued to speed up and he rocked back, depositing her on her butt on the roof.

His smile slipped, though, when he caught sight of Luke and Blue on the last car. Rather, Luke, sitting and holding Blue's motionless body.

His heartbeat roared in his ears, drowning out the noise of the train. He dropped the last parts of Kitty's sling and ran, low to the roof, toward them. Had they been attacked? He scanned the area, looking for enemies, wishing he had more of a weapon than the survival knife he'd managed to take from the Laughtons' shed.

He saw no one.

So what the hell happened?

He dropped down beside Luke, his gaze sweeping over Blue. "What's going on?" He reached out, wanting to snatch her from Luke. He gripped her hand instead, not sure where the intensity of his feelings was coming from.

"I don't know, I don't know." Luke held her and shouted over the wind, rocking back and forth, clearly freaking out. "One minute everything was fine. We were lowering down, about to land on the roof, like we planned. Then Blue screamed, and I dropped. It jarred me, man. Knocked the wind out of me. I lost hold on her, and she fell. She managed to catch that vent"—he nodded to a black metal block nearby—"and then she crawled up that ladder." This time he motioned to the emergency ladder next to him.

"But it was rough, and she hit her head." He lifted his hand and blood stained his fingers. "Holy shit."

Needing to touch her and unable to resist the urge any longer, Seth reached over and pushed her hair out of her face. Her eyelids fluttered, a good sign. And blood trickled from her nose.

Fear pierced his gut. A nosebleed. From a head trauma?

They needed to get her off this roof. "Luke, do you have her?" When the other man didn't answer, Seth shook his sleeve. "Luke, buddy. You got to stay with me here." He waited until he made eye contact before he asked again. "Do you have her? I'm going to check below."

"Yeah. I'm fine."

Seth doubted it, but he didn't say anything. Instead, he grabbed the emergency ladder and dropped down.

He should have been more cautious, he knew. But Blue needed help. At the bottom of the ladder, he felt around for the emergency exit.

There, to his right, was the latch. With a quick steadying breath, he twisted, pushing it in.

He waited. No one stuck their head out. No shouting. He ducked inside.

It wasn't storage. Instead, he felt like he'd hit the lottery. He stood in what appeared to be a private car. Seth had been on a few Amtrak trains in his time. They were comfortable enough, but they weren't anything like this. This one came with its own minibar and some sort of serious entertainment center, and it was decked out like a celebrity yacht.

Score.

He crept in farther, pulling the door closed behind him. Two doors in the back led to a bathroom and a bedroom, complete with its own bathroom. In the bath, he turned on the faucet. Nothing.

Not in use. He let out the breath he hadn't been aware he was holding. No passenger, then. He closed his eyes, thanking the powers that be.

He opened the emergency door and hustled back up the ladder. Jack, Luke, and Kitty huddled over Blue, who seemed to be blinking. Thank God. The faster they got her off this roof, the better. "Let's go."

"Where?" Did Jack have to question everything?

Apparently so.

"The circus, you ass. Where do you think? Down. Inside."

Kitty immediately crawled toward him and gingerly made her way down the ladder. Of course. She'd know what was below.

Apparently, her easy acceptance made Luke and Jack move, too. Jack fumbled past him, scurrying down the ladder and disappearing inside. Luke crept toward him, cradling Blue. "What about…"

"I'll help you. I'll go first and you can help lower her down. We'll get her in."

Luke nodded. As they lowered her, she moaned.

He cursed, calling to Luke. "Gently."

Gently. Right. Seth went down backward, holding her above him with one arm and balancing with the other. She wasn't heavy, not for him, only awkward. It took some maneuvering, but they managed to get her down the ladder and through the door. Luke came right after, as Seth was lowering her to the plush carpet. "Is she okay?"

She moaned, rolling a bit. He shushed her, squeezing her hand, and tilted her head. Blood caked in her blond hair, garish against the light strands. "Looks like she hit it hard."

"Yeah, when she hit the side."

He needed to fix her up. Every head injury he'd ever seen played through his mind, and the fear threatened to consume him.

She'd gotten hurt. On his watch. After he'd promised her that he'd watch out for her…

To distract himself from the failure, he glanced around. The bar looked stocked. "There any bar towels back there?" He needed to put pressure on the wound, get her cleaned up. He wanted to do it himself.

Kitty scurried around, rifling through drawers. "Here." She tossed him a handful and he folded one up, placed it on the wound and pressed. He tried to be gentle, but Blue still winced. Then she opened her eyes. "Who hit me with a bat?"

The sight of her baby blues weakened his knees, and he could barely think around his relief. You never knew with a head wound. He'd seen guys get hit on the head and never be the same again. "Hey, you." He smiled. "No bat. You took on a train single-handed."

"That was stupid." She tried to get up and groaned. He pushed her back down.

"Why don't you take it easy for a minute longer? At least until you stop bleeding on everything." He glanced at their new digs. "Place is pretty posh. Doubt they'd like you messing it up."

One corner of her lips quirked up, and her eyes closed again. He watched her a minute longer. When he looked up, he regretted that long stare. Jack snorted in disgust before pushing away from where he stood and heading for the mini fridge. Luke busied himself looking around the car. But Kitty met his gaze, hers entirely too knowing.

He looked away.

What was he doing? He was way too invested in this girl, and now wasn't the time to get involved. They were on the run, for Christ's sake. She'd lost her grandmother and left the only home she'd ever known. And him? He didn't know how to be involved with someone. He was a soldier. He got shipped all over the world with little notice.

This was a case of two people being attracted during a life-threatening situation. That was all.

Of course, that would mean she was attracted to him, too. Which he didn't know for sure. Which he shouldn't care about at all, because he'd decided this was a bad idea anyway.

He pulled the bar towel from Blue's wound and replaced it with another. It didn't seem to be bleeding as much now. Still more than he liked. He pressed a little more, and she flinched, her eyes clouded with pain as they met his before she squeezed them closed again.

"Sorry," he whispered. He propped the towel against her head with his knee and yanked his T-shirt over his head. He ripped it, shaping it into a triangular bandage. After a few more minutes, he checked the towel. He wished he had some running water, but this would have to do. He hoped it was enough. He exchanged the soiled towel—not as bloody as the last, thank God—with a new one and fashioned a bandage to hold the towel in place. Almost looked like a head wrap, if you didn't look too closely.

"How'd you do that?" Kitty asked from her perch in front of him.

"I'm about to start Special Ops. This is pretty basic first aid."

"That's great." She nodded to Blue and then glanced at Luke and Jack, arguing behind the bar. Satisfied they weren't listening, she lowered her voice and continued. "I know you've had your doubts." He glanced at her before returning his gaze to Blue. That was a nice way to say he'd considered leaving them this morning. "But I want you to know that you're right. We wouldn't have been able to do this without you. So thank you. For staying. We appreciate it." She smiled and nudged her head toward the other guys. "Even Jack."

"You're a bad liar, Kitty." He looked back at Blue, who was entirely too pale. "But I want to stay. Really."

"Yeah. And Blue's pretty great, too, huh?" She grinned.

"Yeah," he allowed. "She is."

"So." Kitty leaned forward on her elbows. "Now what?"

He glanced around the car, really taking in his surroundings for the first time since they'd boarded. He didn't see any access from the main train. He guessed that anyone who rented this thing wouldn't want to be interrupted by Amtrak's ticket checkers. That was good for them, because they didn't want to be bothered by them, either.

They'd be alone until La Junta, then, which Kitty said was a little over an hour away. He'd hoped to steal a car—er, borrow a car—in La Junta and drive through the night to San Antonio. He didn't have many friends, but he trusted Nick. And since Nick was already expecting him there, he figured he'd stick to the plan. He'd only be arriving with a few more people.

After they got to San Antonio, he had no idea what they would do.

Blue wasn't going to be able to travel like this. Not all night. And if she had a concussion…

"Any idea if there are any hotels near the train station in La Junta?"

Kitty blinked. "How would we pay for that?"

He had no clue. Maybe they could break in somewhere… Even as he thought it, he knew how that idea would fly with Blue. As in, not at all. But, they needed running water. Beds.

"I might be able to help." Luke fiddled with a sleeve of crackers they must have found behind the bar. He swallowed before he continued. "I took my dad's wallet when I was leaving."

Kitty's face split into a huge grin, but Seth didn't get it. No need to rejoice over some spare change and a bunch of plastic he didn't feel comfortable using.

When Luke didn't continue, Jack explained, "Luke's rich."

"My dad was rich," Luke added quickly. "He made a lot of money. Computer hacking, intelligence, stuff like that. He's not going to need it now. Anyway, I've got a few thousand bucks in cash and, if I can get to a computer, I could probably figure out a couple other accounts. That no one could track," he added, as if reading Seth's mind. He glanced down at the crackers in his hand. "So, yeah, money's probably not an issue."

Chapter Eight

The sun was setting as the train teetered to a stop in La Junta.

As soon as they halted in front of the La Junta train station, Jack opened the back door. He slouched out, his backpack on and his earbuds in, like any other college kid coming home from school. Luke and Kitty waited a moment before they followed, standing close, engaged in a quiet conversation.

They were doing great, acting their parts perfectly. They'd agreed that if they paired up, they could look more ordinary. A group of five would draw the eye more than a single kid and a couple of pairs.

Finally, when Luke and Kitty were two car lengths away, Seth glanced down at Blue. She fit perfectly, tucked up alongside his body. But she still looked pale. "Ready?"

Her jaw firmed. "Yeah."

She'd awakened in pain, complaining about the light, the noise when anyone spoke, and the movement of the train. She hadn't thrown up yet, but it didn't look good.

He pulled her closer, putting his arm around her shoulder,

as much for him as for her. Technically, he was holding her up, but he needed to feel her, the weight of her against him. To convince himself that he hadn't screwed up. That his scheme hadn't almost gotten her killed. That she was still alive, if a bit banged up.

It was supposed to look like they were snuggling to the rest of the world. She leaned into his side, tucking her head against his shoulder. No hint of her usual prickliness. That told him all he needed to know about how she really felt. He gave her a quick squeeze.

As he guided them to the stairs, wrapping himself around her felt natural. He did his best to ignore how much he liked the soft press of her against his side, even as his pulse quickened at the feel of her. He needed to be sharp. Just in case.

They stepped down the back stairs and out onto the landing.

Other passengers milled around, some checking their luggage, others meeting family members or friends. Ahead of them, Jack slunk toward the parking lot. That guy could pull off a kid with a chip on his shoulder like an Oscar-winning actor. Maybe because fiction mirrored reality. Kitty and Luke had paused nearby while Luke fumbled with his cell phone. The phone was dead, of course, but it looked convincing, like he was checking his texts or something. Seth didn't know if there would be anyone here waiting for them, but he hadn't wanted to take any chances.

"Do you see anyone?" Blue didn't even look up.

"No." But he doubted he would. Not here. They wouldn't want to stick out. "Keep your head down." He steered her past the station, through the parking lot with its chipped cement, and out onto the narrow sidewalk. The other passengers, getting into their cars, having conversations, provided plenty of cover for them.

Across the street, Jack waited under a lamppost in a park.

Seth glanced up and down, looking for traffic, of which there was little, and then escorted Blue across the street. She'd paled considerably since they left the train. Her complexion looked like milk before; now she was practically translucent.

"You okay?" he asked as he gripped her arm.

"I don't feel so good."

She didn't look so good. "You going to throw up?"

"I don't think so."

Well, that was something. He shuffled her to a park bench and helped her sit. She dropped her head in her hands.

This had to be a mild concussion. He'd had one in high school after getting decked in a fight he didn't start. He remembered how banged up he'd felt for a couple days.

He sat next to her, running his hand on her back. He fought the urge to pull her into his lap, to tuck her in to his body. He really needed to get a grip on this.

"Hey. You kids all right?" An older man paused at the park entrance. His button-up shirt was tucked too tightly into his jeans, his midsection bulged over a large belt buckle, and a cowboy hat sat on his head.

Just what they needed, a Good Samaritan drawing attention to them. The man looked concerned, though, and Seth didn't want him worrying. It was too dangerous.

So he smiled. "She's fine, sir. Had a little too much fun last night, I think." Then he chuckled, like a real asshole.

The do-gooder's mouth thinned, and he tipped his hat. "All righty, then." He continued along without a backward glance.

"If I cared, I might be annoyed that you made me look like a stupid party girl."

"Better he think you can't hold your liquor than that you need medical care. Which you probably do."

"Truth, I guess." She managed to sit up straighter. "I'll have you know, though, that I never get sick when I drink. Not that I drink a lot. I don't. But I tend bar. I have a reputation to uphold."

"You tend bar?" He knew she did. She'd mentioned it before. But he looked her over now, full of fake skepticism, to mess with her. She worked up a weakly haughty scowl, also expected. It was good to catch a glimpse of her old self. It reminded him that she was fine, here beside him.

"Yes, and I'm pretty good. Almost as good as Tom Cruise in *Cocktail*."

"*Cocktail*? How old is that movie? My mother liked that movie." As he said the words, he could feel the smile disappear from his face.

She must have noticed. "You okay?"

"Fine." Yeah, fine. Except he didn't talk about his mother. Ever. Not to his friends and certainly not to some girl he met yesterday.

"All right, then, grumpy." She stood purposefully, as if trying to prove that she could do it without his help. "But your mom's got good taste in movies."

"Maybe so." Not in much else, though. No, that wasn't fair. He didn't know his mother well enough to know her tastes. The court had sent him back to her a few times when he'd been little. She'd put on a good face to the social worker, convinced everyone that she'd cleaned herself up. But it never failed—each time she'd refused to stay clean long enough to take care of him.

When Seth was nine, she'd tried again, pleading to the judge, claiming she'd changed. Again. But that time, Seth refused to go back. Luckily, his social worker had taken pity on him and granted his wish. He'd been living with a nice enough family. Maybe they didn't love him, but they didn't forget to feed him either.

Bottom line, he didn't *know* Vanessa Campbell. But he didn't like her.

Blue watched him, expectant. He shrugged. "I didn't grow up with her." He didn't say more. It already felt like he'd said too much.

She watched him for a long moment. Then she reached out to squeeze his hand. "I didn't grow up with my mom, either. Or my dad, for that matter."

"No?" Maybe that was why he felt so comfortable with her. She reminded him a little of other foster kids he'd grown up with.

"Nah. Gran raised me. She was my dad's mom." She inhaled, and her eyes suddenly were vulnerable. "My dad… committed suicide when I was young." She glanced away. "My mom kind of went off the deep end, dragging me from one commune to another. My gran stepped in to take me."

"Commune? Like religious commune?"

"No. Like anti-government, off-the-grid lifestyle stuff. People who were escaping from society. She was always into that stuff. Hence the name—Blueberry Sky Michaels. Some hippie shit right there." Her lips tightened, and he could tell there was more of a story there, but she wasn't ready to tell it. Finally, she shrugged. "Anyway, last I heard she was living in Idaho somewhere."

She was trying to act casual, but he got the impression she didn't talk about this a lot.

His throat tightened. Then he blurted, "My mom was a drug addict." She tilted her head but remained silent. He looked over her head, unable to watch her as he went on. "She left me in foster care. She'd come back to get me every once in a while, insisting that she'd changed, that she'd gotten herself together. But she never did. I eventually had to refuse to go with her."

He gritted his teeth. God, that sounded awful. What kind of son refused his own mother? But when Blue didn't say anything immediately, he looked down. She squeezed his hand again, this time not letting go.

"That must have been hard."

He nodded.

"It's not your fault," she said. "Sometimes I have to remember that. That it isn't my fault my mom couldn't be strong enough to care for me." She studied their fingers, intertwined, deceptively casual.

True.

Sometimes shitty things just happened.

Luke and Kitty joined them then, breaking the spell between them. Blue squeezed his hand once more before breaking the contact. He resisted the urge to snatch her fingers back.

Kitty dropped her backpack at her feet, and Luke tucked his hands in his jeans pockets. "The hotels are that way." He nudged his head east. "Did you see anything?"

Seth scanned the streets. As far as he could tell, everything was quiet.

They couldn't have lost them that easily. They hadn't boarded the train legally, for sure, but still. It seemed too simple.

The next time any of them used a credit card, accessed their phone, or turned up at a relative's house, they'd be all over them.

Maybe the guys hunting them were banking on that. They were a bunch of kids, after all. With no resources they were aware of. They weren't expecting Seth to be with them.

He only had to figure out the particulars. Where they could go. What they could do. They couldn't hide like this forever.

He'd take them to Nick's, figure it out there. Maybe one of them had other relatives…a cabin…hell, a Boy Scout camp they went to as a kid that might be empty now. Something.

Right now, their priority was food, somewhere to sleep, and showers. If Blue had a concussion, it would be best if they didn't travel tonight. They'd get moving again in the morning.

"I say we head that way and check in. Maybe we should split up. You guys go first, and I'll follow with Blue."

"Dude, I need food. Like now." Jack had one earbud in, the other hanging down his neck. "I'm not going anywhere if there isn't food."

God, this kid was tedious. "Fine, whoever wants food, go with Jack. I'll walk Blue to the hotel."

"I'll go with you, man. I'm hungry, too." Luke pulled a wad of money out of his pocket and handed it to Seth. "Here, that should be fine for a couple of rooms."

Seth looked down at the ball of twenties and handed back a few of them. "We should each get our own room. I'll check in under Peter Richards. Ask for me at the desk."

"Peter Richards?" Luke's nose wrinkled.

"Yeah." Seth smiled. "Should be easy enough for a couple of dicks like you to remember."

Jack shook his head. "You suck."

They all chuckled.

Luke shrugged and took some of the money back.

Seth raised his eyebrows. "This looks like a drug sale now. You know that, right?"

A grin split Luke's face. He pushed up his glasses on his nose. "Yeah, well, I've never looked properly up to no good. I kind of like it."

Seth snorted and clapped Luke on the back as he started down the street. Jack followed with his hands in his pockets and his backpack on his back. But Kitty lagged behind, glancing after Luke and Jack but not immediately following.

"You want to come with us, Kitty?" Blue offered. Seth watched as indecision played on Kitty's face.

He still didn't know what to make of Kitty. Even though it seemed like she and Blue were good friends, she appeared uncomfortable around them. But he didn't think it was because she didn't like them. If anything, she seemed self-conscious. Or plain awkward.

She glanced between Blue and Seth a few times.

She lifted her backpack again and slung it over her shoulder. "I think I'm going to go with them. But I'll catch up with you guys at the hotel." She started walking, waving as she went. "Feel better, Blue."

"What was that about?" Blue asked when Kitty was far enough away not to hear them.

"Dunno." But he did. She'd probably overheard him thinking about her. He needed to be more careful in the future. He hadn't intended to hurt her feelings. "Let's get going."

Blue released her hold on the park bench and promptly wobbled. But her stubborn chin said she wasn't ready to ask for help. She took a few steps before staggering a little. He stood next to her but didn't touch her. "You done now? Between being tired and bashing your skull in, you could ask for a little help, you know."

"Yeah, I don't ask for help well."

"No way. I'd never have guessed."

She grimaced. "Fine. Would you help me?" She paused before she added, "Please."

"See, not so bad."

"You've got a mean streak, Seth Campbell."

"Yeah, I know." He tucked her up against him again, allowing himself to rub his cheek against her soft hair for a moment, and they headed off. "One of my better qualities."

Blue made it a few blocks. That felt like a herculean feat, and she was pretty proud of herself.

Her self-congratulating ended when her stomach heaved. She hustled it to a nearby trash can and tossed up what little she had in her stomach. When she finished, she felt like her head had exploded as well. Rubbing her temple, she met Seth's gaze and wondered if she looked as much like dog crap as she felt.

He scratched his head, putting his backpack down. Reaching inside, he retrieved a towel he must have swiped from the train.

"I see," he said, handing it to her.

"What exactly do you see?" She sounded grouchy. She was grouchy. She accepted the towel and wiped her mouth. The slash on her head hurt, the lights were giving her a raging headache, and she'd puked. In front of Seth. Not exactly her finest moment.

"That you'll go a long way to get a piggyback ride."

She wanted to say something smart. A comment like that, she should have been able to wind up some sort of sassy comeback. But she was too tired.

"Wow." He stepped closer, studying her carefully. "You really must feel like shit." He turned. "Come on. Hop up. I got you."

Blue stared at the wide expanse of his back in front of her and balked. She'd spent the past half an hour or so in close proximity to him, and she hated to admit how much she liked it. It seemed every inch of him was covered in tanned skin and toned muscle. With his gorgeous mouth and his intelligent gaze…she had to admit he was probably the best-looking guy she'd ever met.

She'd known how good-looking he was the entire time, of course. She wasn't blind. But it was getting harder to ignore all that. Because he was turning out to be so much more than some good-looking guy. Like when he was talking about his mother. He hated that he'd had to cut her out of his life. He hadn't said it, but she understood. After all, he'd refused to leave them, complete strangers, behind. If he wanted to, he could have been long gone. But he seemed determined to protect them all...protect her. For someone like that, who didn't give up on people...she couldn't even imagine how hard it had been to give up on his mom. And, thanks to her issues with her mother, she could sympathize, way too much.

The whole thing tore at her heart. And softened her toward him.

He put his backpack on so it hung in the front, and then he glanced over his shoulder. "Come on. Up." Then he gave her that grin. The half grin, the one she found entirely too sexy. "Trust me. I think I can hold you."

She didn't need any more coaxing. If asked to choose between pressing herself against Seth's gorgeous back or forcing herself to walk another block and then probably puking again? Yeah. No real choice. Besides, she wanted to be near him.

She put her hands on his shoulders and hiked a leg up. He did the rest of the work, hauling her up like a rucksack. They set off, and the jerk wasn't puffing at all. As if she didn't weigh a thing.

Well, all right, then. *If he's got this...* Blue tucked her head down, laying her cheek between his shoulder blades and allowing herself to curl against him. She closed her eyes and experienced immediate bliss. Why were the lights so...bright?

Against her face, the T-shirt he had borrowed from Jack was warm with his body heat. She rubbed her cheek against him, allowing herself this moment, without him looking, to enjoy the feel of him. She wrapped her arms around him, holding on tightly.

To the outside world, they probably looked like any other young, carefree couple. Goofing around, a boyfriend giving his girl a piggyback ride so he could hold her close in public.

Blue was surprised by how much she wished that was true. She hadn't had a boyfriend in a long time. Not since her high school boyfriend left for college two years ago. He'd said they'd make it work, long-distance, all the way to University of Colorado in Denver.

But they hadn't. Rather, he hadn't. For her, there was nothing new in Glory. Not many prospects. But for him? When he'd broken up with her—over the phone on Halloween, so he could take his new girl to a party without a guilty conscience—she'd told him she understood. And she had. It must be hard to look back with so much in front of him.

Since then, she hadn't had time to date. Guys at the bar would hit on her sometimes. But they weren't dating material.

Sometimes she missed being young, dating and that sort of thing. But she didn't regret caring for her grandmother. Especially now...

"You okay back there?" She heard and felt the question against her cheek.

"Yeah. And thanks. I felt like holy shit."

"Much more dignified than regular shit, then."

She smiled, despite herself. He was too much.

They walked in silence down the street for a while. Occasionally, she'd open her eyes and see them pass some shops, a restaurant or two. Finally, Seth turned in to a Holiday Inn. Out of sight of the door, he stopped at a bench and put her down.

"Why don't you wait here? I'll go check in."

"You sure?" she asked, even though she had no desire to walk another step. She needed a nap in the worst way.

"Yeah. It's a girl behind the desk. I need to get a room without ID. I'll probably have better luck alone."

She glanced up at him. She expected to see some sort of cockiness on his face. If it had been a lot of other guys, he'd have winked or wiggled his eyebrows, or done some other arrogant thing as if to say, *Hey, did you notice I'm incredibly attractive?*

But there was nothing. Only a matter-of-fact *there's an issue, and I know the best way to fix it*. In this case, he was probably right. If he applied that flirty grin, he'd get what he wanted.

She realized at that moment that this was one of her favorite things about him. No bullshit. See a problem, fix it. Do what needed to be done. She appreciated that in people.

"Okay."

He nodded. She closed her eyes. She must have dozed off sitting there, because he was back before she knew it with a few folded-up pages and a couple of swiping door keys.

"Everything all right?" Was that her voice? Her words were too slurred, for sure.

"Jesus." He didn't say anything else, only leaned over and scooped her up into his arms, tucking her head under his chin.

She didn't argue. And for a moment, she pretended. She pretended she was one of those girls who had a reliable boyfriend. For once someone was taking care of her.

Maybe it made her a wimp. But it didn't matter.

He carried her up a flight of stairs. There was a swish and then the door closed behind them, and then he was laying her down.

On a bed. Sweet God above. A bed.

He took her Converse off and pulled the sheets over her. Then he smoothed her hair out of her face with a soft touch.

She closed her eyes, her face pressed against the most comfortable pillow she could remember. The shower turned on in the bathroom, and she decided that she might have been wrong about him. Seth Campbell was someone she could depend on after all.

If she was in the market to depend on someone.

Which she definitely wasn't.

Jack was pouting. Again.

All they have is Subway. I hate fucking Subway.

His attitude grated on Kitty's nerves. Having everyone's thoughts in her head was tough enough, but his negativity would test the patience of a saint.

She'd wanted to stay with Seth and Blue. But they were so…cozy together, and she didn't want to feel like the fifth wheel. She'd tagged along with Luke and Jack instead.

She regretted that decision. At least in Jack's case.

When did they even cut those tomatoes, anyway?

"You know, Jack, we could keep walking. Find somewhere else." Even as she offered, she knew what he'd say.

"No way. I'm starving." *Besides, not many choices in this little hellhole.*

So pleasant.

She turned to Luke behind her. He was pondering his dinner options. *Cold cut combo is always a good choice, though.* She smiled. Now, this was more pleasant.

"I like the cold cut combo, too."

He blinked, his glasses making his eyes even larger. She got a quick flicker of *What the…* before he tapped his chin in mock consideration. "Yeah. A solid choice. But the meatball…"

She grinned. If she only had to listen to Luke… Or the nice elderly woman behind the counter. The tenor of their thoughts was…nice. The sandwich maker, she was thinking about her grandson who'd started walking two days ago. She hadn't seen him do it yet and planned to visit tonight. Thinking about seeing the little boy made her happy. And her happiness filled Kitty with happiness.

This part of her new…gift was fine. She found that some people—like Blue, Seth, and Luke—didn't fill their minds with nastiness. People like that, even when they were inappropriate or having an errant bit of meanness, they weren't inherently mean. But Jack...

Wish I was alone. I'd be in Mexico by now.

He had his moments. When he was thinking about his family, she caught flashes of awful pain and sorrow. Worse even than the others. When he thought about his aunt in Trinidad, his worry and guilt were so consuming she wanted to cry with it. But when he was in these kinds of moods... Kitty sighed, rubbing her temple.

There must be some way to block out this stuff. Currently, she was at the mercy of whoever stood nearby. And right now that meant Jack.

It wasn't fair. It was her head. She should be able to control what came in and out of it.

Doesn't she know the mayonnaise goes on first? God, what an idiot. Jack snorted next to her.

What a jerk. Enough. She couldn't take any more. There had to be something. She stared at him, focusing. All she wanted was to put up a wall between him and her. Just not him, not him, not him...

He turned then, catching her looking at him. *Why's she staring at me again? She's so weird.*

Anger exploded in her. How dare he? She scowled, concentrating hard, determined to put a barrier between them if it killed her.

She should have stayed... And with that, he was gone. His thoughts had been there and then they weren't. She smiled. She wanted to taunt him. He couldn't poison her with his pessimism.

"Kitty?" Luke touched her sleeve. "Are you all right?"

"Never better." Because she was in control again, control of herself, of her own thoughts. "Why?"

"Your nose. It's bleeding."

Chapter Nine

When Kitty returned, Seth left her with Blue and went to get food. He tried to keep the door from making noise as he closed it. Luckily, it latched behind him with only the faintest click.

He paused in the hotel hallway, listening at the door. Blue must have slept through his departure. Good.

Shoving his room key in his back pocket, he jogged to the stairwell, took the stairs down two at a time, and trotted outside into the night air.

He needed to hurry and get back fast. Even though Kitty was there, he didn't want to be away long. Taking off at a steady clip, he hustled down the street to the Subway. Probably the best place to get something for her.

Christ. This entire situation was fucked. It wasn't until he'd tucked her into that bed, safely away from danger, and climbed into the shower that the true weight of it all hit him.

Blue could have been killed. Fallen from a train, crushed under its wheels, dead. Luke was blaming himself. Even Blue had mumbled about her own stupidity. But Seth knew who was to blame. The whole stunt had been his idea. He'd pressed her to levitate Luke, even though he'd known she was nervous. Hell, both Luke and Blue had been as skittish as cats with ADD. But he'd pushed and cajoled. His plan, it would work, his mind said. It was their best option, his mind said.

If she'd died, it would have been his fault.

Pissed, at himself, at their situation, he threw open the door to the Subway. The little bell jingled in protest. The petite older woman behind the counter looked up from the sandwich she was making, her hands up to the elbows in plastic gloves. He smiled in apology and got in line.

As he waited his turn, he took a deep breath. Not again. He wouldn't be responsible for another innocent death again.

An innocent he cared about. Like Bobby.

He'd been part of the detail in charge of keeping Bobby alive. Bobby was one of only a few civilians who traveled with them in Iraq. He was a photographer, a complete artistic geek. He'd come along to take pictures, part of some propaganda about the state of affairs in the Middle East or some other nonsense. They hadn't seemed like they'd be friends. Bobby mostly kept to himself. But one night, Bobby offered him a Milky Way from his box from home, and they'd bonded over a love of caramel. Before long, he was keeping the guy company during his cigarette breaks, and they were chatting during long drives. Seth liked his dry wit and the fact that he never missed an opportunity to make fun of himself.

He learned to not take himself quite so seriously from Bobby.

When Bobby returned to Afghanistan for a second trip, he'd requested Seth. Old friends, reunited.

They'd been bullshitting when the first shells hit that day. While Seth hit the deck and returned fire, Bobby had been clicking pictures. Seth wanted to fall back, to get Bobby to safety and out of the way of the fighting. But when he'd made to shove Bobby behind him, the other man resisted. "No. I need these shots, man."

While the doubt nagged at him, Seth had backed down. This was what Bobby had come for, these shots. He'd thought they were safe enough.

He'd been wrong.

He should have insisted. Protected Bobby when his friend wasn't as concerned about his safety as he should have been. It had been his job to keep him out of harm's way.

He failed.

All these kids from Glory...the whole lot of them kept looking at him, expecting him to make the right decisions, the hard decisions. He did what he could; he didn't want to let them down. But he wasn't perfect.

If he kept going like this, out in the open, running from Goldstone, sooner or later he'd make a choice that got someone killed.

Again.

Blue had no idea how long she'd slept, ten hours or ten minutes, but she felt a hundred times better when she woke. Her mouth felt dry, and her head still ached, but she didn't have to puke. At least not right now. That was something.

"Hey, there, sunshine." Seth lounged at the standard-issue hotel room desk, studying a map. Leaning back from the paperwork, he made studious look pretty hot. He smiled at her. "Why don't you grab a shower?"

A shower. Never had such a simple thing sounded so amazing. She searched the room, located the backpack they'd brought with its spare set of clothes. Grabbing them, she hurried into the bathroom. The mirror proved she was a hot mess. Blood on her T-shirt, crazy hair sticking out of her makeshift head wrap. She pulled the bandage off, checking for bleeding. It had stopped, thank God. That probably meant the cut wasn't too deep. Her head still ached, especially if she moved it too fast, and the lights hurt her eyes, but for the most part, she felt a lot better.

After the best shower of her life, she changed into a fresh pair of jeans and one of Kitty's T-shirts with a picture of Hello Kitty on it. A funny one, that Kitty.

She stepped out of the bathroom minutes later, feeling like a different, cleaner, all around better person. She rubbed her hair with a towel, careful not to reopen her wound.

Seth looked her over with a smile that warmed her. She flushed and looked away. The atmosphere in their little room felt too intimate, like they were sharing the hotel room instead of being stuck together.

Now, after some sleep and a shower, she forced herself to be honest.

She liked him. A lot.

It didn't hurt that he had one of the hottest bodies she'd ever seen. God, when she'd awakened after her little fainting spell on the train, he'd been half naked in front of her, and now all she could think about was the sight of his muscled chest.

Plus, he'd used his own shirt to bandage her. Did it get hotter than that?

She didn't think she imagined that he seemed to be into her, too.

But what did that mean for them? It's not like they had anything in common besides the situation they were in. Thinking too much about this stuff was stupid. A bad idea.

So why did his approval of her, fresh out of the shower, mean so much? And why had she hurried through what had been the most amazing shower she'd had in years to come out here and be with him?

"I brought you a gift."

She tried to be casual when her entire body tingled. "Oh, yeah? You shouldn't have."

She flopped down on the bed and immediately regretted the decision. She put her hand to her throbbing head.

"You'll like this." He tossed her a bag with a Subway logo on it. "Veggie Delite. You're welcome." Then he threw something that landed next to her. A couple of travel packs of Advil. "And this."

He handed over a soda.

She gazed at it as if he'd offered her flowers, taking it slowly from his hand. She ripped open one of the packets of pills and popped the contents in her mouth, and she took a long drag. Coke never tasted so good. "I take back all the bad things I said about you."

"Good to know."

"Seriously," she said, motioning to the sandwich. "Thank you."

He nodded.

She pulled the sub out of the bag and unwrapped it. Oh, man, he even got olives on it. She loved olives. "What's with the map?"

"Phones with batteries in them are traceable. So, I'm going old school." He patted the map in front of him. "Trying to find the best way to get to San Antonio from here."

She took a huge bite and finished chewing before she answered. "What's in San Antonio?"

"My friend. Nick. He's waiting for me."

The last word—"me"—lingered in the air. She paused, the sandwich on its way to her mouth.

Did he mean only him? Or all of them? Had he decided to leave them now? After they'd come all this way together?

Forcing herself to take another bite of her sandwich, she chewed as she processed that. If she thought about it, she supposed she expected they would split up. Eventually. She hadn't expected it to be this soon.

But now, faced with his leaving, it bugged her more than she'd expected.

Just because Seth helped her get out of Glory, that didn't mean he wanted to stay with her.

Them. Stay with them.

Determined to remain casual, she blotted her mouth with a napkin before she asked, "What's he waiting for?"

"I'm supposed to show in North Carolina in two days. For Special Ops training. Nick and I were going to ride together."

She gave up on the sandwich, laying it on her lap and rubbing her hands together to dust the crumbs off. "You can't expect to go there now, can you?" Yeah, he'd had special training. "Had" being the operative word. That was two days ago, before he could outrun her Cavalier. Everything had changed since then. "It's not safe. You must see that."

"To Special Ops training? No. I don't expect to go there now." He grimaced, glancing at his hands. As if the thought of missing it pained him. "But I do want to go to North Carolina. To the army." He looked up. "I think you should come. All of you."

Their eyes held as she processed that.

He didn't want to leave them. Irrational joy exploded in her chest, followed by immediate confusion. "You want us to go to an army base? And tell them what happened to us?"

He nodded. Then he waited, as if he knew she had more to say.

"You can't be serious." The words exploded out of her. He was going to turn himself over to the military?

"I knew you would say that."

"How'd you know I'd say that?"

His eyes narrowed. "So you don't think I'm stupid for wanting to tell the army?"

"Oh, I do. But I don't know how you knew that." She folded her arms over her chest.

He exhaled. "Listen, we can't do this by ourselves. I think it's smart to get them involved."

"How do you know they aren't already involved? How do you know they didn't have something to do with this?" Blue knew she sounded paranoid, but she didn't trust the government. If it hadn't been for the government—the IRS, in particular—her father might still be alive. An audit led them to suspect money laundering in her father's landscaping business. When her father confronted his partner, the other man confessed, but her father could never prove him guilty. After the partner skipped town, and it became clear that her dad would lose everything and go to prison, her father shot himself in the head.

If the IRS hadn't pushed so hard, or if they'd listened to his explanations, investigated the partner further…something, well, maybe her father would be alive today. Maybe her mom wouldn't have gone off the deep end. Maybe Blue would have grown up like a regular kid.

No, no government involvement. As far as she could tell, going somewhere to hide was their best option. Away from the public eye. After a while, they could slip away, out of the country. Canada or Mexico. Something.

"I don't know they aren't involved. But if we keep going like this, someone's going to really get hurt. Or taken." He pressed his palm into the desk and stood, pacing beside the bed. "You guys. You aren't prepared for this, to be on the run. You must know that. Everyone keeps looking at me, but I don't know what I'm doing. My fool plan on the train almost got you killed." He stopped, his hands on his hips. "Can't you see that? I almost got you killed. Someone's going to die, and it's going to be my fault."

She might have shot back at him except she saw real fear

in his eyes. Her mouth snapped shut. He was genuinely afraid. For her.

That sucked the wind out of her, like a deflating balloon. She revisited their entire time together. If anything, Seth had kept them alive. All of this, everything he was saying, it was all wrong. He'd twisted everything. He wouldn't be responsible for their deaths. He was the only reason they'd made it this far.

Some of her anger faded. But before she could come up with a response, a new argument, a knock sounded. Seth stalked over and looked through the peephole before opening the door.

The others trooped in. Luke sprawled across the bed, Kitty sat on the edge, and Jack slumped next to the door. Like he had something better to do.

She took a deep breath and folded her arms over her chest. "Seth wants to go to San Antonio, to meet up with a military friend. Then he wants us to turn ourselves over to the army."

From the other side of the room, Seth let out an exasperated sigh. "Come on, Blue. It isn't like that."

"You want to go to the army?" Luke asked, lifting onto his elbows. "Huh. I'd expected the newspaper."

"The newspapers?" What were these people thinking? Now wasn't the time to talk to anyone. Now was the time to run away. "We can't go to the newspaper, either. The military is bad enough. We're scary. We can do things that other people, *normal* people"—she stressed the word "normal"—"can't do. You think the general population is going to be happy knowing we're out there somewhere, on the loose?" She shook her head. "If you do, you all give people a lot more credit than I do. What we need to do is find somewhere to hide."

"I know." Luke glanced away, obviously not willing to

argue with her.

"I'm going to Mexico. With or without any of you." Jack shrugged. "I don't give a shit what Seth does."

"What do you mean, you're going to Mexico?" That was news to her. She'd thought they would talk about this.

"I'm going to get him there." Luke shifted to sit. "I want to go, too. We're leaving in the morning." His shoulders hunched a little, his shirt dwarfing his slight frame, and he looked away again. "It's as good a place as any to hide."

What was happening here? She looked back and forth between them. Luke still wouldn't make eye contact, and Jack looked belligerent, as always. Had they planned to abandon them the whole time, too? "When did you guys decide this?"

"Over dinner."

"When did you plan to tell me?" They'd sat over crappy fast food and decided to split up? The least they could have done was let her in on their plans. They'd all grown up together. It wasn't like they were great friends, but they were in this together. Weren't they?

"You were sleeping." Jack rolled his eyes. "You can come, too."

"To Mexico?" Why Mexico?

"There are a lot of beaches in Mexico. With half-naked girls," Kitty explained, clutching the edge of the bed, staring at the ceiling.

Half-naked girls? Blue wrinkled her nose. That was definitely Jack. Right up his alley. But Luke? She thought more of him.

"You said it yourself, Blue. Go far away and disappear. Before someone finds us." Jack pushed away from the wall. "Come, or don't come. I don't really care. It's not like there's anything keeping us together. We all got shit on by circumstance. We're not like a family or anything. Our families are dead. And frankly, the faster I leave anything that reminds me of Glory behind, the better."

Yes, that was what she proposed. Run, hide. Get away. Yet she didn't want to go to Mexico. Not if Seth didn't come, too.

Almost against her will, she turned to Seth, who glowered at Jack, his jaw clenched. Having him pissed at Jack, too, made her feel better somehow.

She didn't want to leave him, she realized. She wanted to stay with Seth. So, even as her instincts screamed to run and hide, to follow the others to Mexico, she refused to leave him behind.

"I'm not going with them, either," Kitty said into the awkward silence.

"You aren't?" Luke piped in. He sat forward, studying Kitty as if her mutiny surprised him. Which wasn't unrealistic. Kitty was no rebel.

"No." Kitty shifted, finally meeting Blue's eyes. "I'm going with Seth, if he'll have me. I want to know what happened to us. And I want to figure out how to make it stop. If the army can do that, then that's where I need to go." She came to stand next to Blue and addressed the boys. "Maybe you guys think this is cool, super jumping and running really fast. Moving things with your mind. But I hear everything everyone is thinking, and it's awful. I couldn't go and lie on the beach with bikini-clad women and pretend there isn't anything wrong." She glanced pointedly at Jack. "There is no escape for me."

"Besides," she continued. "After the nosebleed, I'm afraid."

"What nosebleed?" Blue asked.

"I think you're blowing that way out of proportion."

"Shut up, Jack." Seth hadn't involved himself until now, but he sounded as if he meant business. "What nosebleed, Kitty?"

Kitty turned to him. "I tried to use my power...but in reverse, I guess. I wasn't trying to hear anyone..."

"You were trying to shut someone out."

"Yes."

No one looked at Jack. It didn't take a genius to figure out whom she was trying to shut out.

"Well, it worked, but then Luke noticed my nose bleeding. And I ended up with a bad headache."

Dread filled Blue's stomach. A bad headache? Nosebleed? "When I stopped you guys in the tree. My nose bled then." She looked down. "And...on the train. I was trying to keep Luke still. The wind caught him, and I thought I'd lose him over the side. It took so much concentration. And then my head...it exploded."

"Wait." Seth grabbed her wrist, turning her toward him. Not rough, only insistent. "Is that why you got hurt?"

He looked so intense, she backpedaled. "Not exactly. I must have dropped Luke, and then he dropped me. I rolled, couldn't get my grip. It's all a bit of a blur."

He snorted. "I bet."

She hurried on. "The important thing is that it seemed to be when I was trying to use my power. When I was trying really hard, when what I wanted to do was harder than what I'd ever done before. Like I pulled a muscle."

"So you think that's what caused her nosebleed?" Seth motioned to Kitty before turning to Blue. "And what made you pass out?"

"I didn't pass out from that," she pointed out. It was true. She'd passed out later. "I got a headache." She wasn't good at soothing him, but she hated how upset he looked.

"Fine. A headache. You think you got a headache from that?"

Jack scowled. "I haven't had problems. Neither have Luke or Seth. Maybe it's because you're chicks." He smiled, goading.

Misogynist. Though she couldn't exactly rule it out. So she answered sweetly, "You're so charming, Jack."

"That's wrong, actually," Seth added, staring at the floor. "My nose was bleeding after the helicopter. I thought I got it after falling that far. Maybe not."

"I don't know if using my power caused the nosebleed, but what's to say it didn't?" Kitty's hands fisted at her sides. "How do we know it isn't going to get worse? They put something in our water. It killed everyone else, and we drank it. What if it's only a matter of time before it kills us, too?" She waited a beat to let that sink in. "I'm going with Seth. We have to find out what's happening to us."

They all stared at each other. Jack remained silent and belligerent, but Luke looked uncomfortable. Blue didn't know how long the standoff would have continued. But Seth scrambled to the door and killed the lights, effectively ending their conversation.

"What the hell." Jack's annoyed voice filled the darkness.

"Shut it," Seth hissed. "I heard something outside. Everyone down."

Kitty's gasp echoed as she dropped to the ground next to Blue. "We have to get out of here. Now."

"What's going on?" Seth whispered.

Her answer was ominous. "They're here."

Chapter Ten

"It's Goldstone. Like you guessed." Kitty's voice cracked with terror.

Shit, shit, shit. How had they found them? Seth hadn't sensed them or seen anything. Surely he couldn't have been so careless.

He had to get them all out of here. In a hunch, he grabbed his backpack and went to the door, peeking out. Same hallway as before, floors covered in nondescript maroon carpet, walls adorned with cheesy wall sconces. Blessedly empty. "Let's go."

"Where are we going?" Luke whispered back.

"Out."

"Wait. My money. It's in the room."

Of course it was upstairs. In their room. Not with him. Seth fought back his frustration. He needed to have a long talk with these guys about vigilance. Weren't any of them in Boy Scouts or Girl Scouts? Hell, he'd take a troop of Brownies with their preparedness badges over this crew.

"Fine. We'll go get it. If we get split up, though, meet back at the park across from the train station." He hoped they all remembered where that was. More, he hoped they didn't get split up.

Luke nodded. Seth opened the door, ushering them out. He followed backward, watching their backs, until they reached the stairwell door. He waved them through. "Go. Up."

The others ran up the stairs, some of them taking them two at a time. Blue looked a little peaked, but she hustled pretty well for a girl with a concussion. They stopped at the door to the second floor. Seth passed them to check the upstairs hall before waving them through again.

So far, so good.

They quickly found their way to room 214. He and Luke slipped inside without turning on any interior lights. The room was also empty. This was almost too easy.

"It's over by the window." Luke hurried with the grace of someone born without natural athleticism. He leaned down, grabbed the strap, and slung the pack on his shoulder. His shoulders relaxed, and he smiled. "Got it."

The window next to him exploded with a loud crash. Luke flinched, covering his head, as glass shards exploded around him. A soldier dressed in black camo swung in, landing on the carpet beside him, a rifle in his hands.

As it had every time something like this happened, time slowed. Seth easily calculated the distance between himself and the other soldier. He would disarm and neutralize. Come in low, grab the rifle, take out the left knee, return to standing, and bring the butt of the weapon down on his face. All could be accomplished in less than a minute.

The plan took less than a second to formulate. The soldier didn't even have his bearings yet. Seth tensed to spring. But by then, he wasn't needed.

His opponent flew backward, out the way he came in. Surprise and fear registered before he fell, leaving a strangled cry in his wake.

Seth jerked around to find Luke pale, his hands up. "I didn't think. He was there." His face wore the horror of someone who had just killed someone. Pity swept through Seth. Except there was no time. "Out."

Luke hiked the bag onto his back, and they hustled out the door. The others waited in the hall, and Seth tore past them. "Go. They're inside."

Seth didn't look back, grabbed Blue's hand. He wanted her close. She wasn't well. The rest of them would be fine. He expected her to shrink away. She'd been frustrated with him a few minutes ago. But, instead, she squeezed his hand and followed him, her mouth tightened into a straight line.

He pulled her close to his side. They might disagree on where they were going next, but right now, he knew they were better together.

He stopped them at the stairwell and pulled the door open before sticking his head in to listen.

Faint shoe scuffs echoed off the concrete walls.

"Shit." He turned to the others. Jack, his shoulders hunched and defensive. Blue, pale and determined, clinging to his hand. Kitty, her eyes wide and fearful. Luke, his misery so clear it didn't take Kitty to know what he was thinking.

Christ. He really was going to get them all killed.

Maybe they should stop right now. If they went with the Goldstone guys, they would be captives, but they'd be alive. If they ran now, who knew if the organization wouldn't kill them to gag this whole fiasco? They'd fucked up, it was clear. There would come a point when they would cut their losses, realize it was easier to erase them than to chase them all over the country, and call it a day.

As they stared at him, he felt the burden of their trust.

Was this what his mother felt when she looked in his eyes? The unbearable weight of responsibility to someone who couldn't look after himself? The errant thought made his decision easy.

No way would he buckle under duty. Not now, not ever. But once they were out of this, he was moving on. They deserved a better leader than him.

"We go back. The way we came. We're going out that window."

He passed them again, in no rush. No need to hurry now. They couldn't get in front of the soldiers. They were going to have to go through them. What they needed now was a plan. "Jack," he called behind him.

"Yeah."

"You're with me."

He caught up, walking beside him. For once Jack didn't look so pissed off. If anything, he seemed eager for what they were about to do. If he had the same gift Seth did, he had a good idea what was about to happen. "What's up?"

"We're going back inside your room. Once we get in, if you're like me, your mind will give you plenty of time to think through the fight." He glanced to the side, to see how Jack accepted their inevitable fight. He looked solid, so he continued. "Try not to do major damage if you can avoid it. Broken arms, legs, noses, all fine. Watch head injuries and avoid blood. No weapons." The conversation he'd had with Blue yesterday, when she'd chewed him out for not caring about whether the soldiers lived or died, replayed through his mind. Maybe he had been too quick to do harm. These guys weren't in charge. They were following orders. Killing them probably wasn't necessary.

Jack nodded once.

He spoke over his shoulder this time. "Jack and I will go out the window first. We'll neutralize the men on the ground while Blue sends Kitty down. Luke, you paralyze as many as you can. Just hold 'em still. You guys figured out how not to suffocate them, right?" Luke nodded. "Good. Then Blue will send you out, before you bring her down." He could have tasked Luke with more of the work, but after he'd freaked out and tossed a guy out the window, he wasn't sure Luke could manage himself.

Then again, Blue probably had a concussion. He turned to her. "Are you okay?"

She nodded. Good, she was solid. He squeezed her arm, needing to touch her, to feel that she was really fine.

Still touching her, he made eye contact with all of them. "Do you all understand the plan?"

"Yeah. Fight like freaks while the other freaks fly out a window." Jack pressed the room key card into his hand.

That about covered it. "Right. Let's go, then."

And with that, they were all business. Beside him, Jack cracked his neck. Behind him, he could feel the others tense. He thanked his stars that no one was freaking out.

He swiped the card and swung the door open in one movement, so fast anyone inside wouldn't hear the lock. Then he flung himself through the door.

The three men inside 214 didn't have time to react. He dived on two, taking them to the ground, leaving one for Jack. He rolled to the right, planted his elbow in that guy's face, and then gripped the other by his jacket. The fight almost didn't seem fair. Three easily calculated blows—kidney, throat, and nose—and the guy went down. The other had cleared the blood from his face, when Seth knelt over him. He planted a head butt square to the bridge of his nose. It broke, he could feel it, and then he went down, too.

It was so easy it scared him.

Beside him, Jack grappled with his man. Kid could use some hand-to-hand training. He had lots of strength but no finesse. Seemed like he fought with anger alone. Finally, he maneuvered enough to catch the guy in the balls with the kind of kick no man wanted to receive. It worked, though. The soldier flopped around on the ground like a fish out of water.

The others came in as another soldier flew through the window, feetfirst, still holding onto the rope hanging outside. He stopped, though, hovering half in and half out of the window, his muscles still flexed, his mouth open in what had probably started as a battle cry but wasn't even a whisper now. The soldier floated past him, suspended in midair, frozen in place.

Seth studied him then turned to Luke, whose eyebrows were dropped low, concentrating. Man, that trick never got old.

"Time to go." Blue nodded at the window. Shards of glass spiked from the sides. She frowned, and then the remaining glass exploded out, leaving the frame clear of sharp edges. Blue smiled, all smug. He couldn't help but grin in return. She really was too much.

If they got out of this...no. Not if, *when* they got out of this, he hoped she'd come with him. He couldn't imagine leaving her now.

With that errant thought, he dived out the window. As he flew through the sky, ropes dropped off the roof, signaling the arrival of at least two more soldiers. Above him, Blue's brows dropped in what looked like concern. For him. He didn't have time to think about what that meant, because shouts came from above and below. Something whizzed past him, and he twisted to avoid them. Were they shooting at him?

"Tranquilizers! Not bullets!" Kitty's answered yell came from inside.

That was something. At least they weren't trying to kill him. The ground raced to meet him, and he landed in a squat without breaking his foot, thank God. He was in the middle of a small squad, only five. Jack landed ten feet away. He paused a split second to calculate his next steps.

This had to be fast, after all. Kitty would be out in a minute. He sprang.

Arms spread, he knocked two to the ground, using his hands on their throats to smash their heads on the concrete. They groaned, but he knew they wouldn't stand again soon. No way to avoid it. These weren't good odds, even with his strength and speed, so he had to take his advantages where he could. He dived up and to the right, dropping another with a punch to his throat. Two faint pops sounded behind him. He had enough time to bend backward as the tranquilizer needles flew over him. He saw them as they passed above his face. Two tiny darts.

He landed on his hands in a back bend and sprang into a full back handspring, landing on his feet behind the remaining two opponents. A spiral kick knocked out their knees, and then he crashed their heads together.

Jack stood nearby, four bodies littered at his feet.

Kitty landed next to him, surveying the damage they'd done. She looked impressed. "You guys are really something."

"Thanks." From the roof, shouts rang out. Men looked over the edge and ropes dropped over the side. Soldiers spilled from the side door, probably the ones who'd been in the stairwell inside. "Looks like we'll have company soon." He cupped his mouth. "Hurry!"

Damn these ropes. Annoyed, she shoved them away.

Blue watched Kitty land next to the others from the window. Another one, safely out. She sighed in relief, but the feeling was short-lived. Men in camo covered the ground around them. Seth and Jack braced themselves.

They had to hurry. She spun to Luke. "Your turn."

"What should I do with him?" She looked back to find

Luke still holding the soldier who'd come through the window in midair.

Good question. "Can he breathe?"

He snorted at her. "Of course he can breathe. We practiced that a million times. I got it, Blue. Look"—he motioned to the frozen soldier—"his chest is rising and falling, and he doesn't look blue."

"Fair enough."

"So what should I do with him?" Luke's voice went up a little when he panicked. "I can't exactly put him down. He'll try to shoot us."

"Right. How about we put him in the hallway, then?" They sounded like they were discussing rearranging the furniture.

"Good idea."

She took the three steps to the door, opened it enough to look outside. Clear for now. She swung it the rest of the way open and waved her arm, like Vanna White. "After you."

The man in camo sailed through, as if he'd been tossed out like trash. He hung, suspended in the air in the hallway. Blue stuck her head out again. A woman in her bathrobe stood with an ice bucket four doors down. Blue couldn't imagine what the scene looked like, so she wiggled her fingers in a small greeting and slammed the door shut.

Outside, she heard a soft *oomph* and the unmistakable sound of a two-hundred-plus-pound man hitting the floor. A moment later, loud banging on the door, as well as some colorful cursing, filled the room.

"Let's go, Luke."

"Right. Ready when you are."

Out he went, the same as the others.

Her turn.

She glanced at the window. Luke wouldn't be able to see her. She stuck her head over the edge and whistled to Luke below. "I'm going to jump. Catch me."

He nodded.

She moved the end table over a little and stepped on top as two more ropes dropped over the side of the building. Standing on top of the end table, she glared at the offensive ropes.

Anger welled inside her. Why were they making this so difficult? Couldn't they see she and the others wanted to be left alone?

On the heels of her anger, though, she realized she could do something about it. After all, what was the point of these powers if she couldn't use them?

Before she could look down or give herself time to second-guess that she was about to jump out of a window, she dived forward into empty space and spun in midair to face the roof. Two soldiers were already rappelling over the side.

She felt the now familiar tug in her stomach and knew Luke had her. Then she smiled, focusing on the soldiers above her.

Sorry, guys, but gravity isn't going to work out for you today.

Chapter Eleven

How many of these guys were there? After he and Jack disarmed a handful of them, Seth watched two more rappel down. They had to be coming close to the end of the group, didn't they? Goldstone must have sent more than one team this time. His stomach hurt. It was only a matter of time now. This run-in…it hardened his resolve to get them to Bragg, to turn the responsibility for this mess over to someone else, someone smarter than him. They were too visible as a pack. At this rate, Goldstone was bound to catch up with them, and, with the group following him, it was going to be his fault.

He glanced toward the parking lot. It was empty now, but they needed to move.

Blue shot out of the window, twisting in the air so her back faced the ground. She free-fell for a long moment. Seth's heart jumped into his throat, and it felt like a lifetime as he watched her tumbling through the air.

Then she jerked to a stop, beginning to float. Luke had caught her.

He breathed again.

His mind ran through possible strategies to neutralize the latest guys coming down the building. Strategies to keep Blue safe.

But then, they weren't coming down any longer. First, one lifted back up and over the side, arms flailing as he made *whoa* noises. Then, the other followed. They went so fast, Seth imagined they'd have a headache when they landed.

He glanced over. Sure enough, Luke still had Blue. Which meant she'd moved the soldiers. While floating backward through midair.

"Wow," Kitty breathed beside him.

Exactly. Pretty impressive.

The ropes started to move then, twisting like snakes. They slipped through the air, coiling around each other, until they dropped, and he saw her handiwork.

Knotted in three spots. Of course. No ropes, no rappelling.

She touched down next to him, staring up. Her brows had dropped as if studying the results and finding them unsatisfactory.

"Nice touch."

"I was angry."

"So, Windsor knots?"

"Yeah." She shrugged, managing to look sheepish. He smiled.

Two heads popped over the roof above them. Blue sighed. "I didn't hurt them. Only delayed them."

"Humanitarian and all."

She rolled her eyes.

Seth lifted his hands. "No offense."

"Yeah."

He grinned. Without thinking, he folded himself around her in a quick hug, to soothe himself with the feel of her against him. He rubbed his fingers over her hair, and to his surprise, his hand was shaking.

Unwilling to think about that, he pulled away, scanning

the nearly empty parking lot. They needed a car fast. He wouldn't take any more chances. Didn't look like the hotel was very busy tonight, though. He wrote off anything that had been made before 2010 and settled on a Maxima a few cars down. Not his first choice, but it would have to do.

He trotted over. The parking lot remained blessedly quiet, free of soldiers. For now. It wouldn't be long before Goldstone recovered, though.

He lifted the handle on the Maxima. No alarm. Thank God for small towns where no one locked their door.

"What are you doing?" Kitty looked scandalized, glancing up and down the street. Like it was okay to beat the hell out of a bunch of soldiers, but carjacking was beneath her.

"Getting us out of here." He opened the car door, scooting under the steering wheel. He made a few adjustments, stopping the alarm. A few more tweaks, and the engine purred to life. He smiled and unlocked the rest of the doors. "Get in."

Blue studied him. "How'd you learn to do that?"

"Foster kids have eclectic educations." He shrugged. "Time to go. We can travel together to San Antonio." He nodded to Luke and Jack. "A little closer to the Mexican border anyway, right?"

As they all slid into the car, Blue caught him by the sleeve. "Seth." She stepped closer. She didn't even come up to his shoulders, but he felt her presence like a weight. "Thank you. For staying calm and getting us out of there."

Her eyes were so blue. When she looked at him like this, exposed, he had the strongest urge to pull her into his arms again. He resisted this time. They didn't have time.

As the moment stretched, she looked like she wanted to say more. When she didn't, he opened the back door and swept his arm to motion her in. "Yeah. No problem. Let's go."

They turned onto Route 50 going east and headed out of town. It didn't take long, because Seth was driving. Good thing it was flat here. Maybe they wouldn't get killed. But flat meant easier to spot from a helicopter. She wasn't the only one peeking at the rearview mirror, checking for followers.

As the car ate up the miles and the inhabitants sat in silence, Blue replayed the conversation at the hotel room.

What Kitty said changed everything.

If they were suffering from physical problems, then none of them—not even Jack and Luke—could afford to run. They probably should be checked by a doctor. But they couldn't exactly show up at a hospital.

She gritted her teeth. Goddamn Goldstone. What had they done to them? It was all so unfair. No one in Glory caused problems for the corporation. And now they were all dead. Hell, with her health issues, she could be dying, too.

Seth had a point. She'd come to rely on his judgment. If they went to the army, as he'd suggested, they would have access to medical care. Goldstone wouldn't mess with the army.

Would they?

While a kernel of doubt niggled at her stomach, she couldn't deny that the nosebleeds and headaches were unsettling. She hadn't connected her headache and nosebleed on the train to the drug, but if Seth and Kitty had side effects, too… She couldn't ignore that. They should stay together.

That she *wanted* to stay with him, that leaving him now hurt in a spot she didn't want to poke too hard, well, that wasn't important, was it?

His voice cut into her thoughts. "So, who did it?"

"Did what?" She glanced at him in the rearview mirror.

"Someone tipped them off." Seth met her eyes, his brow low, and she nodded, amazed again at how easily she understood what he meant.

Of course. It was the only possible explanation. How else

would they have known they were there? "Someone used a phone or their credit card. Called someone. Something."

"No one called. You made us all take the batteries out of our phones, remember? You said batteries make them traceable." Next to her, Luke looked genuinely confused. Not him, then.

"Yes, but someone had to have reached out," Seth pushed from the front. He didn't bother to signal as he wove around a lone car on the empty highway. "I didn't see anything. There wasn't anyone following us. We'd lost them. Then suddenly, they were there."

"I've never even had a cell phone." Kitty stared out the window. "And I wasn't allowed my own credit cards."

Not Kitty, either, then. Blue turned to Jack in the passenger's seat.

"Oh, so it has to be me?" Predictably, his chin jutted out, and he glared at Seth. "Maybe you're not as good as you think you are, Seth. Did anyone consider that maybe he's giving us away for his own purposes? You guys are so quick to trust him, but what if army boy here is involved in this?"

Blue opened her mouth to light him up when Kitty cut her off.

"He did it." Kitty didn't even turn. "Called his aunt in Trinidad from the hotel phone. He was worrying about her."

"Thanks, Kitty." Jack crossed his arms over his chest, sulking.

"You were worrying about her?" Blue didn't know whether she was more surprised that he cared enough to check on his aunt or if she was more pissed that he'd jeopardized them all.

"Yeah." He said it grudgingly, as if she'd caught him with porn instead of being nice to his relatives.

"Well?"

"Well, what?" he grumbled.

She rolled her eyes. "Well, is she okay?" She didn't like the idea that other people would be hurt because of them.

He looked like he didn't want to answer. Finally, he nodded. "Yeah. She's fine. They asked her where I was, and she didn't know. Then they asked her a bunch of other questions about me and my family. About everyone in Glory. Nosy bastards."

Seth slammed the butt of his hand on the steering wheel. "Damn it, Jack. You don't think."

"You're not my mom. I can call whoever I want."

His defensiveness was getting old. She swatted him on the back of the head. "Maybe you're the shit at USC, maybe your football buddies kiss your ass, but here we all need to work together. You're not the only one you affect with stupid behavior." Next to her, Kitty covered her ears and curled in on herself, but Blue was too angry to stop. Jack needed to hear this. "What if they had caught us? Do you have any idea what they plan to do with us? They killed everyone else. Do you think they'll ask us some questions and let us go?"

He spun in his seat and gritted through his teeth, "I didn't ask for this to happen. All of this. Being stuck with you guys. Losing everything. Did you know I would have started this year? Next year, I could have been drafted. I could have been rich, damn it." His voice had risen, and now, he shouted. "Instead, I come home, my family dies, and my whole life gets ruined. You guys just don't get it."

He breathed heavily after his outburst, staring at her. And she realized he was right. He hadn't asked for this. None of them had. It wasn't fair, and he had the right to be mad. They all did. Lord knew she was pissed off, too. But it wasn't useful. It didn't change anything.

Ahead of them, each dotted line in the center of the road faded as the car ate up the highway. Finally she spoke. "You know, Jack. I get it. You're mad. So am I. Maybe I wouldn't have ever been rich. Maybe I wouldn't even have gone to college. But this wasn't how I'd planned things, either. I'm sure Seth and Luke and Kitty feel the same. Bottom line, though? You need to think of someone besides yourself sometimes."

She fell back against the seat and crossed her arms over her chest. Of all the people to get stuck with, why did it have to have been him? The Murphys were gone, the Keilmans. Jack's little sisters. Yet he remained, jerking up the works.

"Stop it, Blue. I can't take any more." Kitty's whispered plea sounded like she would cry at any second. "Seth, please. Pull over."

Seth must have heard her desperation, because he pulled the Maxima onto the shoulder. Kitty tugged on her door handle, spilling out onto the concrete.

Blue leaned over to check on her, only to find her kneeling on the pebble-covered concrete, retching.

Oh, God. What happened? Was this related to the nosebleeds, the headaches? She scurried out to sit next to her, rubbing her back and whispering soothing words. When the heaving stopped, Kitty started to sob.

Blue put a hand on her shoulder. "Kitty?"

"All of you...you need to stop. You fill my head. I can't take it. But when I try to stop it..." She pressed her hands against her ears, her eyes clenched tightly. A bead of blood trickled from her nose.

"Oh, God. I'm sorry, Kitty." Blue rubbed her hand across her back, making soothing noises and feeling awful. Kitty was suffering because of her, because of her stupid outbreak. She'd probably tried to shut her out and couldn't.

All of this stuff sucked, but Kitty had it the worst. Listening to the lot of them... She'd lectured Jack a second ago about being selfish, but maybe she should take her own advice. She hadn't been thinking of Kitty when she'd let her anger at Jack run wild in her head.

She needed to try harder, for Kitty, especially until they could figure this stuff out a little better. They all did. "Hang on one second."

Blue scooted into the car and rooted around in the backpack Seth had dropped on the floor in the back. She found a bottle of water. But before she rejoined Kitty, she addressed the guys, piercing each of them with an I'm-serious-and-won't-take-any-crap glare. "Listen. Kitty's sick of us clogging up her head with our bullshit. I'm as much at fault as you guys. But I'm going to get her settled down, and then we're going to spend the rest of this trip thinking about puppies and rainbows. Me included. Okay?"

She met each of their eyes separately. Seth and Luke looked appropriately chagrined. Even Jack nodded. Good. She ducked back outside and handed Kitty the water. "We're going to be better. I swear."

Kitty looked at her, her eyes still watery. But she nodded and took a sip of water, spitting it out, before drinking heavily, her hand pressed against her forehead.

Then they both climbed back into the Maxima.

Seth started them off again, quickly accelerating to his characteristic light speed. The silence became heavy and remained so for long minutes. Finally, he spoke. "Thanks for not throwing up in the Maxima, Kitty. I think I can safely say—from all of us—that it's much appreciated."

Kitty sputtered and then gave a shaky laugh. The rest of them joined in, the tension broken. Blue met Seth's eyes in the mirror. She tried to convey her thanks, to let him know that she appreciated him trying to soothe her friend.

But when the laughter subsided, they lapsed back into silence and remained that way through the night. Blue tried to think about puppies and rainbows. She really did. Exhausted, she drifted in and out of sleep, though, and she couldn't help what happened in her dreams.

Chapter Twelve

The trip to San Antonio took the rest of the night and half of the next day. Blue hated it. Long car trips weren't her thing. They reminded her of the summer after she turned seven. She and Gran drove to Utah to see her mom on some commune. Mom had been calling and begging Gran to bring Blue to visit. Telling Gran that she'd cleaned herself up, and she was ready to be a mother. Gran had been so hopeful. The trip there had been great. They sang along to the radio and played I Spy.

When they arrived, though, they never got unpacked. They stayed for an hour before Gran decided she'd had enough. She tucked Blue back in her old Buick Skylark, and they headed home. Gran remained silent the entire trip, a real feat as the ride took more than eight hours. Blue sat next to her in misery, afraid she'd done something wrong. Years later, she realized Gran's silence probably had little to do with her and everything to do with her mother being high and exhibiting a distinct lack of clothing. As in, no clothes. On anyone. But for a long time, all Blue remembered was wishing she could sink into the front seat and disappear.

This silent trip wasn't much better. They took turns driving and sleeping, except Seth cut Kitty's turn short, asking her if she might need a break. She scowled at him but agreed. Didn't take a mind reader to see that Kitty's strict adherence to the speed limit made him itchy.

They stopped at three rest stops and hit two different fast food restaurants. Luckily, one stop was breakfast and she could get an egg sandwich, which left her only one run-in with the lunch/dinner menu. The trip was bad enough. Being forced to eat French fries for two meals might have been the tipping point. She'd be barfing outside instead of Kitty.

At midafternoon, they crossed the San Antonio city limits.

They abandoned the car in the parking lot of a H-E-B grocery store then walked a half a mile before stopping at a coffee shop in a sketchy part of town.

Seth nodded toward the corner. "I'm going to use the pay phone."

Amazing in this day that pay phones even existed. At least here, in a major city. She scanned the street, with its graffiti and broken sidewalk, the trash in the gutters. Then again, maybe folks here couldn't afford cell phones. After all, she couldn't afford a cell phone, either.

The rest of them nodded and trudged inside without another word. She scowled after them. They were heading for the air-conditioning while Seth went to make his call? Didn't seem fair. Someone should have to tough out the Texas heat with him.

Blue looked up at him. How'd he look so good after being stuck in a car all day? Aside from some stubble on his face, he looked gorgeous. If anything, the stubble made him look even more yummy. It was really quite frustrating.

"I'll go with you."

"Thanks."

She fell in step beside him. "You're welcome."

"You can go with the others, you know. I can do this by myself."

"You're not eight. I know you can use the phone." She put her hands in her pockets, wishing she had some shorts. She was sweating in places she wished she wasn't. "I thought you might like some company."

Okay, so fine. She'd rather be with him than the others. Since their change, the rest of their ragtag group…they were falling apart. Seth was changed, too, but he seemed to be holding it together, for them. She admired that kind of strength. The kind of strength that made someone put aside their own bullshit to do what had to be done.

He reminded her that she was a fighter, too.

He glanced sideways, not breaking stride. "All right. Suit yourself." It might have been her imagination, but she thought he sped up a little. She picked up her own pace to keep up.

Blue took a breath and began. "There was actually something I wanted to talk to you about. What you said at the hotel, about feeling responsible for us…"

"Yeah? Hold that thought," he said as he stepped into the booth. He didn't shut the door, probably to keep a breeze going in there, and she was tempted to follow him in. She might have, if it wasn't so god-awful hot.

He picked up the phone and dropped in some coins, effectively stopping what she'd say.

Well, if he thought this would deter her, he didn't know her very well yet. She wasn't going anywhere.

She sat on the bench next to the phone. She fingered the carvings in the wood. Someone named Shandra loved Darnell. The idea of the couple sitting close on this bench, digging their names out together, was sweet. The possibility of either Shandra or Darnell alone, memorializing an unrequited love, made her sad.

"Hey, it's me." Inside the booth, Seth greeted his friend. "Yeah. I know. Man, I know. I'm sorry, I got held up." Sounded like Nick was giving him an earful. "No, it's a really good reason. I can't explain over the phone."

He turned around, his movements jerky, clearly agitated. "Yeah, I know I'm late, and yeah, I know this isn't my cell. I know. But, listen…can you come pick me up? Yeah, I know. Please, Nick, it's important. I need your help." Seth blew out a relieved sigh. "Thanks, man. Really."

It seemed Nick could hear the seriousness in his friend's voice and had given in. Blue's regard for him increased. A friend who set aside his own gripes to help out with no explanations, even when he was pissed? That was a good friend.

"Can you bring something to carry six people?" A pause. "I know your car doesn't have enough room. Is Jeremy there? We need his Tahoe. They don't care if they're uncomfortable for a few minutes. Trust me." Another pause. "No, I'm not smuggling illegals. Christ."

Blue smiled. She might like this Nick. And if Seth trusted him, then maybe she could, too. Maybe. She was still thinking about it.

She listened while Seth rattled off their location. "See you in fifteen, then. And Nick? Really, thanks. I owe you big-time."

She heard the phone hit the cradle and then a moment later, lift again. Who was he calling now?

"La Junta Police Department," he said, speaking slowly. "Connect now."

Was he talking to 411?

"Hello. I wanted to report a stolen car." A pause. "Yes, it's in the parking lot of the H-E-B in San Antonio, Texas, on Nogalitos Street. It's a Toyota Maxima, black. Thank you very much."

Then the phone dropped heavily into the cradle again,

and he stepped out.

"You called in the car?"

He shrugged. "Yeah. I thought they should come and get it before someone stripped it bare tonight." He tucked his hands in his back pockets. "What, you thought you were the only humanitarian here?"

She squinted up at him in the sunshine. He oozed defensiveness, and she took a fortifying breath. "I'm coming with you. To North Carolina or wherever."

He opened his mouth to talk, and she barreled forward, not giving him a chance. "You're right. We need to find out what's going on. With the headaches and nosebleeds… Look at what's happening to Kitty. Both of us have had nosebleeds, too, and after what happened to me on the train…" She shook her head. "We can't afford to ignore this, go hide somewhere, and pretend everything is going to go away."

He crossed his arms over his chest. As he gazed down at her, his eyes were in shadow, the sun directly overhead. She couldn't see what he was thinking, but she figured now was as good a time to air things out as any.

"Seth… About what you said at the hotel…about how you're afraid you'll get us killed…"

He glanced away, his arms falling. "Listen, Blue, I don't really want to talk about this…"

She ignored him. "None of this is your fault. You're the only reason we've come this far. You have to see that. You aren't going to let us down." She wanted to add that she believed in him. But she already felt like she'd said too much.

"Just wait. It's only a matter of time." He tried to brush by her, and she grabbed his arm.

"What happened to you? You can't believe that."

His mouth opened, and his eyes…they were a mosaic of emotion. "I told you about my friend. The one who died? Right?" She nodded, her throat tight. "I was supposed to be protecting him," he said, through gritted teeth. "Instead, he died. On my watch. Because I made a mistake."

She shook her head. "No…"

"Yes." He nodded. "And he died, Blue. He died."

"That wasn't your fault." There was more to this story. She knew it. She knew him.

"You weren't there." He clasped her arms, as if trying to get through to her. "Every day I regret that decision. Every day, I think of his wife and his son."

"No." She gripped his forearms. "This doesn't make sense. You wouldn't have put anyone in danger on purpose."

"Of course not. But he was in danger, because I underestimated the danger." His eyes became knowing. "Like the train."

"The train wasn't your fault. My headache—I was the one that slipped. I was the one that hit my head."

"I didn't even consider the headache, what using these powers might do to us. I have this new ability to see ten steps ahead of us, and I never saw that coming. And you almost got killed."

"No." He was twisting this around, not seeing it clearly. "We didn't have any other choice. You did what had to be done. We needed a plan, and you gave it to us." He was being too hard on himself. Why couldn't he see himself like she saw him? "We wouldn't have gotten out of there if it hadn't been for you. You're a hero."

"I'm no hero." He rubbed her arms, as if to soothe himself more than her. "You don't get it." The low timbre of his voice sent heat rolling into her chest, and goose bumps erupted on her neck. "Do you have any idea how many times I've considered leaving you guys? If I had been smart, I'd have let you go back in Glory. If I'd been smart, I'd have taken off on an ATV at Kitty's house or snuck out of that hotel room while you were sleeping or in the shower. None of you know jack shit about protecting yourselves and you know even less about survival. If I'd been smart, I'd have left you all two days ago."

His words stung, and her mouth felt dry as she pushed the sweaty hair from her forehead. Had he really come this close to leaving them? Her? The line of his jaw said yes, but the softness in his eyes said something else. The traffic on the street continued, cars honked and pedestrians passed. But it felt as if they were alone, in their own little space.

"So why didn't you?" Her voice was a whisper.

"Because I couldn't," he growled. "And…because of you, Blue."

She saw truth in his eyes. This close, with his face inches from her own, she couldn't pretend she didn't see it. Still, she asked. "Me?"

"Yeah, you. You and your stupid way of making me feel like I'm better than I am. They train me to kill people. For a living. But I throw some guys out of a helicopter, and you have me second-guessing everything. You and your vegetarian, do-gooder ways." He let her arm go, as if he was disgusted by himself.

The words weren't romantic. They weren't even true. But something about them had her stepping forward, putting her hand on his chest, right over his heart. Every self-preserving instinct she possessed told her to step back. That this was incredibly dangerous territory.

She ignored them all.

"You wouldn't have left us." She shook her head. "Maybe you thought about it, but it isn't in you. I trust you."

"Well, I don't trust myself." She didn't understand what he meant, but as his hands cradled her elbows and then slid around her back to press against her spine, she didn't overthink. He didn't push, only held her.

"Then you're an idiot." She took the last step into his

arms, curling her hand up to his neck to coax him down to her.

Turned out he didn't need much coaxing.

Their mouths met, him hunched over her, her on tiptoes in her Converse sneakers and Hello Kitty T-shirt. The kiss happened next to a graffiti-ridden pay phone and a wooden bench with Shandra and Darnell's love note on it.

She couldn't think of a better spot.

The touch of his lips sent tingles of awareness arching through her. As his tongue swept in, she sighed, trembling against him. It wasn't the hot sun that warmed her skin and sent heat racing through her body. That was definitely Seth's warm mouth.

His arms circled her, pulling her closer. He lifted her a little, her feet off the ground. As if she was floating. With her feet dangling, her entire body held against him, they touched from chest to thigh. In his tight embrace, the warmth seeped into her, filling her, chasing away the shadows. He was so tall, the shift brought their mouths closer, and he tilted his head to gain better access.

Seth didn't kiss her rough or fast. He didn't kiss like it was a step he needed to pass in order to get to the next base. No, he kissed like he knew exactly what he was doing, without a hint of swagger or arrogance. Only the straightforward way he seemed to do everything.

It completely worked for her.

He nipped at her bottom lip, and she pressed her fingers into his back, pulling him closer, gasping. She allowed herself to cling to him, to fall into him as the delicious waves of fire raced through her, lighting her up from the inside.

They kissed until they were breathless, and she had no interest in stopping. She was hot, sweaty, and the street smelled like exhaust. But everything about their kiss was perfect.

"What do we have here?" The voice, right next to them, broke them apart. She dropped to the ground, irrationally annoyed at the interruption. A small man stood next to the bench, smiling under a hairline mustache, his pants too big for his body and bagging at his knees. "You two in the wrong part of town?"

Seth's mouth firmed as he moved to tuck her behind him. "We don't want any problems. Just using the pay phone."

"And getting some action." Two men nearby chuckled, one in a wifebeater and another with his hat pulled low. Their man wasn't alone. "But we don't care about that, do we? Nah, we want your money."

"We don't have any money," she piped up. If Seth thought he'd give these guys a dime, he was nuts.

"You two? I don't believe that at all." He lifted his hand, still tucked into his San Antonio Spurs jacket. The unmistakable shape of a gun disfigured the pocket.

She was getting sick of people pushing them around. Who did these guys think they were? They'd taken out a helicopter and stopped an entire company of private military men. She glanced at herself, at Seth. They looked innocent enough. That was probably their greatest allure. Two young kids, a little dusty but pretty put together considering what they'd been through. They were perfect targets.

Seth pulled at her arm again, moving her entirely behind him. His body tensed, and she could see him eyeing the three men. No doubt he had a plan, had figured out how to take them all down.

Anger burst through her. If they were anyone else, they'd be at these jerk-offs' mercy. Yeah, well, they weren't anyone else. And she was going to make damn sure these guys didn't forget it.

She froze their talker's gun-wielding hand and stepped from behind Seth. "You interrupted my first kiss in a long time."

The man's eyes widened. "What the hell?"

Her anger blazed, burning a hole in her stomach, and she stopped him talking. She'd be quick. He didn't have to breathe for the next minute.

Out of her peripheral, she saw the other two men tense. She froze them completely as well. Served them right for scaring innocent people. *Wonder how many times they've pulled this stunt before?* On that thought, she tightened them all up, putting a little pressure on their chests.

In a far reach of her mind, she realized this was the first time she'd split her focus in three directions. She noticed it was getting easier to use, this power of hers. Then she stepped forward, meeting her tormentor's eyes directly. "Now, you listen to me. Here's what's going to happen. My friend was about to completely ruin your day. But I thought I'd give you the chance to prove you weren't only meat with eyeballs. We're going to leave"—she nodded down the street—"that way. And once I get down so far, I'll let you go. Then you three are going to find something productive to do with your day. Go volunteer at a soup kitchen or something. Donate something to Goodwill. Give a kid a candy bar. Something."

Seth yanked on her arm, and she followed him, walking backward, still holding the three men with her mind. When they reached the end of the block, she released them, watching as they caught deep breaths, holding their throats and gasping.

Their panic made her triumphant, and she experienced a brief pang of discomfort. She probably hadn't needed to scare them so badly. The fight had been so one-sided. She'd been a bully. Did that make her any better than them? She shook her head. It was different. She had defended herself. She hadn't picked the fight.

They ducked into the foyer at the coffee shop, and Seth turned on her. "Volunteer at a soup kitchen?"

"Why not? Better than what they're doing right now." She glanced back down the street to find the threesome huddled together, staring after them, clearly spooked. They slunk off in the other direction, whispering, as if they'd seen a ghost. She sighed in relief.

"I could have helped." For a guy so adamant that he didn't want to take care of them, he sounded pretty irate.

"I know." She glanced at him. "But your help makes people bleed. I didn't want to cause a scene. You can do it next time."

"Deal."

They smiled. He touched her chin, and the air between them heated up. Memories of their kiss wound on replay through her head.

Was this what she wanted? He was a soldier. A killer, by his own admission. She could be making a huge mistake.

But as his eyes lowered to her mouth, she shivered. Huge mistake or not, they might die tomorrow. She had no idea what was going to happen. For the first time in a long time, she was living in the present. And it wasn't half bad.

Chapter Thirteen

Kitty recognized Seth's friends as soon as they walked in, even before she could hear their thoughts. They were both muscular with short hair, like Seth, but that wasn't the giveaway. They carried themselves like soldiers, as if they meant business. With the confidence that came from meeting obstacles in their life—physical or mental—and overcoming them.

She was immediately jealous.

When they stepped into her hearing, though, she could tell they were much different from each other.

Campbell brings a bunch of people back and only two girls? Typical. The blond one was checking them out. He oozed charm and of the two, he was better looking. Seemed he knew it as well.

Little one is cute. Got that funky thing going on. Like the sneakers. He was correct, though. Blue *was* cute. And funky described her perfectly.

Then his eyes met hers. *Well, hello there, beautiful. Just my type. Pretty hair, pretty eyes, and petite. Come to Papa.*

She blinked. Was he talking about her?

Really big eyes. Very nice.

He was talking about her. She immediately glanced away, dropping her head. No one checked her out. No one had had a chance. Her father had been incredibly strict. She didn't do after-school activities or sports. She didn't even have close friends. Oh, she'd tried. But most people didn't want to be friends with the creepy girl with the really religious mother. And once they were subjected to her father...well, they didn't usually agree to come over again.

And boys? Please. What boy wanted to deal with her parents? They steered far and wide.

But her parents were gone now. These men didn't know anything about them.

The true weight of that settled around her. She was alone. There were no parents left to enforce frustrating rules or stifle her with their restrictions. If people didn't like her, it would be her own fault. Thanks to this power, she would know exactly why they didn't like her, too.

She wasn't the same girl she'd been two days ago.

She'd focused on how awful her new power was. She had to listen to everything. But...on the flip side, she got to listen to everything. No more guessing what people were feeling or thinking. Her whole life she'd lived in terror of her father's next mood swing. She'd always wanted to know exactly what was going on in her mother's mind. She'd felt beyond helpless not knowing, being at the mercy of decisions they made based on thoughts she wasn't privy to.

Well, now she was privy to everything.

Maybe she'd been looking at this all wrong. She might hear them, but their thoughts didn't need to affect her mind. Her brain *was* still her own. There was just more information available. That might not necessarily be a bad thing.

Seth stood, shaking hands with the two newcomers.

"Guys," he motioned to the group. "This is Nick," he said, pointing to the tall one with dark hair. "And Jeremy." This time he waved toward the good-looking blond.

Kitty offered a small wave. No one paid her much attention, and Seth spoke quietly to the pair.

Unnoticed, she listened, determined not to fear what she heard. Fearing their thoughts would be silly.

First, the blond one. Jeremy.

Not too tall. But a nice ass.

She'd never get used to everyone's cursing, though. Jeremy thought she had a nice butt. How…interesting. Did other people think she had a nice butt? How strange to think about it.

Uncomfortable with Jeremy's attention, she zoned in on the other man with him. Nick. He was worrying about traffic laws. *Glad I brought Rickles, even if the guy's been acting strange lately. The Tahoe fits nine. I wouldn't have gotten seven of us in my car.* Then his thoughts switched. *Who are these people? What's Campbell gotten himself into now?* She could feel the older brother vibe oozing off him. The tenor of his thoughts wasn't as strong as Jeremy's. Softer, but pleasant, too. *Seems taken with the blond girl. Hope that isn't what this is about.* He didn't sound angry. Only concerned.

Finally, Nick addressed the group. "We brought the Tahoe. You guys ready to go?"

"Yeah, man. Thanks. We have to get the tab." Seth stood, cleaning up their table, and Luke rose to go to the counter.

She listened to Luke as they walked out. *Wonder if they'll know if that guy lived. Wonder if he'd even show up on a Google search. Secret soldier, killed after falling from second floor.* The soldier in La Junta. He hadn't stopped thinking about him. Poor Luke.

She followed the others outside, listening as an older couple complained in their minds about the younger set, how loud and rude their generation was. She turned to them and smiled in apology, mouthing a sorry. They glanced back at the muffin they were sharing and didn't make any more eye contact.

Outside, the heat hit her like a cannon blast. She gasped.

"At least it's a dry heat." Jeremy appeared next to her.

Remembering the things he'd thought about her, she smiled. "That's what you tell yourselves?"

"Been reciting it the whole time I've been stationed here." He leaned closer and continued in a stage whisper, "It's not working." He offered his hand. "I'm Jeremy Rickles."

She took it. "Hello, Jeremy. I'm Kitty."

Kitty. Sexy porn star name.

That made her grin.

Nice smile. Score. She shook her head, laughing.

His grin widened. "What's funny?"

She continued out the door he held for her. "You wouldn't understand."

"Well"—he offered his arm to her—"we have the entire ride back to the apartment for you to explain."

She looked at his arm and then up at him. After a moment, she looped her hand around his and allowed him to escort her toward his SUV.

"Front seat for you, pretty lady."

Behind them, she could feel Nick's disapproval, even though his thoughts weren't pointed enough to put them into words.

As Jeremy helped her in, and she listened to him appreciate her behind again, she decided to enjoy the attention. What harm could come of it?

The trip across town took twenty minutes, weaving in and out of traffic. Beside Seth, in what passed for third-row seating, Blue dug her fingers into the leather armrest with one hand and cut off blood flow to his arm with the other. She mustn't like Jeremy's driving, either.

But the touch of her hand both comforted him and made him want to pull her into his lap. A simple connection, but it had his whole body ready. He wanted to wrap his arm around her. To run his hands all over her. He rubbed his palms on his thighs, forcing himself to stay still, to not reach for her.

He'd kissed her. Bad idea, even though he'd wanted to do it since he met her. Maybe it was a reaction to the extreme circumstances.

Yeah. Right.

What the hell am I doing?

You're an idiot. That was the only explanation. He'd let her—and that smart mouth of hers—get close. He had a few good friends, like Nick, and Mark, who was stationed in Germany. They were work buddies. They shared beers and a few laughs. He would trust them with his life on the battlefield. But they didn't know about his mom or Bobby.

Yet Blue had the whole story.

Why her? She made him laugh, and she was easy to talk to, yes. She was also sexy as hell, but that wasn't all of it, either. She seemed to understand where he was coming from.

That kind of thinking was dangerous. And he sure as hell shouldn't be kissing her.

If he gave in to his feelings, it would put her in danger. People did stupid things when they were emotionally involved.

He only had to hold it together—remain aloof enough to keep her safe—until they made it to Bragg.

Determined to keep things in perspective, he scanned the car. Luke and Jack stared out opposite windows in the middle bench seat. Luke hadn't been the same since La Junta.

Seth didn't push, though. He remembered his first casualty too well.

And Jack? In the rearview, he caught Jack's reflection. Looked pissy like he always did.

Between them, Nick looked grouchy but remained silent. Thank God he wasn't hounding him right now. He deserved an explanation. But Seth hoped he'd be able to put it off until some of them split up. Luke and Jack said they'd only stay the night. If Seth only had to convince Nick to let Kitty and Blue tag along to North Carolina, maybe he'd be more receptive.

Too bad he had to include Jeremy. Not that he was a bad guy. But he always watched out for number one. Even now, he'd zoned in on Kitty. Probably saw an opening and decided to capitalize. That was the kind of guy he was.

He'd have to keep an eye on that. Kitty could hear him, sure, but he still didn't trust the guy.

Finally, Jeremy stopped outside an apartment complex and swiped a key card. The gates swung open, and the Tahoe pulled through, following the curving roads around cookie-cutter buildings until he stopped at the one marked with the three hundreds.

They crawled out of the Tahoe, and Seth looked at his troops. Luke's hair stood in every direction, and the circles under his eyes made the grief in them even starker. Even the chip on Jack's shoulder seemed less pronounced when he was tired.

They needed some shut-eye.

But as he stepped onto the sidewalk, Blue stopped him.

She waited until the others began walking toward the buildings, far enough that they wouldn't overhear. "I don't trust that Jeremy guy. He's too smooth. I mean, Kitty? She's not…I mean, I don't know if she'd…" Her brow furrowed.

"She's not experienced with guys?"

She nodded. "No. Not at all."

"I'd already planned to say something." She nodded, but her brow remained scrunched. "What?"

"You'll want to talk to them alone."

"Yeah." Already seeing the fight, he mounted his case. "Listen, they know me. I think they should hear it from me. And they're sticking their necks out for us. It could be dangerous, us being here. They deserve an explanation."

"Yeah. I know."

"And they…" He stopped when he realized what she said. "Wait, you know?"

"Yeah. I think you should talk to them by yourself, too. As you say, they're your friends. They should hear it from you. Maybe it'll be easier, coming from you."

"Right."

She folded her arms over her ridiculous Hello Kitty T-shirt, biting her lip. She wanted to be in on that conversation, it was written all over her face. But she was doing her best to believe in him.

Her faith in him meant the world. It shouldn't, but it did.

Before he second-guessed himself, he cupped the back of her head and pulled her close, kissing her full on the mouth. She stepped closer and wrapped her arms around his waist.

His body tightened, and his stomach coiled as her curves pressed against him. Warm, pliant, she fit him perfectly. He shouldn't have done this—any of this—but at that moment, all of his determination to remain impartial flew out the window. And he didn't care. As he pulled back, he gazed down into her beautiful eyes. His breath came faster than normal. "Thank you. It's important."

They might have continued like that if not for the wolf whistle. Seth pulled away but still held her next to him. Then he turned to glare at Jeremy. "Shut it, Rickles."

Jeremy flipped him off, grinning. "Whatever, man." He grabbed one of their bags out of the backseat and chuckled, going inside.

Guy really was a douche bag. He squeezed Blue's arm. "Come on."

Upstairs, Nick's apartment looked like standard-issue bachelor's pad. Two bedrooms, two baths, no real decor to speak of. He'd lived in numerous apartments like this. Beer can chic.

Nick's bags were by the door, and one of the bedrooms had been stripped clean. He was ready to go to Bragg. Seth stifled his pang of guilt. They should go on to Bragg. But none of them had slept more than an hour or so in two days. They needed to stop.

"So, what's going on?" Nick asked through the cutout to the galley kitchen. He was pulling bottles of water from under the counter, lining them up.

Seth glanced at the rest of them. They looked exhausted. "You got any food in this place?"

Nick lifted his brows and didn't immediately comment on his non-answer. "We had Chinese last night, and there are some leftovers."

"We'll have to order out, then. Good pizza?" Seth dropped his stuff near the door. Not that he had much. None of them did.

"Yeah. Sal's Pizza. Down the road."

"They deliver?"

"Yeah."

"Good."

Seth looked around, took a deep breath. "We'll need to stay here tonight."

No surprise, Nick's patience expired. "Fuck, Seth. You know we can't do that."

"I'll explain. I swear. It's only for tonight. We'll leave for Bragg tomorrow. But we've been on the move for two days now. We need a good night's sleep."

"You need to tell me what the hell is going on. Now."

"Fine." There wasn't any putting this off, it seemed. Seth sighed. The conversation was exhausting, and he hadn't even started it yet. He turned to Blue. "You guys get settled, get some showers, and order some grub. You got a house line, Nick? We had to lose our phones."

Nick said nothing, only jerked his head to the kitchen.

"I'll take care of it," Blue said, squeezing his hand, her eyes full of trust. His chest swelled with her support even as he turned away.

He opened the patio door and stepped out, Nick and Jeremy following him without a word.

Outside, the hot air hit him like a fist to the face. He crossed their tiny apartment patio to lean against the railing. He glanced around. No one. Their place wasn't next to the parking lot, which was good. They shouldn't be overheard.

Nick sat at the patio table, putting a Monster drink beside him, tucking his ankle on his knee. He nodded toward the door. "Strange collection of folks you got there, Campbell." He popped the top on his drink. "Seem close to the blond girl."

Seth avoided his friend's eyes. He didn't want to explain what Blue was to him yet. Because the truth was that she was too close. He cared about her too much. He didn't need his friend to remind him of that.

Jeremy stretched out, hands behind his head, kicking his feet up on the chaise lounge. He nodded toward the sliding door. "Yo, next time leave the douche canoe where you found him."

"Who, Jack?" Not that he had to ask, really. "He's not that bad. Just having a rough week." Was he really defending Jack?

"Whatever. Seems like a dickhead."

Couldn't argue with that. "You got neighbors?"

Nick pointed up. "One older lady upstairs."

"She the nosy sort?"

"Nah. Thinks we're sweet boys. Makes us cannoli. Watches *Jeopardy* and goes to bed." Nick crossed his arms. "Talk."

Where the hell to start?

He looked between them. He'd known Nick for years and trusted him with his life. Jeremy? Well, he'd have to take a chance.

He inhaled. "I stopped in Colorado, two nights ago, to sleep. At a bed-and-breakfast. Podunk town in the middle of nowhere called Glory, and I was poisoned."

The story came out in fits at first, but his friends stayed quiet, and he hit his rhythm. The details were crazy—even he had to admit that. Spiked water and superpowers. Private security corporations and helicopters. He sounded like he was telling them about some movie he saw.

The story wound its way out until he finished with, "We assume Goldstone is watching. We've decided to go to the army in Bragg. We need help, both with the medical problems and to stop Goldstone."

He looked between his friends. Jeremy had dropped his hands, blinking at him. Nick's face had stormed over.

"So you are, what, like Superman now or some shit?" Jeremy's face split into a smile. "Are you afraid of kryptonite, too?"

Seth scowled at him. "No, fuckwad. I'm not Superman."

"Are you kidding me, Campbell?" Nick jumped up and grabbed Seth by the front of his shirt and got right in his face. "I'm two days late getting started—three by tomorrow—because you've lost your goddamned mind?"

Seth broke Nick's hold on him and glared right back. "I haven't lost my mind. I'm dead serious. I can run, like forty miles an hour. And jump two floors up. Maybe more. I get hurt when I fall, so I haven't tried. I heal fast, and I can punch like some sort of heavyweight fighter." He put his hand on his hair, pulling at the strands. "Blue? She can move things with her mind. So can Luke. Jack's like me. And Kitty? She can read your mind. Anything you thought in front of her, she heard." He snorted at Jeremy, looking him over. "Hope you were a gentleman, asshole."

Jeremy laughed, standing up. "This is rich. Seriously, Seth, I didn't think you had this kind of stunt in you. You're usually such a stiff."

He gritted his teeth. "I'm not joking."

Jeremy opened the screen door, stepping in where the rest of them were having pizza. They all looked up at him. The whole group of them looked rough, wrinkled, and tired.

"Hello, band of freaks!" Jeremy greeted them, opening his arms wide. "I'd like to welcome you, and Superman here, to our home."

Seth glanced around him. The kids from Glory stared back. Luke had paused with his pizza on the way to his mouth. Kitty's eyes were wide, frantic. Probably everyone's brains had kicked up, giving her a good dose of all of their reactions.

Then he met Blue's eyes as she dusted her hands on her pants.

Uh-oh.

"I see," she said, crumpling her napkin up and putting it on her paper plate. Jeremy didn't know, but her calm didn't bode well for him.

It surprised Seth that he knew her that well. "Blue..."

Slowly, Jeremy lifted in the air. He wheeled his arms, going, "Whoa, whoa, whoa," before he tilted onto his stomach above their heads. Then he swept from one end of the little living room to the other, cursing and carrying on, while Blue gathered her empty plate. "Who's doing that?"

"That would be me." She looked up and wiggled her fingers. "Now who's Superman?" Suddenly, he dropped until he was a few inches from the ground. He stayed there for a long minute before he fell, flat on his face. Seth knew she could have laid him down gently. She was just being mean.

Jeremy sprang into action. "Jesus Christ!" He scuttled back until he hit the wall, his eyes wide and freaked out. His head swung between them all, as if he half expected one of them to jump out and bite him. "What the hell are you people?"

"I'm the same guy. Remember, we went to Vegas last year for Charles's bachelor party." Afraid Jeremy would do something rash, Seth stepped between him and the rest of them. "I told you. We were poisoned. Goldstone wiped out the town. And now we're...different."

"Shit." Jeremy fell back on his butt, rubbing his head with his hands.

Silence fell over the little living room as they all stared at each other.

What the hell was he supposed to do now? This wasn't how he'd planned the conversation to go. But still. These guys had seen some crazy shit before. Surely they would be able to get their heads around this.

"Well." Kitty stood, smoothing out her clothes. Somehow, she made standing in the middle of a lame two-bedroom, wearing dirty jeans and a wrinkled T-shirt, look very proper. "It's been lovely meeting you both. If you wouldn't mind, I'd really like to take a shower, please, and find somewhere to sleep. I'm exhausted."

Everyone seemed to hold their breath. Then Nick sighed. "Sure. Follow me." He started across the room before turning back to him with a scowl. "Seth. We're not done here."

As he stalked from the room with Kitty trailing behind him, Seth wondered again whether he was doing the right thing.

Chapter Fourteen

Kitty followed Nick into an empty bedroom. As he looked around it, his frustration spiked again, but his voice remained calm. "You can sleep here, if you like. Let me get you some sheets."

"No, no," she added quickly. "No need. I'll crash on the floor."

He ran a hand over his head, rubbing the short-cut dark hair. His thoughts flitted across the subject. *Can't let a girl sleep on the floor in my home... My mom would kill me. Don't know where the sheets are... Maybe the pullout sofa has sheets, if she can wait...*

"It's fine. Really. I don't want to be trouble."

His guilt lingered, but he nodded. She expected him to leave, and she wanted him to. She was exhausted. Large groups were particularly exhausting. She could usually manage when she had only one other person's thoughts to contend with. But in a large group, the thoughts came at her like ice shards, each one pricking and hurting until she was overdone, an open wound.

All she wanted to do was lie down and tune all the voices in this apartment out.

But Nick didn't leave right away. His thoughts were filled with conflict.

"Is there something you need?" She was trying to be polite. She really was.

"I'm not sure anyone else will say this, but..." *Don't sound like a dickhead.* "My roommate. He's not the kind of guy that...well...that's friends with girls." *Yeah, that made sense, Degrassi. Try again.* "I mean, he's the kind of guy that hooks up with girls at bars and then never calls. I mean, he's not an awful guy. He's just not boyfriend material. I thought you should know."

"You are warning me against your roommate?"

"I guess." *Yeah. How is this any of your business? She seems so nice. And pretty.* Again the thought—that someone thought she was pretty—startled her. *But some of these girls are so young and naive. I feel bad.*

He felt bad for her? Thought she was naive? She smiled tightly. "Thanks for the heads-up. But this isn't any of your business."

His mouth tightened. "I don't want you to get hurt."

"Thanks. But I'm a big girl. I can take care of myself."

"Can you now?" He touched his eyebrow. *So be it.* "Then forget I said anything." *When am I going to learn that not everyone wants my help? Stupid hero complex.*

"I'm sorry I snapped," she sighed. Everything felt raw tonight. "I know you're only trying to help."

"Let me know if you need anything else. Good night."

With a pang of guilt, Kitty watched him go. She forgot that other people's behavior might not have anything to do with her. It sounded like Nick had his own demons. She probably hadn't needed to snap at him that way. She was so tired of people making decisions for her.

She sighed, dropping her backpack on the ground next to the bed. She punched at it with angry stabs, trying to make it comfy, before dropping her head on top. Curling into the fetal position, she closed her eyes. In the other room, the sounds of six other people's thoughts filled her mind. Again, she turned to her prayers for comfort.

She must have dozed off, because she was awakened later by someone putting a blanket over her. Through blurry eyes, she saw Nick duck back out of the room.

Seth came inside from the porch, shutting the slider and finding Blue rubbing a towel over her short hair. Their eyes met. She looked sexy and appealing, freshly scrubbed from the shower with no makeup on. The leggings she wore clung to her legs, to her butt, and he liked the way all of those curves looked. The pull was there, the attraction he had for this brave, impulsive girl.

These were things he shouldn't be thinking at all.

He'd spent the past fifteen minutes letting Nick chew him out. Not that Nick didn't deserve an explanation, but he couldn't help thinking the entire situation could have gone better.

He glanced away, digging into his backpack.

"You know, I could have handled Jeremy." He kept his voice low, trying not to be overheard. "I had it."

"They're going to help us, aren't they?" she whispered back.

"Yeah, but you agreed to let me handle it. You made that much harder on me than it had to be."

"Maybe I did, but your way wasn't working." Her jaw clenched. "That guy wasn't going to help us unless he saw proof. I gave him proof."

He might not like it, but she probably had a point. He changed tactics. "You don't like him, and you lashed out. If I can't trust you to do what you say you'll do, how is *this* going to work?" He didn't know what he meant by "this."

Her eyes widened, and she jerked back a little, surprised. "You're right. I don't like him. And yes, I did lash out. He was being a jerk, and it wasn't necessary." Her eyes softened, and he could see the hurt.

She glanced away, the towel gripped in her white-knuckled fingers. "My father killed himself when I was very young. And my mom went off the deep end because of it. Stuff like that…well, it's a big deal in a small town." She shrugged one shoulder, busying her hands with drying her hair again. "So, when people look at me like that…like I'm strange, well, it bothers me. A lot."

As he stared at her downturned head, he felt like a jerk. He understood how it felt to be different from the other kids. He'd grown up in foster care, always the outsider.

He groaned, unable to stop himself from stepping forward and pulling her into his arms. "I'm sorry." She stiffened and then softened into him, wrapping her arms around him, the towel dropping to the ground. "I know Jeremy's an ass. And I'm sorry he made you feel like that. I get it. I really do." He tucked her head under his chin and allowed himself, for only a moment, to find comfort in the warmth of her against him.

He forced himself to step away from her, even as his body immediately missed the warmth of hers. "But if we make a plan, I need you to stick with me."

"Even if the plan doesn't work?"

"The plan might have worked if you'd stuck to it."

Her brow dropped, taking on the mulish look he was coming to equate with her when she dug her heels in.

This. This was exactly the problem. How could he expect to keep her alive if she wouldn't even listen to him? She needed to see him as the leader, too, like the rest of them.

"I shouldn't have kissed you, Blue." Oh, man. Her eyes, so blue. He could see everything in them, and he tried not to gag on his own words. "It was a bad idea, and I shouldn't have done it."

She jerked back, as if he'd slapped her. "You think…it was a bad idea. To kiss me." It was a statement, not a question.

"I gave you the wrong idea. We need to focus on getting to Bragg. That…" His hands fisted at his sides to keep from reaching for her. "Was inappropriate. I'm sorry. Stuff like that…it makes people lose perspective." Like him. He was losing his grip.

"You're sorry you kissed me."

He gritted his teeth to stop himself from recanting and nodded, even as he wanted to pull her back into his arms. To tell her that he lied, that he wasn't sorry at all, that he wanted to kiss her again even now.

He had to do this.

Betrayal swept across her face, and it struck him in the gut like a punch.

Better to hurt her now than get her killed later. "I'll get you and Kitty to Bragg, if you'll let me. I promise I'll do whatever I can to keep you as safe as I can. There will be doctors there that can help us."

"And no more kissy distractions." The sarcasm wasn't lost on him.

"No." He said it even as a voice in his head screamed.

She nodded and avoided his eyes when she shrugged. "Fine. If that's what you want."

This was for the best. *Keep telling yourself that.*

She gathered her things as his fingers practically ached to reach for her. When she turned and walked into the room where Kitty and Jack already slept, her back was rigid. He immediately wanted to call out to her, to apologize. He wanted to tell her he was stupid and scared, but he forced himself to let her go.

The door closed softly behind her.

He didn't know how long he stared at that door before Luke stuck his head out of Jeremy's room and interrupted his thoughts. "Seth. I found him."

About an hour ago, Luke had decided to jack into Goldstone's infrastructure and see what he could find out. Seth hadn't known if he'd be able to get in. Goldstone was an elite private security firm. They would have serious firewalls. But Luke found some back alleyway in. He'd also managed to transfer money from his father's account to an offshore account in the Caymans with almost frightening ease. Seth would hate to see what the kid could do if he had malicious intentions. He followed him into the bedroom, sitting down heavily on the bed next to the computer.

Jeremy stretched out behind him, flipping channels on the television, as if none of this concerned him. Nick leaned against the wall at the door, his face unreadable.

He inhaled a steadying breath. "What's up?"

"This has to be him. Dr. Fields. Lots of letters after his name." Luke jabbed a finger at the screen, swiveling the desk chair a little to face him. "The guy's a chemist in Goldstone's R&D department. Or at least he was." He glanced back, tapping away at the keys a bit more. "He was working on a compound to enhance agility." He snorted. "'Enhance.' Great word."

Yeah, great. After spending time with them, he could see how their new talents were enhancements. Kitty's sensitivity and inherent intuition. Blue and Luke's persuasiveness and force of will. Which meant he was like Jack in some way. He wasn't sure how he felt about that.

"Good job." He squinted at the screen. "What else can you tell?"

"Lemme see..." Some clicks and he scanned down. "Days before the drug was supposed to go to clinical trials, the funding was cut to his program. Two months ago." His brow furrowed. "The official reason: too dangerous."

Right.

"This Dr. Fields...he went missing. Over a month ago. There's a police report, too, filed by his sister. Wait, two reports. One about him going missing, and another alleges he stole top-secret property from his employer, Goldstone." Luke glanced up from the screen. "Stole property?"

Seth shook his head. Stole from Goldstone? He allowed that to twist in his mind. It put all the pieces together for him. "That has to be why it took so long for Goldstone to get to Glory, after our flu. They didn't do this to us... Fields must have done this. He must have stolen the drug or research on it. He decided to continue with his clinical trial, funding and safety be damned. I bet Goldstone swept in to clean up the mess."

"He worked under Pike, a retired major in the marines." His face suddenly split into a smile. "Hey, now we're talking. Look at this. One of the trials on the drug. Solvimine." He paused, scanning, and his smile faded. "Oh."

"What?"

"Rats. He tested it first on rats." Luke pushed back from the computer, considerably paler.

When he didn't continue, Seth jumped up, reading the report on the screen.

Twenty rats injected with the drug. Twelve dead the next day after serious illness and seizures. Of the eight remaining, a variety of results. Two of the rats rearranged the objects in their cages with their minds, including an alarming incident in which one of the mice threw the other against the bars, fracturing its spine. Three of the mice exhibited no visual side effects, but there was unusual social behavior. The rat who'd been the pack leader suddenly became more docile. They stopped showing normal rat hierarchies and moved toward an egalitarian society. Their grooming patterns became more predictive and whole pack oriented, as did their eating patterns. The remaining three rats were the most bothersome. Their cages had to be reinforced in new and increasingly sophisticated ways in order to prevent the rats from escaping.

He scowled. That sounded about right.

But as he continued, his amusement faded. The next paragraph chilled him.

At the month mark, only three rats remained. As the animals' behaviors became more pronounced and sophisticated, they suffered seizures, growing in intensity until some of the reactions actually killed the subjects, all deaths marked by blood from the nose and ears.

He looked at Luke. This was bad.

From across the room, Nick piped up. "What?"

Seth stood, pushing away from the computer desk, not sure what to make of all of this. The rats' skills increased along with the side effects. Until it killed some of them? But those were rats, not humans. They were smarter than that. They could control their new talents, right? Most of the time, anyway.

Who was he kidding? None of them seemed to be able to control anything.

Was that their fate, then? Survivors destined to dwindle by another half or more over the next days or weeks? They already suffered nosebleeds, headaches. Would seizures be next? Would they be forced to watch one another die?

No. No way. There had to be something else. He refused to admit that there was nothing else.

Except he couldn't think of anything.

He turned to Luke. "You know what this means, right? This means you guys should come to Bragg. With us."

Still pale, Luke shook his head. "I don't know, man."

Luke was having a rough time, Seth got that. He didn't push. "Think about it. Okay?"

Luke nodded, and Seth left him alone, going out to the living room to collect his thoughts.

As far as he knew, Jack and Luke hadn't experienced any side effects. Yet. Though, with Jack, Seth didn't put it past that kid to keep it to himself. He hoped they would both come to their senses.

But he'd had the one nosebleed. Kitty, too.

And Blue…

He squeezed his eyes closed.

No way could he have driven a wedge between them to keep her safe only to find that nothing would save them. He wouldn't accept that.

They needed to get going, with or without Luke and Jack. First thing in the morning. They were running out of time.

Chapter Fifteen

Kitty woke full of optimism. Amazing what a full night sleep would do. Sure, her bed could have been more comfortable—the carpet in this apartment didn't offer much barrier between her and the concrete floor—but at least she hadn't slept in a cold tent or crammed in the back of a Toyota, catching a half an hour here or there on a long car ride. She'd take it.

She got up, went to the bathroom, and splashed water on her face. She brushed her teeth and felt like a million bucks.

When she stepped out into the living room, she found Blue staring at a piece of paper. Her thoughts were stormy. *Fools. Cowards. They said they were going, but they could have at least said good-bye. What if we're sick? What if we're dying? How are we going to help them in Mexico?*

"What happened?" Kitty asked.

Blue turned over the paper she was holding. "See for yourself."

She read: *I'm so sorry. I know we should stay, get help, too, but we're heading for Mexico. Wishing you both the best, but I can't do this anymore. If you need me, email the address below. Please be careful.*

Luke had signed it, including a generic Gmail address at the bottom.

"I see."

"They're stupid. I expected something like this out of Jack. But Luke? Don't they know we're stronger together?" Blue stormed into the kitchenette, took out a bottle of water, and slammed the fridge door shut. "How are they going to get out of the country without Goldstone finding out about it?"

Kitty didn't know. But unlike Blue, she couldn't work up the same level of outrage. Who was she to know what was best? When she listened to Luke or Jack talk about getting away, she couldn't fault their reasoning. If she could escape this new power, she'd do it in a heartbeat. But for her, it wasn't that easy.

And Seth's concerns about their side effects were valid, no matter what any of the others said.

She wondered if Blue was aware of the fear that tinged her reactions. Probably not. She shied away from thinking of herself like that.

She looked at her friend. They'd been close in high school. But since they graduated, they'd drifted apart. Her parents had never liked guests, after all, and Blue worked long hours.

Her friend was vivacious, outgoing. She spoke her mind, didn't care what other people thought. More naturally introverted, Kitty preferred to blend in. To her they'd always seemed a classic case of opposites attracting.

But now that she was privy to her thoughts, Kitty could see they weren't all that different. At least, not in some important ways. Neither of them wanted to be alone. They didn't think Goldstone should get away with what they'd done. And more importantly, they were afraid of what they would become. None of the guys thought about it, that this new normal could be dangerous, life threatening. But she and Blue thought about it. A lot.

Kitty put the letter down, shaking her head. "It's not as easy as that."

Blue huffed. Her mind filled with betrayal, and Kitty steeled herself against it. And when she inspected Blue's emotions further, it wasn't Luke and Jack that bothered her. She was thinking about Seth, and the pain there hurt Kitty more than she could handle. She tried to drag the conversation back to Luke and Jack. Easier that way.

"Luke needed to leave." She wouldn't explain Luke's state of mind last night. It seemed too personal. He'd replayed the soldier in La Junta's fall over and over, the man's face becoming more and more gruesome with each mental retelling. He'd turned himself into a monster in his mind—that's the word that screamed out over and over—and to him, he'd become someone unfit to be around others. How could she explain to Blue that he didn't trust himself anymore?

"That's idiotic."

Kitty shrugged.

When she didn't get any fight from Kitty, Blue's anger faded, and she sighed. "Well, at least he left us an email. And a huge chunk of the cash he had. That's something, I guess."

"Yeah."

Jeremy stepped out of his room, his hair still wet from his shower. In low-slung jeans, a tight gray T-shirt stretching over impressive muscles, he looked like any girl's dream. He smiled at her, a charming smile, and she tucked her hair behind her ear, looking down. She could feel the heat on her face.

She really is hot. Hope she'll come with me.

"I'm going to run out to get bagels. Anyone want to come?" he asked, looking directly at her, hope in his expression.

She watched visions of herself—a prettier version of her, a version she wished she could be—flash through his mind, and her face heated further. When that vision became more and more scantily clad, she looked away.

She shouldn't go with him. Even his roommate had warned her against him. The memory of that conversation pricked at her, and she wasn't sure why. So why was she even considering this? His thoughts were vulgar. She should do as her mother would advise: take the road of chastity and modesty and remain far from him. All she knew was his head was full of dirty—if vaguely flattering—thoughts.

So why wasn't she declining?

When she didn't answer, he stepped closer. "Come on, Kitty. Take a ride with me."

I need to get her to go. Come on, cutie. Say you'll go.

His green eyes bored into hers, and she found herself drawn to him. He really was incredibly attractive. And he was staring right at her—her!—with that hot look. Her stomach fluttered, and her gaze dropped to his mouth. He had a really strong jaw, a really nice mouth. With two perfectly shaped lips.

Blue stepped closer, shrugging, a fake smile on her face. "Kitty and I will hang out here. But thanks, Jeremy, for the offer." *Back off, pal. You're not her type.*

Kitty scowled at her. What exactly was her type? She'd never been permitted an opinion about boys. Always from her mother, how sexual fantasies were the work of Satan and led down the road to ruin. And her father? Please. If she wanted to leave her house at all, the topic of boys was never to cross her lips. Ever.

She stared at Jeremy's muscles and enticing grin. Maybe she did have a type after all.

When he didn't move to leave, Blue tucked her arm around Kitty's waist and her thoughts turned darker. "Scurry along now." *You douche. Leave the innocent alone.*

That was enough. Kitty shrugged out of Blue's hold. Was that what she thought of her? That she was some innocent who needed protection? Well, she'd been protected her entire life. She was eighteen years old. She'd always let everyone push her around, make decisions for her. Blue was overreacting, afraid again, that was all. She needed to calm down.

She looked at Jeremy, considering. What harm could come of it? It was a quick trip out. For bagels, for pete's sake. He seemed good-natured enough. A little arrogant, but look at him. Besides, he was Seth's friend. They could trust him, right?

Come on, baby.

Why not? "To the bagel store, right?"

His face split into a grin. *Awesome.* "Yep, down the street. I'll even let you pick the music station. You strike me as the country music kind of girl."

She wrinkled her nose. "Too much twang. Jazz?"

"Deal."

"Kitty." Blue's concern washed over her. *He sees her as an easy target. He'll take advantage.*

Was it too much to consider that he might really want to get to know her? Did it have to be that he meant to take advantage? And how much advantage could he take at the bagel store, for goodness' sake? She wasn't a child. "It's fine. We're going for bagels. You like bagels, right?"

"Sure."

"Great."

Jeremy swept the door open and ushered her out. When he stepped in front of her, leaving her to follow, she experienced a moment of doubt. But he opened the front car door, helping her in, before he went around. The show of manners made her feel a little better. Her mother used to say that good manners were the mark of good raising.

Only a couple blocks away. Not far. The thought flitted quickly and then was gone. Wonder what that meant. But when he turned the car on and smiled at her, she forgot about it. *She really is a cute girl.* "Radio's all yours."

"Thanks." She twisted the volume knob. "And thanks for asking me along."

He chuckled. "No problem." *None at all.*

She felt her face flush again. His appreciation was incredibly flattering. "So what kind of music do you like?"

"Whatever you like, baby." *Just something to listen to on the way.*

She pushed the seek button, stopping when she found a suitable jazz station. He smiled encouragingly but didn't say anything. For someone who'd wanted her to come so badly, he was being awfully quiet. Oh, well. There were worse ways to spend an early morning than seated next to a handsome guy who thought you were pretty.

As he pulled the Tahoe into the parking lot of a small strip mall, he searched the cars parked there, taking note of their make and model. How strange. He must really like cars.

They pulled into a spot directly in front of the bagel store, and she let herself out, jumping down from the high SUV. He opened the door to the store for her, and she listened as he appreciated her rear end. *Seriously, so cute. Such a shame.*

A shame? What did he mean?

Then a hand was on her arm. Confused, she shook at it, turning to find a man in a dark suit and sunglasses. "Excuse me, sir."

He didn't let go. Only tightening his grip. Another man, dressed similarly, appeared on the other side. "Ms. Laughton. I'm going to have to ask you to come with us." *We are armed, ma'am. Please do not resist. There are innocent people here.* His thoughts sounded as if they were spoken directly to her. *My name is Agent Poole. I work for Goldstone.*

His thoughts were directed at her, then.

Fear sliced through her. How had they found her? She jerked her head, meeting Jeremy's eyes. He shrugged, his smile only vaguely apologetic. "Sorry, love."

Then all of it crashed down on her. Jeremy's call to the former colonel at Goldstone, who had offered him a golden career opportunity. How he'd focused on her to keep her from seeing his true intentions. She'd listened to his eagerness to go without searching for an ulterior motive. A huge mistake.

Sickness settled in her stomach. He'd set her up. And she'd fallen for it, completely and totally. Like a naive child.

She glared at him, continuing to fix her eyes on him as she allowed the two men to turn her and lead her outside. He followed, standing on the sidewalk as they escorted her along. His half smile mocked her, but she wouldn't turn away, even craning her neck to find him. She wanted to remember this moment. To embrace it, to breathe it in.

As they tucked her into a nondescript sedan, her mother's words—so often tossed out when she believed her daughter was being willful—echoed through her mind.

It was a passage from Proverbs.

You have never wanted my advice or paid any attention when I corrected you/So then you will get what you deserve, and your own actions will make you sick.

Some things were true, harsh or not.

She shouldn't have left Seth and Blue. Not to go with anyone. She'd allowed herself to be separated. Now she was captured. And it was all her fault.

As the sedan started and pulled out into traffic, she closed her eyes. She felt sorry for Blue. She'd take this personally. Her captor's thoughts drifted to her, vague and indistinct. Utterly terrifying visions of hospital tables and padded, empty rooms. Folding her hands in her lap, she knew she should pray. But no greater power had made her leave her friends. She'd made that foolish decision all by herself.

Now it seemed she would pay dearly for it.

Blue shoved the clothes she'd worn yesterday into her knapsack. She still wore the leggings and T-shirt she'd put on after her shower last night, but they would need to either stop and buy something new or find a Laundromat. The few things she had—these clothes and the jeans and Hello Kitty shirt—would start to stink soon. No one wanted that.

She packed it all in the bag with vicious pushes.

What was Kitty thinking? Didn't she see what a scumbag that guy Jeremy was? He was good-looking, with his slick clothes and cocky smile. She saw guys like him at the bar. Those weren't guys interested in *knowing* girls. They were interested in conquering girls. Then they tallied them up like the keepsake plates Gran collected from the places she'd been.

That's all Kitty would be. Some other place Jeremy had been.

Hopefully she'd be back soon. Before he got in the shower, Seth had said he wanted to leave immediately. He'd seemed upset, in a rush.

Seth.

Her head dropped, and she gripped her pack tighter. She should have listened to herself sooner. Before she kissed him. For some guys, kisses meant nothing. Hell, for some girls they didn't mean much, either. But she'd seriously thought this had been different. There had been something underneath their words, something unspoken. Something important.

Or so she'd thought.

He'd been right, though. She shouldn't have done that to Jeremy. The guy was irritating, but she'd been heavy-handed in the way she dealt with him.

She flopped on the bed. The guy hadn't believed Seth, and so she showed him. Maybe she'd gone too far, but there had to be more.

She was missing something. Sometime between their kiss in the phone booth and his conversation with Nick and Jeremy, Seth had pulled away from her. She didn't know why and she didn't want to be so upset about it. But she was.

He and Kitty thought that going to the military was the best idea. That it would help them figure out what was wrong. And Blue couldn't refute that they needed medical attention. But she also couldn't shake the kernel of doubt.

It was the army. The army was secretive.

There were other hospitals, even quiet, private ones. Surely there were other places they could get help, right?

She could go to her mother…

The thought barely crossed her mind before she discarded it. No. She hadn't spoken with her mom in years. She didn't know why she'd think she'd be helpful now. She finished packing her things with a vicious tug to her zipper.

Nick's phone buzzed on the coffee table in the living room. She turned, slinging her pack on her shoulder.

Where the hell were Kitty and Jeremy? They'd left over twenty minutes ago. A long time for a bagel run.

The phone buzzed again, vibrating across the wood surface, and a sick feeling started to settle in her stomach. Nick strolled in and snagged it. He read and scowled. "Jeremy says I should get out of here."

"What?" Seth stepped in from the bathroom, his own pack on his back. His hair was wet, and his shoulders looked insanely wide in a soft blue T-shirt. She tried to temper her stupid stomach flutters. She wasn't successful. For his part, he ignored her, and she glared at him. He didn't notice as he read over Nick's shoulder. "'Leave while you can.'"

Blue's heart picked up, her anger at Seth forgotten. *Leave while you can.*

They were coming.

Seth's eyes met hers, and understanding flared between them, their disagreement of yesterday forgotten. Then they were in motion, in complete harmony. Time to go. Now.

She scanned the room, searching for anything she'd left behind, her heart yammering in her ear. She grabbed Kitty's knapsack and tossed it on over her own. She slipped her feet into her sneakers, and she was ready. Seth returned from Jeremy's room, tucking Jeremy's laptop into his bag along with its power cord. Nick stood in the living room where they'd left him, his phone in his hands, looking shell-shocked.

When he saw Seth hijacking Jeremy's computer, it seemed to jolt Nick to life. "Hey, man. You can't take that."

"We're going, and I'm not leaving this, with any trace of Luke's info on it, behind." He finished zippering the bag, meeting her eyes again. He put his hand out to her. "Ready?"

She stared at his upturned palm. Part of her wanted to shrug it off, to push him away. Instead, she put her own hand in his, squeezing. Because even though he'd pushed her away last night, right now she didn't care. She didn't get his thinking, why he thought their kisses were nothing but an unwelcome distraction. But she didn't care now.

If she'd learned anything from Gran's death, it was that things were uncertain all the time. They were better together than apart. She wouldn't let her pride get in the way of that.

He squeezed back, and they moved toward the door.

Nick followed, putting himself between them and the exit. "No way. I'm coming with you." He kicked into moccasins by the door, grabbing his keys. "I'll drive."

Seth shook his head. "It's bad enough we involved you. You don't have to do this."

Blue rolled her eyes. All this unnecessary regret and guilt... And then... "Where's Kitty? She went with Jeremy. Where is she?"

Nick shook his head. "He didn't say."

He didn't say? Blue tried not to panic. Maybe Kitty had heard something and they'd escaped. Kitty had her own defenses. Maybe she'd gotten them out.

Maybe.

Antsy, unable to meet Nick's eyes, she glanced away, her gaze falling on the patio slider. That's when she saw them.

A line of soldiers in black, their guns in front of them, running crouched along the sidewalk outside. She shifted away from the window and caught sight of them arriving from the other direction. There had to be at least fifteen she could see.

"They're here." Her heart picked up, and she joined Seth's side. "They're coming up the stairs. Is there another exit?"

"Windows in the bedrooms." Nick grabbed his keys and wallet, tucking them in his pockets. He disappeared into Jeremy's room.

She nodded at Seth. "I'll send you guys out while they come in the door."

He shook his head, already scanning the room with that look that said he was planning his attack. "There'll be some downstairs, Blue."

"Fewer than at the door."

He finally met her eyes. "Luke's not here to send you out. How are we going to do that?"

She didn't know. She tried for bravado. "Let me figure that out."

Obviously he wasn't convinced, because he snorted. They followed Nick into Jeremy's room. "You guys are the superheroes. How are we doing this?"

Blue had already opened the window. A big one, thank goodness. Nick and Seth weren't small guys. "We're going out the window." She exhaled. "Seth first. He can deal with whoever is below."

She briefly considered asking him for permission. She

knew he would hate that she made the decision by herself. But they didn't have time to consult the committee. They needed to get out of here.

She lifted him in the air, and his face stormed over. "Blue. No. This is what I mean. We need to talk. There's got to be better way."

"Is there? A better way?" She lifted her eyebrows and waited a moment.

"The door... Maybe the roof..."

"Those are other ways. Are they better?"

His jaw tightened, but he said nothing. So this was the best, and he knew it. He just didn't like it.

"Right." She glanced out the window, happy to find a tree next to them and a pretty dense cropping of shrubbery beneath. Some cover. Finally, a lucky break. From the living room they heard the sound of banging on the door.

He complained as she moved him out the window, and then he cursed before falling silent. She knew he was preparing to take on whatever met him on the ground. She sent a silent prayer that he would be fine, hating how much she worried about him, how much he'd come to mean to her.

Nick raised his eyebrows. "He's going to be pissed about that, you know." It wasn't a question, and it was said with a helping of respect.

"I know." She sighed, but there was no time for remorse now. "You ready? Seth'll keep you protected below."

Nick tucked a pistol in his waistband. "I'm sure I'll be fine."

She paused and then nodded toward the gun. "Put that away, please."

"What?"

"They don't have bullets. They're only trying to capture us." At least that's what Kitty always said, and Blue had come to count on that. "They have tranquilizers. You don't need a gun."

"You've got to be kidding."

"Not in the slightest."

When they started shooting at these guys, when they aimed to kill them, something would change. Until then, it was a step she wasn't willing to take.

He shook his head. "I can't leave it behind. But I won't use it unless absolutely necessary. You're going to have to believe me."

They were coming. She couldn't wait any longer. He held her gaze, steady and certain.

She exhaled. "Fine." His promise would have to be good enough.

She picked him up and moved him as slowly as she could, what with the racket and sounds of impending entrance coming from the other room. With his jaw tightened and fists clenched, she could tell he wasn't happy about this mode of transportation, but he was toughing it out.

She dropped him down behind Seth, who stood next to three crumpled-up soldiers.

Then she looked around the room. Now for her. She had no idea what she was going to do. Short of stringing together some sheets, like old-school prison breaks, she was out of ideas.

She scowled. This would be so much easier if she could move herself. Why the hell could she move everyone and everything else without a whole lot of effort, and yet she couldn't move herself? It was a real black mark on an otherwise cool power.

By the sound of it, she only had a minute or two before the soldiers broke into the living room. Upstairs, she could hear Nick and Jeremy's neighbor banging on the floor, hollering that she'd call the cops. If she didn't want to live in a cage, she needed to figure something out.

She broke out in a cold sweat. The answer was in front of her, inside her. She only needed…

The desk chair.

She could move the chair. If she sat on the chair, she could move it. She'd only have to stay on top of it.

Brilliant.

It was big, one of those large, cushy leather desk chairs. A nice chair, but too big for the window. With a quick thought, she ripped the wheel contraption off the bottom of it. It took some effort, but in a matter of moments it was gone, leaving only the cushioned section in a heap on the ground.

She swept forward, positioning it for her to sit down. She closed her eyes and focused on the chair beneath her. When it lifted, she laughed. She might not be able to move herself, but she could move something else. All she'd have to do was ride along.

The door to Jeremy's room burst open. She turned the chair to ease it through the window as the soldiers filed in, shock on their faces. She could only imagine how she looked, hovering on a busted chair in an open window.

But they didn't remain paralyzed long.

The one in the doorway motioned to the one near here. "Trank her!"

Panicked, she spun the chair, ducking. Two thuds shook the back of the seat and a tranquilizer needle embedded in the armrest next to her.

Desperate to escape, she dropped the chair under her. But when it plunged too fast, she realized she'd miscalculated. She found herself free-falling through the air. Tamping down on her terror, trying to regain control, she reached out with her mind, searching for the chair, trying to move it underneath to catch herself. There. She recovered it, still falling, and pulled it to a halt.

Her momentum didn't stop, though. She hit the immobile

chair with an *oomph*, pain spreading from the impact at her hip, up and down her spine. She gritted her teeth as she forced the chair to remain still. Then something hit her thigh, leaving a sting. She grimaced, swiping at it.

She came away with a little dart.

Not good, was her last thought before she faded away.

Blue fell through the air like a stone.

Seth had heard the other soldiers pounding down the stairs, out of the apartment. He'd dispatched the three he'd encountered, and Nick had stood watchful, aware that he couldn't compete with what Seth had going on.

Seth glanced up to see what was taking her so long. Then she shot out of the window. On a chair, it looked like. Whatever it was, it fell faster than she did and then she plummeted, like dead weight through the sky, as the sun reflected off the windows.

His stomach twisted. He didn't think; he just ran. In his mind, everything slowed and he calculated how fast he could realistically go. His brain said he would fail, that he wouldn't reach her in time, but he refused to accept that. As his feet tore across the pavement and he dived through the manicured landscaping, he poured on the speed. He needed to reach her. There would be no excuses. He wouldn't accept logic.

He dodged the falling chair seat, and then he slid, like a ballplayer, to put himself under her.

She hit him from above like a grand piano. He could feel his rib crack under the force of her fall. But he didn't care. This was Blue.

He pulled her against him, her soft, slight frame a dead weight, and rolled. A quick pat down proved her fine, only unconscious. He patted her face. "Blue?"

Nothing. Fear, stark and cold, roared through him. It had been hard pretending he was unaffected by her all morning. Now, he was too afraid to pretend.

"Tranked, probably." Nick's face was grim. "We need to get out of here."

He was probably right. On both counts. "Which way to your car?" He scurried to his feet, pulling Blue against him. He scanned the parking lot. No Goldstone right now, but they were coming. He could hear them.

Nick nudged his head toward the right. "Second row. Over there. Let me take her. I think you're better with your hands free."

Seth pulled her inert body closer as his ribs complained. The logic was sound. Even his superhuman brain agreed. Why, then, didn't he want to turn her over to the very capable hands of his friend?

Nick held out his hands, moving his fingers in a "come on" kind of way. "You're wasting time."

"Right." Seth relinquished her, casting a last look at her unconscious face. "Let's go."

Though he was the better choice to ward off attacks, Blue's weight slowed Nick down more than it would have slowed Seth. He scanned the area. Nothing. Must be regrouping. They took off through the parking lot, Nick huffing beside him, sweat dripping from his forehead and his hair wet. He knew his friend didn't have his strength or speed, but it was hard for Seth not to get impatient.

He ran backward, watching for soldiers following them. He heard shouts in the distance but didn't see anyone yet, thank God. They reached Nick's car, a beat-up old Civic, and Nick dropped Blue unceremoniously in the backseat.

"Careful with her." Seth said as he opened the passenger door. "She probably still has a concussion."

Nick slammed the door shut, scowling. "Now you tell me."

"I drive."

Nick didn't bother to argue, only grimaced and handed over the keys. Seth settled him in the passenger seat and then rolled over the roof, landing on the driver's side. In less than a second, he opened the driver's side and starting the engine.

"The stuff you can do…it's pretty creepy-ass."

Seth sighed. "Yeah. I know."

Pops sounded behind them, and he felt something hit the open door beside him. Holes peppered the door.

Gunshot holes.

They were really shooting at them now.

He hit the gas and peeled out, the Civic's fan belt squealing, and only when they turned the corner did he slam the door shut.

Chapter Sixteen

The car stopped at a small airport an hour or so outside San Antonio. Kitty knew they were to meet a small airplane that would take her to a Goldstone research and development facility in Virginia. She'd considered escape, but they kept her locked in the car, in handcuffs, like a criminal. She didn't have her friends' powers, and these guards had real guns. Her options were severely limited. She decided her best bet would be to run when they got to the airport.

The two men in front got out, and then they opened her door, assisting her. Not an easy feat as her hands remained bound behind her back. But they managed it fine, considering. They were actually being more polite than she'd expected. She wasn't certain why that surprised her, but she supposed even villains had the right to manners.

They escorted her toward a small passenger plane, and she followed, scanning the area.

There was no one around. No one to help.

Was it worth the risk to run? Would they just shoot her and be done with it?

As she debated, a man stepped out from the hatch, and her guards stopped, pulling their weapons from their pockets. She tensed. What was going on?

"Please. Gentlemen. No need for that. I'm harmless, I promise."

"You are not permitted on this aircraft, Dr. Fields. Please stand down." The man beside her knelt, his pistol still raised. *I don't want to shoot him. Please don't make me shoot him.* How odd. This man knew Dr. Fields personally.

Curious now, she reached out to the doctor. *She looks young. It does seem that the younger recipients managed the effects of the drug better. How interesting. I hadn't considered that age would be a factor.*

So this was the scientist who'd done this to them. He was different than she'd expected. Less…maniacal-looking than she would have guessed. Maybe she'd watched too much *Scooby-Doo*.

Why were the two guards pointing their guns at him, though, if they were all from Goldstone?

"I'm sorry, but I've come to retrieve Ms. Laughton."

"Me?"

"Yes. I'm in need of your assistance, my girl. Will you please come with me?" he asked her kindly, as if she had any choice in where she went.

"Stand down!" The guard on her other side was getting twitchy, his finger flicking on the trigger.

"Now, Carl. You know you won't shoot me," Fields chided. "Why don't you both put your weapons away, before someone gets hurt."

The two men glanced between themselves, and she could hear their confusion. *Is Fields armed? That isn't his style.* And… *Surely he wouldn't risk hurting us.*

Kitty narrowed her eyes, trying desperately to catch up.

"Ms. Laughton. Will you please accompany me?" Dr.

Fields started down the stairs from the hatch. She wanted to call out to him, to tell him how serious her guards were, but the words got trapped in her throat.

"Fields, stop!" And then Carl fired, one, two, three rounds.

She cried out. But it wasn't Fields who fell—he continued moving toward her as if unconcerned about the gunfire. Carl went down first, then her other guard. Carl clutched his calf; the other man groaned over his thigh. She stood, gasping, crying between them.

Fields stopped in front of her. He held out his hand. "Please. If you will."

"You..." Her brain spun. "You're like Blue. You can move things."

"Why, yes." He smiled as if approving of her deduction. "There is another of you who has that capability?"

She nodded, dumbly. *Great. Now I've outed Blue. Think before you speak.*

"How extraordinary." He took her arm. "We must go, though."

"Where are you taking me?"

"Why, we have research to do together, Kitty. May I call you Kitty? I feel as if I know you, having researched all the people in your town before choosing it for my experiment." She only stared at him like he was crazy. Maybe he was. He smiled. "What are your new skills, if you don't mind?"

She didn't want to tell him.

"Now, now." His hand tightened on her arm, almost becoming painful, and she gasped. "I will find out anyway. It would be more...pleasant if we could get along." The pressure on her arm eased, but the message was clear in his mind. *Do not cross me, little girl.*

"I can...read minds."

He smiled. A few minutes ago, she might have found it calming. But now the expression chilled her.

"You don't say? How…extraordinary."

She woke up with a headache.

Again.

Recent events were fuzzy, but even in the fog, she knew this wasn't the first time she'd awakened with a headache lately. And she was certain it was getting old.

She rubbed her temple, struggling to sit in the backseat of what looked to be a vintage Civic. This car and her Cavalier could have dated. "Ugh. What happened?"

In the front seat, Nick turned, concern on his face. "Good. You're awake. I was starting to worry." He studied his watch and turned to Seth, who was driving. "Half an hour. Long enough for whatever they needed, I suppose."

Seth's jaw clenched, and he nodded, but he said nothing, as if it didn't matter to him at all. But his knuckles whitened on the steering wheel.

She furrowed her brows as things returned to her. Seth apologizing for kissing her, for letting them distract one another. The apartment. The chair. Losing control. The tranquilizer needle. "Oh."

Damn. She'd been so afraid, all she could think about was getting away. She hadn't paused to think, or she would have frozen the soldiers in the room before she went out the window.

That mistake had gotten her tranked.

No wonder Seth seemed upset. She'd done exactly what he'd said she shouldn't do. She'd been so worried about him, she'd jumped right to doing whatever it took to keep him safe and nearly gotten herself killed.

She wanted to ask how they'd saved her, but now probably wasn't the time.

With a pang in her stomach, she realized Seth might be right. Maybe what she felt for him was a distraction. Maybe it kept her from thinking clearly. But while he seemed to have no problem putting their kisses and talks aside, she couldn't pretend she didn't care about him. That she wasn't falling for him.

Correction. She's already fallen. Hard.

"Yeah." Nick's mouth tilted up. "Oh." He nudged Seth and pointed. "Over there."

She followed his finger, still rubbing her head, to a car parked in the corner of what looked like a Home Depot parking lot. The car was a flashy red Tahoe.

Jeremy.

She shook her head but stopped when it started to throb. "No. Seeing Jeremy is a bad idea."

Seth turned the wheel. "We have to talk to him, Blue."

He was probably right, but there had to be a better way than this, out in the open, making them perfect targets.

"He knew they were coming for us. How could he know that and still be free?" No way Jeremy got away from Goldstone. He was an ordinary guy. He didn't have their skills. Goldstone would have picked him up, if only to cover their bases.

If he was here, then he wasn't safe. And Kitty... So help her, if he'd hurt Kitty in any way, he'd pray for mercy.

Seth met her eyes in the rearview mirror, iron gray and full of understanding. "I know what you're thinking. And I agree. But he contacted us. We need to know what he knows. Besides, we need to get Kitty back." He seemed wary, too. Good, he should be. "Better a public place than a private one."

She wasn't sure about that. At least somewhere private they could fight properly. There were so many people here. It wouldn't be safe for anyone.

"Besides," Seth said with a sigh. "They're shooting at us.

Real bullets." He motioned to the door beside him. Tiny holes peppered the interior of the door. "Best to meet somewhere public."

A rush filled her ears. Really shooting at them? Until now, she'd been able to shrug off Goldstone's pursuit. They wanted to capture them. That was dangerous enough. But shooting? To kill? She couldn't pretend they were safe any longer.

This changed everything.

She leaned around them to scan the area. She didn't see any soldiers, but she saw Jeremy behind the wheel of the Tahoe. Alone.

"No Kitty." It was an obvious statement, but she had to make it anyway. And if Kitty wasn't with him, she was with Goldstone.

Her fist clenched. Why hadn't she put up more of a fight this morning? If she'd been more forceful, maybe her friend would have listened to her. Maybe she would be safe now. If Kitty had been taken, it was partly Blue's fault.

Anger exploded in her. Damn Goldstone. What they'd done in Glory. Her gran. All these changes, these side effects. Now Kitty. She wouldn't let them get away with this. She had no idea how, but she'd make sure they were stopped. Somehow.

Seth pulled the Civic behind Jeremy's car, leaving it in park with the motor running. Smart. In case they had to get out of here fast.

Seth turned, then, and looked at her, holding her eyes. "No. No Kitty." His brows dropped. The distance that had been in his face faded a bit, and his eyes softened. "I'll find her. I swear to you, I'll find her."

He held her gaze, steady as a rock. As if they hadn't had that conversation last night. And she wanted to believe him.

He took a breath and held it. "I want you to stay here."

She jerked back to glare at him. What? "Absolutely not.

If you're going, I'm going." Who else was going to keep him safe?

"Right." He sighed. "Because why would you listen to me?" He got out without letting her answer, slamming the door closed.

Blue watched him step around the car, trying not to feel hurt. Why didn't he see that she needed to protect him as much as he wanted to protect her? Why couldn't he see how much she cared about him?

The big jerk.

Tired and wearier than she could ever remember, she unfolded herself from the car.

As the driver's door of the Tahoe opened and Jeremy climbed out, her anger at Seth refocused on him. This guy had something to do with all of this. Seth and Nick were right. They needed to know what he knew. If it helped get Kitty back, she'd stand by and hear him out.

She stepped out, staying back while Seth and Nick moved forward. They stopped only a few feet from him, their legs apart. This wasn't a conversation; it was a confrontation. Good. He had some explaining to do.

She scanned the two exits, watching them both as she listened in. This part of the lot was secluded, tucked away from the more frequent traffic. It made her nervous.

"Where's Kitty?" Seth folded his arms over his chest.

"Gone. With Goldstone."

The words echoed through Blue's head. *Gone.* She'd suspected, but hearing it confirmed…

Jeremy's body language didn't suggest guilt. His posture was loose, arms at his sides. She didn't trust him one bit. "Where are the other two guys?"

"Gone." Seth didn't elaborate. "What happened to you?"

"They were waiting for us."

"Waiting for you? At the bagel shop?" Nick piped up, full

of skepticism. He leaned against the Civic as if he didn't give two shits what Jeremy had to say.

"Yeah, they were there, at the bagel shop, when we got there." He shrugged. "I think they followed us."

"Why would they follow you first and not come in to get us?" Seth didn't give him a chance to answer. "How did they find us, then?"

"I don't know. Maybe Luke's sleuthing around last night tipped them off." It was a plausible explanation...if you didn't know Luke. But there was no way Luke left any trail behind. He and his father were *the* go-to computer nerds in Glory. Hell, people came from across the state to talk to them about technology-related issues, and that didn't include emailed or phoned-in issues. Blue had heard that Mr. Kincaid did secret work for the government. He was brilliant and so was his son.

It didn't matter. Bottom line? Luke hadn't left a trail. Jeremy was full of shit.

"Didn't Kitty hear them? She didn't say anything?"

Jeremy shook his head. "Not that she said."

That was the part Blue didn't understand. How had he fooled Kitty? If he'd been involved, if he'd had something to do with her capture, why hadn't his thoughts tipped her off? It didn't make sense. It was one of the main reasons she remained silent, listening.

"So what happened, then?" She could hear Seth getting impatient.

"They stopped us. Took her away. That was it."

"Just like that?" Nick remained leaning against the car, his ankles crossed. "What did you do? Stand there and let them?"

"Listen." Jeremy didn't back down. "They had guns. I'm not going to get myself killed over some chick I just met. These people aren't my people."

"They aren't going to ask her questions and let her go,

you asshole," she gritted out. He had some nerve, with his blasé attitude, while who knew what was happening to her friend. But Seth was watching her, and she knew he expected her to fly off the handle. She gritted her teeth. If she was going to find Kitty, she needed to hear what this jerk had to say. "She deserved a fight," she couldn't help adding. "Watch the way you talk about her."

Jeremy sneered. Seth stepped forward, partially concealing her. "Why didn't they take you?"

This was the question, the most important question they'd asked. From Seth's mouth, it sounded sweet. Exactly. Why didn't they take him? Even to question him. It was why he was so damned in her mind.

"I don't know."

Complete bullshit. She turned sideways, to obscure her face.

"I see." Seth's mouth pursed.

"Why did you text me? Why didn't you call?" Nick pushed away from the car, stalking toward his roommate. "Something as important as 'get out while you can' probably deserved a call, don't you think?"

Jeremy must have sensed he was running out of time. He took a couple steps back. "You guys got out, didn't you? I wanted to give you some time. Come on. You know me." He lifted his hands in the universal sign for innocence.

Nick and Seth looked at each other. Nick nodded. Then Seth stepped forward, his voice low. "How much are they paying you?"

"What are you talking about?" Jeremy didn't sound as confident anymore.

"Goldstone. Did you contact them or did they contact you? What do you get out of this?"

Jeremy's jaw worked. Bingo. Blue smiled.

He stepped back farther, then, as if he was going to run, and his hand dropped into his pocket.

She froze him where he stood. She'd had enough of this. Seth and Nick couldn't get any more out of him. Now it would be her turn.

Seth laid his hand on her arm. "Don't." She could see his wariness. This was what he meant when he said that she didn't listen to directions. So be it. Maybe she didn't. But she had as much right to this guy as they did.

"I'm fine. We're going to talk, that's all." She stepped closer, removing the gun from his frozen hand. She handed it to Seth. Seth looked at it, surprised.

So he hadn't believed his friend would pull a weapon on him. She lifted her eyebrow at him. See? This was why they were better as a team.

She smiled at Jeremy, her anger right below the surface. "Isn't that right? I only have a few questions. Should be easy. First, I want to know exactly who you called."

She unfroze his head, but the rest of him remained paralyzed.

"I'm not telling you anything." He spat.

"Then you don't need to breathe." She squeezed him, to illustrate her point, and then released his breathing. A flash of fear entered his eyes. There. Maybe they'd get somewhere. "Now. Who did you call?"

He seemed to consider. He must have decided the information wasn't that important. "Pike. He's in charge of the Goldstone operation—"

"We're an operation, then." How clinical.

"He needs to round you guys up, and he's trying to track down their doctor. The guy with the drug is AWOL."

They knew that already. "What did Pike promise you?"

Again, a delay. "I'm going to work for him."

"Congratulations. Your parents must be proud. Where is Kitty?"

"I don't know." She squeezed him again, but he shook his

head. "I'm serious, I don't know. They said they were going to take her somewhere she would be safe."

"If you believe that, you're dumber than you look." She stepped back. Only a couple more things. "I imagine they're waiting for us."

"Watching right now."

She nodded, expecting that. "They're shooting at us."

"Yes. You guys have killed five men. They're through taking chances with you."

She wanted to defend them. Those deaths had been self-defense at best and accidents at worst. But she didn't bother. "Do they know about Seth and Nick?"

"Yes. Both." Jeremy paused.

She supposed it was a matter of time. But it still pissed her off.

She glared at him, this piece of shit who'd turned on them all, on his own roommate, his friends. What kind of person did that to his friends? If it had only been her and the other kids from Glory, that would have been one thing. But this? Where was his loyalty?

And Kitty... How could he have done that to Kitty? He'd used her. Blue wanted him to pay for the things he'd done. He didn't deserve to have friends as nice as Seth and Nick. And Kitty had been way too good for him.

A piece of garbage like this...he didn't deserve to live.

Her anger increased, becoming almost unbearable. She could do it. She could make him cease to live, if she wanted to. It was right here, inside her.

A hand on her shoulder distracted her. "Blue?" Seth met her eyes. It was hot, noon, and the light made his gray eyes murky. "This isn't what you want."

Staring at him, she realized her breath was coming fast, shallow, and her heart was pounding. But while her mouth worked—opened and closed—no words came out.

He was right. She didn't want to do this, whatever this would have been. With complete certainty, she could feel her future regrets. She might not know what she was now, but she knew for sure that she wasn't a murderer.

Three days ago, she never would have pictured herself cutting off someone's oxygen. She didn't believe in violence. She'd considered the Peace Corps, for Christ's sake. She didn't eat meat, had volunteered at the animal shelter throughout high school, until she started working too much to swing it.

How had she come to this? Maybe Seth was right. How was he supposed to trust her if she couldn't even trust herself?

She held his eyes. There was no judgment, only his guarded concern and a tenderness that filled her with warmth. He believed in her.

She backed away, dropping Jeremy on the ground. He scurried back, ran around the side of his car and dived inside. They could hear the locks catch. He was trapped, of course, unless he wanted to take his precious Tahoe off-roading. He cowered down in the front seat.

She turned away, not wanting to look at him. "Can we please go?"

She could feel Seth's eyes on her for a long moment, before he removed his hand from her shoulder. He stepped next to her. His closeness soothed her. Did he know how much she relied on his support? Did he know that if he hadn't stepped in, she might have done something she'd never have forgiven herself for?

When she glanced up at his face, he was scanning the parking lot, purposely avoiding her eyes. Detached. She wrapped her arms around herself.

She looked out, trying to see what he might be seeing. A small group of men with sunglasses and grim faces, in front of the store, wearing more clothes than necessary in this weather. Another group near the parking lot entrance. A quick glance revealed a dark car blocked the exit. As she watched, the men started toward them. She stepped back, her heartbeat picking up.

They were from Goldstone. She didn't need any experience detecting undercover operatives to figure that out.

They were trapped.

But there were shoppers everywhere. The place was packed. Goldstone couldn't shoot at them here. Could they?

Seth reached for Blue's hand. He was all business again. With his hand in hers, though, her anxiety ebbed. Seth would have a plan. He'd get them out of here if he could.

Seth turned to Nick. "Sorry, man. We're ditching your car."

"Awesome." Nick rubbed his face. "Where to, boss?"

"In," he said. Blue tripped along beside him as they headed toward a side door. He kicked the door a few times before it flew open. Inside, plenty of orange carts and a line of tractors. Yep. Definitely a Home Depot.

They swept through, greeted by welcoming air-conditioning. They passed a helpful-looking associate, in her orange apron, and didn't stop, half walking and half running straight through the store. They followed the back wall into the hallway toward the bathrooms. They passed them by, into the swinging doors that concealed the back storage rooms. Seth hung a sharp right and turned to the stairs leading up.

"Where are we going?" She panted, trying to keep up with his longer strides as he took the stairs two at a time.

"We're getting out of here."

Nick gestured behind them. "Um, there were a few more exits down there than there are up here."

"Yeah. But every one of them ends with us getting tranked. Or shot. Besides, we don't need an exit. We can make our own." He threw open the door marked ROOF ACCESS. Then he turned to smile at them. "We're jumping off the building."

Of course. This was the one way out that Goldstone

couldn't follow. Unless they had a plane. She smiled back. See a problem, solve a problem. That was her Seth.

"Wait, what?"

They ignored Nick as they stormed up the last few stairs, throwing open another door at the top. Black tarmac coated the rooftop, and Seth trotted over to the edge of the building, briefly glancing over the side. Checking if it was still a two-story drop, maybe. Then he moved back a few paces and shook a thumb over his shoulder. "Blue. You climb up. Can you get both of us?"

"Absolutely."

"Put me down in the field, over there." He pointed. "So you don't have to hold us both for long."

"Will do."

The beat of propellers sounded in the background.

Not a plane. A helicopter.

"Seth…" Blue's terror colored his name.

"I hear it." His mouth tightened. "Let's go."

Nick lifted his hands, shaking his head. "Listen, I didn't sign up for this."

She lifted him off the ground. "Sorry."

"Not this again," he mumbled. She might have smiled at another time.

She climbed on Seth's back, and he spoke over his shoulder. "Keep him close to us, in case."

"Got it." She didn't want to think about the "in case."

She held Nick beside them, her head turned so she could watch him, all the while holding tight to Seth's shoulders. He was solid beneath her. She leaned her head against him for a moment.

She should have felt some form of panic. But she didn't. She trusted Seth. If he thought this would work, it would. He'd make sure they made it. "No worries," she told Nick. "I got you."

"Wonderful."

Seth broke into a run, barely slowed by the weight of her on his back. He dived off the roof of the Home Depot, sailing across the parking lot behind the building, as if he'd jumped a puddle on a rainy day.

She kept Nick right at her side. She didn't hear his cry, but she saw it on his face.

In midair, she took a deep breath and split her focus, catching Seth as well. Her brow furrowed, and the ghost of an ache pressed against her forehead. But she continued to breathe and relax, guiding all three of them into the field that Seth had pointed out.

It was getting easier to use the power.

As soon as she released him, Seth started running. She continued to hold Nick, and he flew along beside them, stoically silent now.

The helicopter sounded louder, and she turned to see it coming around the side of the Home Depot. A helicopter. At a Home Depot. It was so out of place, it felt surreal.

"Seth!"

Seth's pause to look was enough time for her to jump down and lower Nick to the ground.

They were in the middle of a field between the Home Depot and a Best Buy. Even though she wasn't the one with the massive analytic brain, she knew they couldn't outrun a helicopter. And there was no other escape around.

She stopped and turned slowly to face the helicopter as it dropped farther. From across the field, she could see the armed men inside. Seth said they were shooting real bullets now. They were trying to kill them.

No. That wasn't going to happen.

Seth yelled at her from somewhere far away, telling her to stop.

But she could save them now. Save Seth.

So she braced herself. As the helicopter sped toward her, the propellers' beating vibrated inside her, she focused on everything she'd seen and done the past few days.

She thought of Gran with a hollow ache in her chest. She thought of Kitty, of Luke and Jack. Of how they were captured or on the run. Of how they would never see their families again and that the people they loved were gone from the Earth as if they hadn't mattered at all.

She thought of Seth.

None of them would ever return to their old lives. She held the injustice of it in her chest and lifted her hands.

Then the sound of metal grinding and creaking filled the air. The first propeller spun off with a squeal, twisting through the air like a feather on the breeze. It crashed nearby, skidding. The others followed, scattering around the field.

The first panel split from the side of the helicopter, crumbling into a ball and falling to the ground. The remainder of the aircraft pulled apart, leaving nothing but a few seats and the floor intact. It all came down, rubble all over the dirty ground.

She grabbed each of the men that had been on the helicopter out of the air, freezing all six of them. Bit by bit, she pulled their gear from their body. Everything. Clothes, weapons, right down to their underwear. All of it flew through the air and landed in the retention pond to the right of them.

Then she dropped the men on the ground, hard enough that some of them looked unconscious and others rolled to their knees, coughing.

When she was done, she realized with a bit of detachment that she couldn't hear anything, only a faint ringing in her head. She only noticed that because Seth appeared to be yelling something, and yet she had no idea what he was saying.

Dizziness washed over her, making her lose her balance. Or perhaps the ground was actually moving toward her, and she wasn't falling. But she doubted it.

Chapter Seventeen

"I'm fine." Blue said the words for at least the fifth time, but no one seemed to hear. Seth's arms remained firmly around her.

Ahead of Seth, Nick swiped the card on another dumpy hotel room while glancing up and down the corridor. He flicked on the lights, and Seth carried Blue in behind him.

He laid her on the bed and sent Nick off to get ice.

Blue could have walked. She'd told him that over and over. She hadn't passed out. She'd only had the dizziness and the hearing loss. Even that had gone away after a few minutes.

Even so, Seth had insisted on carrying her inside.

"I'm okay, Seth. I swear. I told you. I feel fine now." Her voice was weak, though, destroying her credibility. He retreated to the bathroom, and she heard the water run. He returned with a wet washcloth and hand towel.

He sat down next to her, easing her back onto the bed, and proceeded to gently wipe at her face, her nose, her temple. The towels pinkened.

She'd been bleeding. Again.

Her stomach sank.

Nick returned, sparing her from responding. He put the ice down on the desk before he looked between them. Then he cleared his throat before he said, "You know, um, I think I'm going to go, dump the car." He looked at Seth. "Yeah. You got this?"

After he slipped out, she asked Seth, "Can we trust him?" After how things had gone with Jeremy, she couldn't help her distrust.

Seth nodded. "I'd trust Nick with my life. Never felt the same about Jeremy."

Well, that was something. She shifted, trying to get up.

"Lie down, you lunatic." His voice was gruff. "You're a wreck."

She smoothed a hand over her hair. That was probably true. Her clothes looked like she'd rolled in the dirt. She had, technically.

But he didn't seem put off by the dirt. No, he studied her as if she was a precious object that had been mistreated. Outraged, protective. Concerned.

That look made her stomach flutter. That wasn't the look of a man who didn't want to kiss her. That wasn't the look of someone who didn't care. Not that he'd admit it.

She reached for him, cupping his face with her hand.

His eyes pierced her, and she waited, still, expecting him to rip her a new one, to shrink away.

"You're going to get yourself killed," he said, his voice raw, full of emotion.

She'd expected anger. She probably could have handled anger. But this... He sounded destroyed.

So she did the only thing she knew how to do when faced with disaster...she tried to downplay it. "Maybe."

As soon as the word was out, she knew it was the wrong thing to say. He scowled. "What do you mean, maybe? Not acceptable, Blue. I mean, that stunt out the window? What were you thinking?"

He looked so genuinely distressed that she dropped her hand. She didn't know what to say to that, either, so she told the truth. "I was thinking that a desk chair is no flying carpet."

He glared at her. "This isn't funny."

"I know, Seth. It's not funny." She was so bad at this stuff.

"And the helicopter. Jesus Christ."

"Yes. The helicopter. What else could we do? It was going to catch us. Even you can't outrun a helicopter." She knew he wouldn't like to acknowledge he wasn't unstoppable, but it was the truth.

"I would have thought of something. You didn't give me a chance."

She sighed. "But we got away. Isn't that good enough?"

She didn't need a lecture right now. God, he was so concerned with being the one in charge, with trying to control a situation. Didn't he know that sometimes things were out of his control?

She shifted, trying to get to her feet, unable to handle this conversation any longer. She felt raw and antsy. As if she'd had too much caffeine and might explode with the need to move, to walk off the jitters.

No, that wasn't true, either. She didn't want to move or walk. She wanted him to take her into his arms. She needed to feel the strength of him. She needed to know that he was fine, that he was warm and safe.

That even in the midst of these messed-up circumstances, they had each other.

But he couldn't do that, could he? He didn't want to lean on her, too. He wanted to be the strong one, the levelheaded one. The one who wasn't distracted.

She pressed her lips together, determined to stop their shaking, and swallowed hard.

He stood as well, stopping her as she tried to step around him. "It's not good enough, Blue." He gripped her arm, forcing her to look at him. She tried her hardest to shield her feelings, to keep the hurt out of her eyes. She always gave everything away on her face.

"Luke found out the name of the doctor who created this drug," he said. "Fields. He did tests on rats. The drug killed half of them, but the remaining survivors, they exhibited side effects, too. Similar to all of us. Moving things, strategy, stuff like that. And as their powers grew, half of the remaining rats died. Seizures and blood and pain." He pulled her closer. "Do you get it? Even though they lived, they died. If you keep pushing…if you keep risking everything…"

"That helicopter was going to catch us, Seth," she whispered at him. "I know you think you have to protect me, but what about me? Don't you think I feel the same way? Don't you think I need to make sure you're okay, too?" Didn't he know how much she cared about him yet?

"I need to keep you safe," he whispered.

"And I need to keep you safe, too. You jerk." Her teeth gritted together, and she held onto her anger. Because otherwise, she'd lose it completely. "You don't have the monopoly on trying to protect the people you care about."

He stilled. As if her words had paralyzed him. Oh, God. But she'd never been the kind to pretend she didn't care. There were so few people she'd really cared about, and she'd lost them all. At least Gran had known how much she loved her. Blue had told her every day.

Seth needed to know, too. He didn't want to feel anything for her, but she wasn't going to bother hiding. With the way things were going, she had no idea how much longer they had together.

He didn't say anything, just stared at her like she had two heads.

Then he pulled her against him, and she found herself crushed against the wide expanse of his chest. She inhaled, closing her eyes, cherishing the feel of him, letting it wipe away the terror of the day.

"God, Blue... You... I'm..." He swallowed, and she listened to his quickened heartbeat against her cheek. "I can be a jerk. I don't know how to do this stuff with you, and I'm messing it up. I'm sorry, babe. So sorry. I know one thing, though. I wouldn't be able to deal if something happened to you." He cupped her face, rubbing his thumb across her cheekbone. "Watching you fall out of that window... It was... I didn't..." He swallowed hard, squeezing his eyes closed. "I almost didn't get there in time. And the helicopter..." He shook his head, his face full of pain.

"But I'm fine. I'm here." He was here, too, in her arms. No matter what happened next. She leaned forward, touching her forehead to his, trying to prove to him that she was indeed there and alive.

"You aren't going to listen to me, are you?"

It was her turn to scowl. "I do listen to you."

"Yeah, but you're going to do what you think is best anyway. Aren't you?"

She shrugged. He was right. She wouldn't stand by if it meant he'd get hurt. "I don't take directions well."

He chuckled, and the sound vibrated through her. "No, you don't."

"Um, sorry?" she offered.

"No, you aren't." He laughed again. "But I am. I'm sorry I told you I regretted kissing you. I lied. I loved every second of kissing you. I can't stop thinking about kissing you. I can't stop wanting to touch you, to hold you." His fingertips pressed into her back, pulling her closer.

"Seth..." She didn't recognize her pleading voice.

He must have known what she needed.

He lowered his head, and their mouths touched. A shiver raced through her. Her fingers trailed over his chest, his shoulders, up to his neck, urging him closer, unable to get enough.

This was what she needed. Him, in this moment.

His firm lips moved across hers, insistent and warm, stealing her breath.

His mouth tasted so good.

Shuddering, she pulled at him, and they tumbled sideways onto the bed. As their mouths danced, his hand found her hip, and he squeezed, his knuckles brushing her bare stomach. His fingers trailed up under her T-shirt. He waited that all-important second to make sure he had the green light.

In response, she covered his hand, moving it up to cup her breast.

Needing no other encouragement, he pulled at the cup of her bra, finding her hardened nipple. One gentle squeeze, and she came off the bed with a gasp.

God, that felt good.

He dipped his head, trailing soft kisses along her jaw that sent tingles down her spine.

Seth Campbell's mouth didn't only taste good. It performed magic.

As he continued along to nip at the sensitive spot below her earlobe, he nudged the hem of her T-shirt up to expose her to the cool air. Goose bumps erupted on her skin, and then his hand covered her breast, and she closed her eyes, arching against him. Heat spread through her, making her feel like she was on fire from within.

Through the haze of what he was doing with his mouth and fingers, she yanked at his shirt, smoothing it up over his chest. He helped her, only breaking contact when he needed to pull it over his head. Blue used the moment to draw her own shirt off and unsnap her bra. He made quick work of smoothing her leggings down and off her, leaving her completely naked to him. She shivered, both from the cool air and the intensity of his gaze.

As they touched, skin to skin, from thigh to shoulder, she rubbed against him, unable to get enough of the feel of him. Her hand shook as she linked it with his.

"I want you." She didn't want there to be any doubt. "I don't know what happens next, but I want you."

"God, yes," he breathed as he took her mouth again.

Blueberry Michaels didn't do anything passively. Even bruised and exhausted, she didn't hold back. She kissed him with all of her, touched him without hesitation. She told him how much she cared with every move she made.

And he couldn't get enough.

It wasn't only the feel of her, of what she was doing. It was the way she sighed and arched into him. The way she tugged at his hair, sending ripples of need running through him. The way she responded without fear.

She was brave even here, in the most vulnerable of places.

He'd been fooling himself if he thought he could control this situation. And if he couldn't control it, he didn't know why he had to fight it any longer.

He wanted her. So much it hurt.

So he leaned back to kneel between her thighs, determined to memorize every inch of her. Holding her eyes, he ran his trembling hands over her, reveling in the softness of her skin and the strength in her small frame. She managed to be both soft and strong simultaneously without a trace of irony.

When his fingers found the soft center of her, her nails sank into the sheets and her eyes shone the bluest blue.

With the color high in her cheeks and her hair mussed,

she was complete perfection.

He needed more. More for himself, more for her. So he bent his head and replaced his fingers with his mouth.

She cried out. Her heels dug into the mattress beside him, and her hips came off the bed. He trailed his fingers along her sides, watching her up the length of her body. She was breathing fast. Her eyes were closed, and her mouth opened the slightest bit. The sight of her, coupled with the taste of her on his tongue, brought him closer to the edge of sanity than he could ever remember.

He bungee jumped and drove too fast, skydived and BASE jumped, but nothing would ever beat the rush of Blue beneath him.

They didn't have a lot of time, but he used what he had to his advantage. With the blood rushing in his ears, he stayed with her until she gasped, calling his name, and fell apart under his shaking hands. In the aftermath, he gathered her to him and rolled to the side, catching his breath. Gradually, reality returned. He leaned back and pulled away from her, immediately missing her warmth.

"Nick," he offered by way of explanation, not bothering to hide his disappointment. Beside him, the color was high in her cheeks and her hair was mussed. He couldn't resist pulling her close and kissing her again.

She chuckled and then sat up awkwardly, reaching for her clothes. He tugged his own shirt over his head before he moved to sit beside her, trying to get his bearings. In the silence that followed, he closed his eyes, and he could still see Blue, her hands out and feet apart, her bright blond hair whipping in the wind, as she faced down the helicopter and ripped it apart. She'd stared at it, and it had fallen to pieces. Then she'd spilled onto the ground in a heap.

She'd knelt there, making no sense, rambling on as if she was coming out of anesthesia. More alarming was the slow trickle of blood from her ears and nose. He'd stroked her hair, feeling sick.

In that field, he'd realized that this was nothing like Bobby. She and Bobby shared persistence and stubbornness, all right. Two more bullheaded people he'd never met. Took one to know one, after all, and he wasn't exactly mild tempered, either. But Blue wasn't Bobby, not at all. She was worse. Because while Bobby wanted the things he wanted, he would have listened if he'd thought he was in danger. Blue? She would go to any length, risk her own safety and health, push any boundary, if it would protect the people she cared about.

She humbled and terrified him. He had no idea how to guard her against herself. Wasn't sure he wanted to anymore.

"We'll stay here tonight. You need to rest. Tomorrow, we'll leave for Bragg."

They stayed like that for a long moment, neither saying anything. Then, with a deep breath, she said, "I want to contact the media."

That wasn't what he'd expected her to say. "What?"

"I think we should go to the media. With what happened to us."

"Come on, Blue. What would we tell them? We have no proof. Luke couldn't find anything online. I bet Goldstone has covered up most of this already."

"Goldstone took Kitty. Do you think it's going to be easy for us to find her? To get her away from them? The media can dig around in places we can't."

"So can the army. If we go to the media, who protects us while some investigative reporter digs up enough to expose Goldstone? That could take days, weeks, even. That's time we don't have." He shook his head. "No, I think we should go to the army. At Bragg. Now. We'll be there tomorrow night, if I can manage it. They'll be able to help us." They'd need to jack another car in the morning. They'd only driven a half an hour out of San Antonio, because he'd refused to drive too far with Blue barely conscious. But, if they took turns driving, they could make it from San Antonio to Bragg tomorrow. Then they wouldn't be alone. He wouldn't bear all of the responsibility for what happened to them.

She shook her head. "I was thinking about that while we were on our way here. How did Goldstone get a helicopter over a Home Depot in San Antonio? Where were the police? Men with guns were everywhere, and you know some of those shoppers were videotaping it all. But we didn't hear anything on the radio, nothing on the news. Goldstone couldn't cover all of that up, but the government could."

"You think the army knows."

She nodded. "I do. San Antonio is a big city. Not like Glory. Not out in the boonies."

That was true. He debated other possible explanations. "Maybe the police and the army thought it was a training exercise. Maybe they got clearance. Private citizens own and rent helicopters, too. That doctor poisoned a whole town, and Goldstone has been covering that up for days. You don't think they would lie about a helicopter?"

"Maybe. But it feels wrong. Don't you think?"

He had to admit it was possible. Still… "You don't trust any government institution. But your father's experience isn't everyone's experience."

She jerked, as if she'd been slapped. He'd overstepped, mentioning her father. She'd see it as a low blow. But she was being unreasonable. He wasn't going to let her put them in more danger because of her irrational distaste for the government.

Besides, even if the army knew, and they might, he didn't see any other option. The risk to their—her—health was just too great. Her symptoms were getting worse. She needed help, fast.

Her gaze dropped to her hands, and he felt like an asshole. When she spoke, her voice was strong. "I don't want to go. To Bragg."

"What?" His head spun. Didn't she understand the stakes?

She glanced up. "Not until we talk to the media. Can't you see it would be safer if we had someone private, someone with nothing to gain, involved?" When he didn't immediately respond, she pressed on. "Didn't you say that this…what they did to us, was funded by the government? Come on, Seth. They have to know."

"Yes, they funded it. But they pulled the funding when they saw it was too dangerous. They didn't agree to kill an entire town. And we need help. Your side effects? The nosebleeds and the headaches? After that helicopter stunt, you were delirious. We can't exactly walk into any hospital. They aren't going to know what's wrong. They don't have access to the drug. The army is our best bet to get help for that. We don't have time to wait around while the media decides they can trust us or until they can dig around in Goldstone's business."

Today's near misses had sealed that for him. And the effects of using their powers? They'd taken enough chances.

"We could go to my mother's house. While we wait for the media."

"Your mother?"

Blue's face twisted. "Yeah. She's in Idaho, on some commune. We could go. Stay with her. Wait until this blows over. See if the media, or we, can find Kitty." She squeezed his hand. "Please. Let's get out of here. We could go. The two of us. We'll figure out another way, give it some time."

"What about your headaches, the nosebleeds? I bet this commune doesn't even have a first aid box. Come on, Blue. Even you must see we need help." The army would have people who could figure this out. Hell, she might be right. They might already know about Goldstone, the drug. But if the army knew what Goldstone had done, maybe someone had information about the drug already. If there was a cure, some antidote, they might already have it. It was the best chance to get help for her.

"No." She shook her head adamantly. "I won't use the powers. From here on, I won't use them. If I don't use them, they can't hurt me."

But he shook his head. "Yes, you will. If you feel like you have to use them." As he stared into her earnest face, her concern, the naked feeling she had for him ripped at his chest. She would try to protect him, if she had to.

"Please, listen to me. We can't go to them. They'll poke us and prod us. Turn us into lab rats. You must see that. We can't go." Her fingers gripped her knees. "What about Kitty? Who is going to get Kitty?"

She was right. At least partly.

His stomach sick, he kissed her cheek. "Okay. Maybe you're right."

Yeah, she was right. They might study him. They might have to. After all, how else would they find a cure, a way to fix them, if they didn't already have one? But he was going to contact them anyway.

He couldn't see any other way to help her.

She sprang forward and hugged him, laughing in relief. "Oh, God. Thank you. We'll leave tomorrow. Mom lives off the grid. If we want to disappear for a while, that's the way to go. I shouldn't have to use any powers in Idaho." She pulled away to smile up at him. "With the way you drive, we should be there in a few days."

In the face of her teasing, he felt even worse. But he nodded, did his best to smile back. "Why don't you grab a shower?"

She dropped a kiss on his mouth before she grabbed her bag and headed for the bathroom.

The sound of the key swipe sounded, and Nick stepped in. His friend took one look at him and shook his head. "Whatever just happened, it's not good."

Seth shook his head. When the shower started, he exhaled. "I need your phone. You said Major Martins is at Sam Houston, right?"

"Yeah. Why?"

"I'm going to call him."

Nick's eyebrow went up. "Asking him out on a date?"

"No. Ass." Seth exhaled. "I'm going to see if he can help us."

"Seth..."

"No, hear me out. Martins, he's good people. Maybe he can find out something, maybe they have some information about this drug. Maybe he can help us. It's worth a try. I can't let her keep going like this. She's going to get herself killed."

"He's going to want to see you." Nick shook his head. "No way he'll give you anything over the phone. He's no idiot."

"I know. I'll go tonight."

"I'm going with you."

"No." Seth shook his head. "No, you have to stay and keep an eye on her. Take her to her mom's, where she'll be safe. When I find out how to fix what's going on, I'll contact you." It was the best he could do. If he allowed things to keep going on like this, either he was going to get Blue killed or she'd end up doing it to herself. Neither option was acceptable.

"I don't like this."

"What choices do we have?"

Nick didn't answer, only slipped the battery back into his phone and passed it to him.

Seth stepped into the hall, heading toward the snack alcove as he dialed 411. With some finagling, he finally connected to Martins's home number. His wife answered, and after long moments, Major Martins was on the line. "This better be pretty goddamn important."

"I apologize, sir, for calling you at home."

"As you should. Who the hell is this?"

"This is Specialist Seth Campbell, sir. I worked with you a few months back, sir. At training at Fort Hood."

A brief pause. "I remember you. You still better have a good explanation for this call."

A few minutes later, it was arranged. He'd meet Martins at 2300 hours at Sam Houston.

He turned to the snack machine, deposited a handful of coins and stabbed the E7 button. A Twix bar dropped down, and he retrieved it before trotting back to their hotel room.

This was the best thing. He knew it was. It wasn't safe, not at all. But Martins would get them information. He could get them answers.

Blue greeted him at the door with a scowl. "Where the hell have you been?"

He lifted the chocolate bar, waving it at her. "Hungry?"

She smiled, seemed to relax. "You're a good man."

Over her head, he nodded at Nick.

Night fell. They put SportsCenter on. It acted like a lullaby for Blue. She was asleep in minutes.

He waited until he heard her steady breathing before he rose. He stared at her for a long moment, her wild blond curls on the pillow, but he didn't dare touch her. Then he sat at the little desk, wrote her the note he'd been composing in his head for the last hour, and dropped the bulk of the money Luke had left them next to it.

In silence, Nick walked him out to the street. "I hate this."

Yeah. He did, too. But he couldn't think of anything else. "Give her another fifteen minutes, twenty, tops, and get moving. If they talk to me and decide they want her, you'll be long gone by the time they get here. You know how to wire, right?" Nick nodded. "Jack a car and head to her mother's. She lives on some compound, off the grid. Blue will help you. I'll track you down, meet up with you as soon as I can." He cleared his throat. "But if I don't…" He didn't want to think about not meeting them, but he had to be practical. "If I don't, try to find Kitty. She needs our help."

"Of course." Something flashed in Nick's eyes, and Seth wondered if maybe there was more there than he knew about.

Seth stared at him. He trusted Nick with his life, with Blue's life, but he wondered if he was doing the right thing. No time to second-guess now. If this could help Blue, this was what he'd do.

He nodded and shook the other man's hand.

He walked a few blocks before he caught a cab and took it to the gate at Sam Houston. When the MP at the gate stopped him, he showed his credentials and requested to see Martins. The MP went into his booth. Seth watched him as he studied his military ID. He glanced out at him and picked up the phone. When he realized Seth was watching, he turned his back so he couldn't read his lips. He watched as the MP in the booth nodded and hung up.

They knew.

Damn it.

Though he was pissed, he'd known it was possible. He'd committed to this plan. He was going to see it through, either way. But now he had to worry about Blue. He checked his watch—2307. It had only taken him fifteen minutes to get here. He frowned. He hoped Nick didn't wait too long to get moving.

Two other MPs joined the one from the booth, then they all turned toward him. In seconds, he was surrounded. "Please come with us, Specialist Campbell."

Seth nodded. He'd expected as much, hadn't he? "I'm

supposed to see Major Martins. He's expecting me."

"We are to escort you."

Yeah, he'd bet they were.

Together, they all entered the base. It looked like any other hall on any other base that Seth had ever been in. He followed the MP to an empty conference room. They waved him inside and closed the door behind him. The ominous sound of the lock catching echoed through the room.

Where the hell was Martins? His mind told him that it was possible, even likely now that he saw the extent of security here, that the army had known about this whole fiasco—the drugs, the running, Goldstone—the whole time. Probably wasn't a good sign that they'd locked him in, though.

Seth knew someone, somewhere was listening in, so he kept his trap closed and waited.

And waited. And waited. He remained seated, his head in his arms, preferring to remain awake. He didn't want to be disoriented for whatever was coming.

When the knock came at the door, he sat up even as the exhaustion crashed down on him. The events of the last couple days hadn't been kind. The door opened, and uniformed men trooped in. He snapped to attention.

Martins entered, followed by enough brass to remodel a house.

Thank God Blue hadn't come.

"At ease, soldier." The highest rank, a colonel, waved him down. Seth dropped his arm. "Have a seat, Specialist Campbell."

He did as ordered. Martins sat across from him, the colonel—Lloyd, according to his name patch—sat beside him. The others were first and second lieutenants. Seth ignored Martins and met Lloyd's eyes.

"Fine mess you've found your way into, soldier."

"Yes, sir."

"You want to tell us what happened out there, son?" The colonel raised his eyebrows.

Naturally, he'd be skeptical. Who wouldn't be? The stuff he was about to say was incredible. But Lloyd knew something already. He had to. Apparently this would be a game of show-and-tell. And it seemed he'd have to go first.

Still. Blue's health depended on him and what he said here. He wouldn't let her down. He took a deep breath and started. "I was on my way to pick up Specialist Degrassi before heading to training at Fort Bragg. I stopped in Glory, Colorado, for the night and woke up as strong as an ox and as fast as a train."

Chapter Eighteen

A firm hand shook her. "Blue. We need to get moving."
Her eyelids felt like concrete. She finally pried them open and sat up, glancing around at the crappy blinds. Her disorientation cleared. The hotel. But it was still dark out.

"Rise and shine. We need to go."

That wasn't Seth. She sat up, instantly alert. "Where's Seth?"

Nick's smile faded. "Blue…"

"He's gone." Her desperate mind suggested breakfast. Or a trip out for coffee. But she knew better. "God damn him." She threw the blankets off, bounding out of bed and reaching for her clothes.

The feeling of abandonment crushed her. What had happened? They'd talked last night. She'd thought they were on the same page. Hell, she'd thought they'd gotten past his macho Captain America fixation and moved to somewhere better.

Around the crushing pain, she asked, "Where did he go?"

"Blue, come on."

"Tell me."

"He went to Fort Sam Houston. The other side of town."

Her fingers dug into the hotel comforter. Even as every disgusting thing she'd ever read about hotel comforters played through her mind, she had to hold on as the hurt rolled through her.

"Listen, he had to go. He didn't know what else to do. He's terrified of what this thing is doing to you guys. To you."

She glared up at Nick. "Nice of him to leave you behind to explain. He should have explained himself."

But he had tried to explain. She hadn't wanted to hear.

She moved to get up, to flee to the bathroom, where she could be hurt all by herself. But Nick caught her arm. "He left you a note." He nodded toward the desk and studied her for a moment before asking, "Did he tell you about Bobby?"

"His friend, in Afghanistan?" What did this have to do with him leaving her behind?

Nick nodded. "Bobby was a civilian who traveled with us in the 'Stan. A photographer. He and Seth got real tight. But one day, when Seth was on his detail, Bobby was killed."

"He told me that. But it was an accident, right?" It had to be an accident. Seth would never be needlessly negligent.

"Of course it was an accident. But Campbell…"

"He thinks it's his fault."

Nick nodded. "Listen, Campbell…he has reasons for what he's doing. You should know that."

She wasn't sure what she knew right now. "He thinks they can help him."

"You." Nick pointed at her. "He thinks they can help you."

"Me?"

"Yeah, you." He snorted and reached for his bag, stuffing his few items inside.

"Because of Bobby?"

"No." He glanced up. "Well, maybe. Because he doesn't want you to be another Bobby. But that isn't all of it. If you think it is, you haven't been paying any attention." He zippered his bag and dropped it on the bed. "We have to get moving."

"To where?"

"Seth thinks we should go to your mother's. I think it's as good as any place."

"No." She shook her head.

"What?"

"I said no." She stood, reaching for her things, sliding her feet into her shoes. "We're not going anywhere without Seth."

"I told you. He's at Sam Houston. And he'd be pissed at me that we've been so slow getting going."

"Nah, he'll be pissed at me." She smiled. "He knows I'm unmanageable."

Her gaze drifted across the room, the hideous painting of ugly flowers, the brass wall sconces, before falling on the wad of cash on the desk.

A lot of cash. She retrieved the bills and counted. It seemed to be all the cash Luke had left them. She put her hand on her stomach, suddenly nauseous, and reached for the letter beside it all.

She lifted it with shaking fingers.

Blue:

I know you're upset. I'm sorry for that. You're right. If you didn't want to go, you shouldn't have to. But I needed to find out what they know. We need their help.

I've left the money. Go to your mother's, like you planned. I'll let you know when I have answers. I hope they can help us.

Be safe.
Seth

He wanted her to go to Idaho? Now? Did he really think she'd leave him here? Idaho was only a hiding place. She'd thought they could stay with her mom, find some internet access somewhere, and try to figure out where they'd hidden Kitty.

None of that could happen now, not with him at Sam Houston.

She didn't trust the army at all. She certainly wouldn't leave him here to face it alone. It wasn't who she was.

He'd accused her of making her own decisions, everyone else be damned. Talk about the pot and the kettle. She snorted.

She went to the window and glanced out, trying to get her thoughts together, figure out her next steps.

But below, three army utility vehicles were parked at the curb. She stepped back from the window quickly, letting the curtain fall.

A slow smile split her face, and she dropped her bag on the carpet.

"What are you doing?" Nick demanded.

She crossed her arms over her chest and leaned against the desk. "Listen. If you want to go, you can go by yourself. But decide fast, because the military's here to get us. And I'm going with them. I'm getting Seth back."

The questioning had gone on for at least an hour. It had to be after midnight, though he wasn't sure, since the room they'd chosen for this interrogation had no windows. He rubbed his forehead, then his eyes, the exhaustion almost debilitating.

"You can run fast, you say?" the lieutenant next to Colonel

Lloyd asked again. Maybe it was all the hours of questioning, but it came off patronizingly. Seth fought the urge to stand, to pace off his growing irritation. They'd gone over this and over this. He'd explained every minute—well, almost every minute—of the last few days. Twice. Then he'd explained what he knew of his powers. He'd explained about the rest of their powers. He'd told them everything, and they made him repeat himself again and again.

These were standard interrogation tactics. They were waiting for him to make a mistake, change his story. They were testing every facet of his knowledge and looking for holes. When they found one, they would pounce.

"Yes. I've said that already. Three times. I can run fast. But I came because we are having side effects. Nosebleeds. Headaches. Lost consciousness. We need your help." He glanced at Martins, who stared at his folded hands. Damn him. Why had he thought he could trust that guy?

The colonel's face darkened. "You've said that as well, Specialist."

"Beg your pardon, sir, but I thought maybe you were having difficulty hearing." He smiled, but he was walking the thin line between cute and insubordinate.

The colonel opened his mouth to respond, and Seth had no idea what was about to come out next, when a knock at the door saved him. A grunt came in. He stood next to Martins and whispered. The kid obviously didn't want Seth to hear, but he shouldn't have bothered. Seth heard everything. "We have her."

Martins's mouth thinned, and he met Seth's eyes. Seth forgot his exhaustion. "Have who, sir?"

The men sitting across from him said nothing, but their expressions closed, became cautious. Two of the lieutenants began shuffling papers, not making eye contact. That's when he knew. Immediately, he felt ill. "You went after Blue, didn't you?"

Martins's brow furrowed. "I don't like this."

He'd given Nick enough time to get moving. He hadn't arrived at Sam Houston until 2300, as planned.

Which meant the army must have gone after Blue before he'd even spoken to Martins.

The taxi driver. There weren't that many hotels in the area where the taxi had picked him up. They must have questioned the taxi driver before Martins even walked in. And Seth had given them Blue's location.

So, she had been right. They'd been watching Goldstone's activities. He'd known there was a good chance of that, too, but he'd hoped they'd at least want to help them. Apparently not.

He stared across the table. The men in front of him had gone from being wary to suspicious. They hadn't given him an explanation. That was unacceptable. He deserved an explanation. When you double-crossed someone, you should have to stare him in the face while you did it. He glared, waiting. "You have no intention of helping us, do you?"

The particularly smarmy fellow at the end of the table pushed his glasses up his nose and answered, "You all need to remain in our custody. You may pose a danger to society or yourselves. From what you've said, Miss Michaels doesn't have complete control of her new abilities. She belongs here. All of you do."

"I came here so you could help us," he gritted out. "We need help."

"Some things are more important, son." No hint of apology.

He let that wash over him. They were a risk, something the army needed to neutralize.

Blue was in great danger. So was he.

He needed to get out of here, get to her. She needed help

before it was too late. He should have stayed with Blue in the first place. He should have found another way.

More, if he'd explained what he was planning to her, they could have come up with a better option…together. Like the team she'd wanted them to be. Instead, he'd insisted on doing it alone.

And he'd ruined everything.

Glancing around the room, he channeled his anger and allowed his brain to do the work for him. There were five of them, all armed. They really must have thought he was a threat if they had their guns on base. Of the group, only Martins looked uncomfortable. The door was locked. He thought back, his mind replaying their entrance hours ago, and realized the smarmy guy had the keys in his front pants pocket. He decided to go for the door instead and not bother with keys. His brain told him that choice had a better chance of success but remained fuzzy on how much better of a chance.

Before, when he thought through a fight, he would see the final outcome clearly. He'd see how he would manipulate each of the participants for his own gain. Then he would see his ultimate victory.

Here, he couldn't see his victory. He saw numerous outcomes. There were too many variables. There were five opponents. On their breasts, they wore varying ribbons and medals, all boasting additional trainings and advanced valor. These were the army's finest, men who could think and act. Men with no shortage of courage. Men who knew exactly what he could do now, thanks to his own mouth.

There were other men watching, he was certain of it. He didn't know how many or what their roles would be. That added another layer of difficulty to what would already be a nearly impossible escape.

It didn't matter. He had to try. He had to get to Blue.

He spent a fraction of a second calming his mind. Telling

himself that it didn't matter that he was going to lose. Then he sprang forward.

He jumped out of his seat and over the heads of the men seated in front of him. He spun in the air, landing behind them, and pulled two of their chairs backward with quick yanks, sending the colonel and one of the lieutenants sprawling backward. He spun, snapped Colonel Lloyd's face against the table and tripped another lieutenant who had stumbled to his feet.

All this happened in less than a second, but it had been enough time to allow Lt. Smarmy to get his bearings. He'd stood and was in the process of pulling his gun. Seth didn't slow, barreling forward and catching him around the waist. They tumbled to the floor with an *oomph*, and Seth elbowed him in the face. He tried to scramble over him, but Smarmy squeezed. They grappled, rolling from side to side. Smarmy might not look like much, but he wrestled like an octopus. Seth twisted the lieutenant's hand and broke past him.

In his periphery, he watched Martins step back, his hands up. He'd chosen to stay out of the fight.

Smart man.

As he scurried to his feet, his chest expanded for a brief moment. If he could open the door…if he could get out into the hall, he could get going. This closed space…if he could only get out of here…

The door opened, admitting more men, a dozen maybe, before it slammed shut again, trapping him inside. He continued to fight, but hands circled his waist, his arms, so many hands. He shook, tried to break free, but they brought him to the ground.

There was shouting and the sound of chairs scratching against the floor. Feet shuffled nearby and grunts rent the air.

A zip tie fastened around his right wrist. His struggles became desperate, but he was ultimately overpowered. As they took him to the ground, he lay on his stomach staring at the small table that held an ancient coffeepot and a few chipped mugs.

As he heard movement outside—reinforcements, probably—he knew he wasn't getting out of here.

They dragged him to his feet, and his sense of failure was absolute.

Then the door exploded. It didn't open; it flew off the hinges and into the room as if hit by an explosive. The military men cowered, hitting the ground. Everyone but him.

Blue stepped inside, her eyebrows furrowed. Nick stood behind her, pistol raised, guarding her back. Seth glanced at the officers, all in different phases of standing or falling to the ground. Blue didn't look at him, instead staring out into room as if trying to see its entirety at once.

"You ready?" Her tone was mild, but her voice shook. He could see the strain on her face.

And a trickle of blood ran from her nose.

Chapter Nineteen

Blue ignored the headache pounding behind her eyes. So, fine, she didn't ignore it. It would have been like ignoring a battering ram on her forehead. She refused to acknowledge it, to be mastered by it. If she lost control, she'd lose her hold on all of these guys, and she needed to get them out of here. It wasn't only those guys, but the men in the next room who'd been watching the proceedings.

Holding men still through a concrete wall... It was proving difficult.

Nick swept into the interrogation room and used a knife to cut the zip tie at Seth's wrists. Seth was on his feet in a second, snagging the gun from the nearest officer's holster and another from the man next to him. He tossed the spare to Nick, who caught it. "What the hell are you doing here?"

"Saving...your ass." She could hardly talk through the strain of holding the men still.

She couldn't figure out if she was incredibly loyal or incredibly stupid. What she did know was she couldn't leave him here, alone. He belonged with her.

"Thank God you're all right. I'm so glad to see you." His whisper was full of relief. Happiness sailed through her, even as the pain behind her eyes became unbearable. She could feel herself quaking with it. Her vision blurred, and she teetered, losing grip of what was going on. As she lost her hold on the men in the room, the pain released.

In desperation, she dived forward, to shield Seth and Nick. Vaguely, she heard a pop, and then fire exploded in her right shoulder. In her periphery, she saw Seth turn, horror on his face.

She hadn't been strong enough, hadn't held them long enough. She'd failed.

Arms circled her, and then she was moving into the hall at a run, held against Seth's strong chest.

She couldn't catch her breath, and her right arm was completely numb. Had she been shot? It felt like it. God, the burn... She clung to Seth with her left arm as her head pounded with the effects of holding the men for so long, and her body began to go numb. She struggled to open her eyes, needed to get her bearings, to help. But for a few long minutes, all she caught were flashes. Painted cement block walls. Commercial doors. Ugly drop-tile ceiling and fluorescent lighting.

Noises penetrated. The sound of fists connecting, more gunshots. Beneath her, Seth was running at breakneck speed, and she could almost taste his panic, could hear it as he barked commands at Nick.

She dragged her eyes open. "I'm glad."

He glanced down at her quickly, never breaking his stride. "What?"

"I'm glad...I came."

"Oh, no, you don't." He shook his head. "You stay awake. No sleeping." The command was a challenge. As if he didn't think she could stay awake.

She would stay awake. To prove him wrong. But then she

lifted her hand, to touch his face, and she saw blood on her fingers. So much blood.

Staying awake might be harder than she thought.

With Blue disoriented in his arms, the panic in Seth's stomach nearly ate him from within. The wound was bleeding, but it wasn't gushing as it would if it had hit an artery. She had time. Or so his massively logical brain said.

She wouldn't die. He'd refused to allow it, hadn't he? He'd refused to let another person die because of him.

Still, he picked up his pace. He rounded the corner to find men lined up, blocking his path. He halted and backtracked, stopping Nick beside him.

"We need to get her out of here."

"Where's she hit?" Nick asked, checking his pistol.

"Right shoulder. High, I think."

Nick peeked around the corner. "Not this way. Back the way we came?"

"I think we need to find a window." The doors would be blocked by now. If they had any chance, they'd have to sneak out of the building. But they would have to do it fast, while everything was still in flux.

Even now, he heard sirens. Not good at all.

"What is it with you guys and windows?" Nick muttered.

Seth would have smiled if he wasn't so worried about Blue. He nudged his head to the open door behind them. They crept backward, Nick covering him, and into the room, closing the door behind them. He pulled the string on the blinds next to the door, covering the window. It might buy them an extra second or two to get out of here.

They appeared to be in someone's office. He strode forward, swept his hand across the desk, and laid Blue down.

A quick assessment showed both an entrance wound in back and an exit wound in front, right below her collarbone. He breathed a sigh of relief. At least the bullet wasn't still inside.

"Blue?"

Full of pain, her eyes focused on him. "Yeah?"

"I'm so sorry. You need to know that. I'm going to get you out of here."

"Came to get you out." He had no idea how she managed to sound so outraged, but it tugged at his heart like nothing else could have.

He ran one hand over his hair, the other on his hip. He'd tried to avoid this exact thing, damn it. Why hadn't she listened to him?

Even as he stared at her too pale face, he knew why. Blue didn't run and hide. How had he not seen that she would come?

He'd misjudged her, and because of that, she'd ended up bleeding and hurt. The one thing he feared the most.

As he paced the room, he tried to work through what had to happen next.

There was no way they were getting out of this. Sam Houston had amazing security. It was a military base, after all. If they tried to slink out, let alone slink out while carrying a nearly unconscious and wounded woman, they'd be sitting ducks, caught for sure.

He stood, thinking. His brain offered him nothing that got them out—all three of them—alive.

But when he took himself out of the equation, the outcome sifted out easily enough. He would cause a diversion, distract the security detail while Nick secreted Blue out. If they didn't use the main gate, they'd have a good chance. Even going over the wall somewhere. Blue was hurt, but Nick was well trained, competent. He would get her out and to safety.

They would be all right. Without him.

He turned to Nick. "You're going out this window. Head farther into the base. Get over the wall, find a car. Go."

Nick scowled. "I'm not leaving you here."

Blue shook her head, struggling to sit up. "No. No."

He gritted his teeth. "You have to. It's the only way. I'll distract them. You guys get away."

Nick looked fierce, his brown eyes angry. "This is some serious shit."

Seth had to get him to go. It was the only chance. "You have to do this for me," he whispered. "This girl"—he kept his eyes on his friend—"she's special. To me. Get her out. Get her help. Then get somewhere safe." He smiled. "I'll find you when I can."

Even as he said the words, they didn't ring true. He probably wouldn't be going anywhere for a long time.

There was banging at the door.

"Go. Now. I'll hold them off."

"No." Blue stumbled off the desk, standing, pushing off his hands when he tried to help. "No…you don't. Stop right there."

He glared at her precious face. "We don't have time for this."

"Yeah, so stop fucking around. We do this…together." She met his eyes, hers glazed with pain. "You have to trust me. I trust you." She said it defensively, glaring at him. "Now put your big stupid mind to work. You know what I can do, so figure it out." Her grip on his arm was surprisingly fierce. "But so help me God, Seth, if you don't get yourself out of here, too, I will hurt you myself. I won't have…this bullshit."

As he stared into her eyes, met her intensity, he let himself, for one moment, stop feeling guilty, stop feeling like everything was his fault.

Stop feeling like he had to solve every problem alone.

It was heaven. And it allowed him to see the possibilities.

All the possibilities. He might have gotten them into this mess, but he sure as hell could get them out.

He closed his eyes for a long moment, running through the scenarios. When he let himself include Blue, he could see it come together like a puzzle. "The window, Blue. Can you take out the window, make us a hole to get out?"

She smiled, beatific at first and then rebellious, that mix of hers that he found completely irresistible. "Why, of course."

The gun felt heavy in his hand, and he tucked it into his waistband. He hoped he didn't have to use it. He hated where this had come, to him maybe using a weapon against men like him, men he might have served with. But, as Blue had told him, sometimes shitty things just happened. Best to have the weapon, if he needed it.

He faced the door, considering the best ways to slow them down and predicting their next moves. If he was in their place, he'd gas him. They knew how much he could do. He'd been an idiot and told them what he could do. They would want to disable him and then contain him.

Yeah, that wouldn't work for him.

"They're going to gas us."

As the banging continued at the door, louder now, he glanced around the room. A spare uniform jacket hung over the back of the desk chair. He yanked it down, finding the bars of a major. He ripped the back of it into shreds. He threw two pieces to Nick, who wrapped one around Blue's face and the other around his mouth and nose. Seth followed suit. He overheard Nick explain quietly how the gas would affect Blue's eyes.

The door next to the knob splintered, and the door flew open. He didn't wait for the tear gas grenade.

Diving up, he jumped high in the air as the pop of the gas gun sounded. He twisted in a somersault near the ceiling, coming down on the two soldiers in the doorway feetfirst.

Knocking them to the floor, he burst into a whirlwind, moving forward quickly as he punched and kicked his way forward.

"Blue, now," he ordered.

He took down three, four, eight men in quick succession. He buried his fist in one man's stomach and used him as a battering ram to knock down two more.

Behind him a huge explosion split the air, sucking the gas out of the room like a vacuum.

Seemed Blue really could make an escape route.

He was holding his own, but he was taking some hits. A punch to his kidney, a blow to the back of his shoulders. And no matter how many he took down, another soldier took his place. He backed up, spinning, kicking and punching, jumping and fighting. If he'd been the sort to admire his work, he'd be amazed with himself. No fatigue. He felt pain, but it was manageable. He was a machine.

Then a gunshot split the air, and fire burned through his calf. He stumbled but continued, determined to get them out of there. He pulled his own gun from his waist, dropped to his knee, and shot three in the legs. They dropped like stones, making a hole in the horde, and he barreled forward, pocketing his gun again. As he fought, he could feel how fast he struck out, too fast, faster than he'd ever moved before.

Whatever else it was, this drug was really something.

As men dived on him, he was covered for a moment. He should have been captured, but instead he stood, with a twist, and shrugged them all off, as if they weighed nothing. They flew through the air, like trash on the wind. Earlier, he hadn't been able to avoid a zip tie. Now, he was throwing people around like they were paper airplanes.

Something had changed. As if he'd only touched the surface of how strong he could be before and now he finally had full access.

And it was amazing.

He didn't have time to admire his handiwork, though, because then he was running through the hole Blue had made in the wall.

Bullets exploded through the air, all around him, but nothing hit him. He jumped over the rubble of the wall, sailing through the air as if floating.

He landed twenty-five yards away, out of the rubble but not clear of the men. Troops approached, materializing from the darkness like cockroaches. It seemed like hundreds.

That's when he saw Blue, standing in the middle of the grounds a hundred yards in front of him, next to the parking lot. Her feet were spread apart, her arms out, and her hair stood straight up around her face, as if she suffered from serious static electricity. She was covered in grime, and blood stained the front of her shirt, but she still looked like an avenging angel as military men, weapons, and debris swirled in the air around her.

He'd told her an escape route. What was she doing?

Then he knew. She was saving him.

He raced toward her as a rumbling like a freight train sounded behind him. Or maybe not a freight train—more like an…earthquake.

Only then did he glance back to see the building crumble, large chunks crashing to the ground and windows exploding. He'd seen bombs do less damage than Blue.

It would be magnificent if he wasn't scared shitless for her.

On all sides, as men almost overtook him, they would fly away from him, as if they'd bounced off an invisible wall. The few who actually reached him he tossed aside, never slowing. As he sped toward her, she started to wobble on her feet. He overtook her, tossed her over his shoulder, running as fast as he could away from the destruction. Nick knelt next to a Hummer in the parking lot, and he veered toward him. As the chaos quieted behind him, Blue's body went limp.

She wasn't breathing.

Terror coursed through him, making his head buzz, and he wanted to vomit.

He hadn't told her. She wasn't breathing, he might have lost her, and he hadn't told her how important she was to him.

Sweeping into the backseat of the Hummer Nick had hot-wired, he straddled her too still body, leaning over her. He placed his fingers to her neck. A pulse, faint but present. She still wasn't breathing, though.

"Go," he gasped at Nick as the other man slipped into the driver's seat. Nick didn't need to be told twice. They peeled out of the parking lot.

As they drove, Seth wiped the blood from Blue's nose and started rescue breathing.

Chapter Twenty

There was no window in this room. The cement blocks that surrounded her should have kept everyone out. They were thick; she'd felt them under her fingers. But still, she heard everything.

The stupid orderly Dr. Fields had hired to watch her was still here, playing Minecraft. He didn't care at all about the little girl in the room with only a bed and a sheet and a nightgown. To him, this seemed stupid. He fed her and had to go in, every half an hour, and wake her if she slept. Then he had to think of a number and get her to guess. Like she was the bearded lady at the fair. He'd thought the last number—7532—would stump her. But, of course, she'd gotten it. She'd been tempted to pretend. But if she got it wrong, the doctor had told her he'd wake her every ten minutes. She didn't want to be disturbed that often.

The doctor.

His thoughts were the ones that had roused her. She'd only been able to doze since arriving, and it was starting to take its toll. But she wouldn't relax, not enough to sleep.

Now she was glad. She feared what she would miss if she was sleeping. She already felt out of control. She wouldn't allow things to happen without her knowledge.

The door swung open. The doctor stepped in, carrying her food tray. He set it on the ground in front of him. He hadn't gotten close to her since the day he'd retrieved her from Goldstone, and she preferred it that way. He'd put her here, in this cage, after explaining that another survivor had taken advantage of his hospitality already. She could see Parker Sinclair's face in his mind, and she'd listened as his thoughts turned nasty toward the older man.

Interesting. Fields had seen Sinclair as a kindred spirit, a fellow scholar. Sinclair had used that trust to steal Fields's research, including a large supply of his drug.

Kitty had never met the hermit who lived in the hills outside Glory. Word in town was he had left a successful career in academia to retreat into the wilderness. Like Thoreau or something.

She wondered what Sinclair wanted with Fields's research. Nothing good, she imagined.

When Fields stepped back from her food, she watched him before scurrying forward to grab the cup of water, quickly returning to her bed. He rationed all her food, all her drink. Which meant she was constantly hungry, thirsty. The cup was Styrofoam, with a straw. Nothing she could use to hurt herself or anyone else. She drank thirstily.

When he stood again, he smiled at her. She didn't return it, pulling her knees closer to herself on the little cot in the corner. "Good evening, Ms. Laughton."

She could feel the zeal in him, the self-satisfaction. He believed she'd be thankful to him for these gifts. That she would worship him. She had to keep herself from gagging.

"It's evening?" She didn't even hide the disdain. Why should she care? He was going to do whatever he wanted to do anyway.

"It is." He flipped through a chart, considering. He read through the results of the orderly's questions. *She got them all right. Astounding.*

He took credit for her actions. She wanted to scream.

His next tests ran through his head. How strong were her abilities? How far away could the mind be before she could no longer hear thoughts? How much of her brain was used while reading thoughts?

His eagerness was creepy. He considered himself her creator, which was even more disturbing.

"Lovely progress, Ms. Laughton." He rearranged the paperwork again. "I believe we're ready to begin the next phase of our testing."

She got fleeting visions of an MRI tube, of a gurney and different drug cocktails. Of machines she'd never seen before and didn't know the purposes of.

The doctor smiled. "But first you must sleep."

She wanted to laugh at him. Then her eyes began to droop. In his head, she heard him laughing about the water, the sedative he'd put in it. He congratulated himself on tricking her, on figuring out that she couldn't hear thoughts unless they occupied the mind at that moment.

If she'd been inclined, she might have told him that. It was, after all, how Jeremy had tricked her.

She was too trusting. People would use that against her every time.

She'd learn, she thought, as she drifted off to sleep. She'd learn.

Blue tripped out of the darkness in fits and starts.
The first time she could pry her eyes open, she

registered someone beside her, holding her hand. They squeezed so tightly, she thought it might hurt any other time. But it didn't hurt now. Maybe because everything else hurt so much that she couldn't even feel her fingers.

The next time she stumbled forward, she heard voices.

"Her blood pressure hasn't stabilized yet. Kent is trying, but without better equipment there's not much he can do." Nick sounded worried, more worried than usual. Who were they talking about? "The seizures aren't helping anything, either."

"I can go. I'll get whatever he needs." Seth sounded ill.

"I know you don't want to leave her, but…"

"Yeah. I'm the best equipped."

Wait, were they talking about her? She tried to open her eyes, tried to tell them she was fine. But she couldn't move.

It *was* her. The realization terrified her and filled her with defiance at the same time. No way was she stuck here, no way was she as bad off as they sounded. But when she tried to get up, she found herself tumbling into the dark again.

Seth's voice, filled with panic, was the last thing she heard.

Pain became the main part of her existence, until the time that it wasn't. At some point in the seemingly endless agony, peace spread through her. She'd never felt anything so alluring…or seductive. She wanted to stay there in the blissful nothing, but Seth's pleading voice told her to come back to him. He pulled at her and made her push out of it, somehow. Then she was back to the pain, but Seth sounded pleased, wherever he was, and if he was happy, she was happy, too.

Much later, though, she didn't know how long, her eyes opened again.

She was in a bed in a stark room. Nearby, a machine beeped, and needles and lines ran from her arm. In a chair next to her, Seth was sleeping. She turned her head, testing to see if she'd be able to move. She'd been trapped inside her skull for so long, movement felt new again.

Even in slumber, he looked tired. Really tired. As if he'd been the one slipping in and out of consciousness for the past eternity.

"Seth?" Was that her voice? She sounded...wimpy.

His eyes shot open. "Thank God. You're awake."

"Yeah." She licked her lips. "Water?"

He stared at her, not moving, wonder on his face. "You're awake."

He was acting strange. "Yeah," she croaked. "Help?"

"Oh." He hopped up, hobbled out, and returned a minute later with a glass of water. He held it to her lips with infinite care, helping her take sips. She wanted to yell at him for treating her like an infant, but then she realized she didn't have much energy after all. A little help might be nice.

"How long?" The events before she lost consciousness were a little fuzzy. She remembered being at Sam Houston, remembered being shot, remembered running across the field toward the parking lot.

So, fine. Running was probably an overstatement. If she remembered correctly, she'd pretty much stumbled along while Nick dragged her across the grass. Technicalities.

But then she'd heard Seth cry out and turned to see him fall under a pile of soldiers.

Right.

The rest of the details filled in fast. The wash of pure rage. The wave of determination. Then she'd been possessed by that rogue part of her, the part that didn't give a damn about anything except the people she loved.

And she'd made it rain concrete and glass, sent men flying like a house of cards on the wind.

"It's been four days now."

Four days. That was a long time. "Tell me."

"Christ, Blue. What the hell? You took out Sam Houston.

One building will need extensive renovations. From what we've heard, almost forty people needed first aid, at least ten people were hospitalized, and two are in critical condition. No one was killed, but..." He left that hanging in the air.

She looked away. No one was killed. At least that was something.

What a mess she was. She used to know, without a doubt, that violence was wrong. But sometime in the past week, she'd become someone else. Someone who destroyed entire buildings, who hospitalized people.

But she didn't care. She hadn't wanted to hurt them, but they'd shot Seth. They'd shot her. They would have killed them if they'd had to.

Violence to protect herself, to protect her friends...well, it was different.

She was different.

"I was worried. So many of them." She shrugged, even as fire stole up from her shoulder. "I needed to get you out."

He smiled. "So you wrecked a building? Remind me not to get you mad." She chuckled, remembering when she said something similar to him after he took out the helicopter at Kitty's house.

She pointed at herself. "Anger management issues."

"Right. You rage-filled vegetarians, scary things."

"Are you all right?" He'd been shot, at least twice that she saw.

He raised his hands, showing two bandages and pointing to one on his calf, peeking out from his athletic shorts. "Yeah. I heal fast."

She relaxed and smiled, but as she looked at him, she had a lot of questions. "Why did you go? Why didn't you tell me?" It still hurt, that he hadn't trusted her enough to tell her his plans. In fact, he hadn't trusted her at all.

"I'm sorry." He ran a hand over his head. "The nosebleeds,

the headaches. You. I was afraid."

He took her hand. "I told you about Bobby. But I didn't give you the whole story." She shook her head. "Bobby was one of my best friends. We were nothing alike, except maybe we were. I don't know. He was in the 'Stan, taking pictures, and I was in the detail assigned to watch him. He was shooting government propaganda stuff, pretty standard, but he also took other things, candids. Wanted to see what the real experience was like. He was very talented." He stared into space, smiling softly. "The day he died, I was with him. We were attacked, and he wanted to get some shots. I knew it was a bad idea, but he begged. So I let him move closer. I even pointed him where to go."

He swallowed. "I was wrong. A rocket, right where he was standing. He died instantly."

"I'm so sorry." Her heart ached for him. She got the impression he didn't have many close friends.

"I should have listened to my gut. I could have made him move to safety. But he wanted to go. I could have made him stay, but I didn't. If I had, he'd still be here. Instead, his wife and son don't have him anymore." He paused. "And neither do I."

She reached for his hand. Since Gran's death, she knew all too well what it was like to feel guilty for surviving. "If he wanted to go, really wanted to go, do you think you could have stopped him?" She raised her eyebrow. "Short of physically restraining him? Shooting him?"

"Of course not."

"Right, because that's nuts. He was an adult. He made his own choices. We all do. And you cared about him, and you wanted him to be happy. You didn't shoot him with a rocket. You didn't know the rocket was even coming."

"I don't know." He squeezed her hand, not letting up the pressure at all as he continued. "Anyway. I couldn't stop thinking that I was going to get you killed. That once again, I was going to be the reason someone else I cared about died." He lifted his eyes, meeting hers. "Someone I'd come to love."

She inhaled. She hadn't allowed herself to think about how much she wanted his love. She'd been left behind so many times, by her parents, by her previous boyfriend. And Gran. But now, maybe because she'd lost Gran or because she'd seen how fast things in her new reality could go wrong, now she wasn't afraid anymore. "Yeah, well, it takes you longer to figure stuff out."

Seth grinned, his eyes soft. "Of course you had to be first."

"Of course."

"I love you, babe." He reached up and tucked a strand of hair behind her ear. "I only want to be with you, wherever we go. I want to go with you. All this stuff doesn't make sense, but I feel like together, we can figure it out."

"That, Seth Campbell, is exactly the right thing to say."

"It is?"

"Exactly." She squeezed his hand. "I love you."

"And I love you, too." He moved forward, pressing his lips to hers. The kiss held promise, was gentle and full of respect. She leaned into him, wanting to get closer, knowing that the sanity in her crazy world was with him, a breath away. But her shoulder ached, and she flinched in pain. "Ouch."

"You should be lying down," he scowled as he helped her back, tucking the pillow under her. "We can only stay here another day, maybe two at the most, before we need to get moving."

"Where are we?"

"Spare room at a friend's house. A medic Nick worked with before." Seth pulled the blankets over her. "He saved your life, so I guess he's my friend, too, now." He shook his head. "I thought I was going to lose you. I can't…"

"I'm here, though. And I'm going to be more careful. I

swear. Until we can figure out what's going on. Until we can find a cure for this." She didn't mention her experience with the peace. She suspected she was closer to death than she wanted him to know.

"Thank you. We will. We have to." His eyes squeezed shut. "I don't think I can do that again."

"You won't." Her eyelids felt heavy again. Man, she was a big baby.

"You should get some sleep. You've had a rough few days."

"Where are we going to go?" Her words were slurred, but she didn't want him to leave. Not yet.

"To Idaho. I hear there are some anti-government communes there that might hide us for a little while."

"My mom?" Even tired, the horror was clear in her voice.

"We need somewhere to search for Kitty. We don't leave people behind. One way or the other, we're going to get to the bottom of this."

"Now you're talking," As her eyes drifted closed, she couldn't help her smug smile. Yeah, they'd get to the bottom of this, all right. And when they did…

God help anyone who stood in their way.

Seth closed the door to Blue's room, listening for a moment to make sure she was asleep. Across the room, Nick's fingers paused on the keyboard of their friend's borrowed computer. "How is she?"

"She woke up." He grinned. "She's going to be okay." Saying the words made it feel real. She'd made it. There'd been times over the past days he'd wondered. He'd barely slept. Never had he known so much fear. But she'd made it. She'd be okay.

"Good." Nick's smile faded, though. "So, what next?"

Seth sobered. "You're welcome to come with us, to Blue's mom's house. From there, we're going to try to find Kitty."

Nick stared at the computer. "I tried to talk to her, you know. Kitty. About Jeremy. He'd become so unsettled these past months, detached. He got caught sleeping with a subordinate. Was getting an other-than-honorable discharge. I knew he was capable of anything. I should have told her more." He shook his head. "I need to make it right. I hope you understand."

Seth did. There were some things people had to do.

"I need to get her back, Seth." Nick's words were angry, almost violent. "I need to."

Seth nodded. "We will, Nick. We will."

Acknowledgments

Writing these short paragraphs has reminded me how many people have helped me on my path to publication. My heart is full. I can't possibly thank everyone, but know that I appreciate you all and couldn't have done this without you.

First, thank you to anyone who reads this book. Readers are the reason writers write. My gratitude is endless.

To my beta readers, brainstormers, and critique partners over the years, especially Terri, Jessica, Fran, Laurie, Kim, Haleigh, Jordan, and Kate. You all have helped me to grow in so many ways. I wouldn't be here if not for all of you. Big hugs.

Thanks to my super agent, Helen Breitwieser, for all your guidance and support. Also, a huge thank you to my editor, Candace Havens, and the team at Entangled. This book is better because of all of you and your amazing talents.

Thank you to the women and men of the Romance Writers of America. Through that organization, I connected with so many amazing specialty chapters, especially New Jersey RWA, YARWA, the Beau Monde, and Kiss of Death. Through RWA's Golden Heart contest, I met the Dreamweavers and the Dragonflies, the two classes of finalists I'm fortunate enough to be a part of. The knowledge and camaraderie of all of these women and men is humbling and gratifying. Thank you all for your friendship and expertise. I'm a better writer and a better person for my experiences with you.

A hearty huzzah to the pirates of the Romance Writers' Revenge. You girls were my first writing sisters. I wouldn't have kept going through some of those early years if not for you. Thank you all.

To Caroline Linden, who took me under her wing years ago. Your generous advice has guided me through lots of confusing times. I'm so lucky to call you my friend.

I couldn't ask for a better support system than my extended family and friends, especially my two earliest readers, my Mom and my sister, Aubree. Thank you all for wanting the best for me. I love you.

Finally, and most importantly, my eternal thanks to my family. To my husband, George, my rock and the calm in my storm. Nothing I say could come close to expressing how much I adore you. Your faith and support have never faltered. I'm blessed to have you in my corner. Also, thank you to our two sons. You both cheered for me when things went well and cheered me up when they didn't. All three of you shared me with the characters in my head as I chased this dream. I love you all.

About the Author

Two-time Golden Heart® Finalist Marnee Blake used to teach high school students but these days she only has to wrangle her own children. Originally from a small town in Western Pennsylvania, she now battles traffic in southern New Jersey where she lives with her hero husband and their happily-ever-after: two very energetic boys. When she isn't writing, she can be found refereeing disputes between her children, cooking up something sweet, or hiding from encroaching dust bunnies with a book.

Made in the USA
Middletown, DE
20 November 2015